Annie

A Lt. Kate Gazzara Novel

The Lt. Kate Gazzara Murder Files
Book 20

Blair Howard

Copyright © 2024 ANNIE by Blair Howard
All rights reserved.

Cleveland, TN, United States of America
ISBN PRINT: 979-8-9908529-1-4
Library of Congress Control Number: 2024917280

No part of this publication may be reproduced, stored in a retrieval system, or transmitted in any form, or by any means, electronic, mechanical, photocopying, recording, or otherwise, without the express written permission of the publisher except for the use of brief quotations in a book review.

Disclaimer: Annie is a work of fiction. The persons and events depicted in this novel were created by the author's imagination; no resemblance to actual persons or events is intended. Product names, businesses, brands, and other trademarks referred to within this book are the property of the respective trademark holders and are used fictitiously. Unless otherwise specified, no association between the author and any trademark holder is expressed or implied. Nor does the use of such trademarks indicate an endorsement of the products, trademarks, or trademark holders unless so stated. Use of a term in this book should not be regarded as affecting the validity of any trademark, registered trademark, or service mark.

www.blairhowardbooks.com
Contact: blairhoward@blairhowardbooks.com

For Jo
My long-suffering but oh-so-supportive wife.

Chapter One

July 13, 1986

White knuckling the steering wheel, he made a hard left, bouncing the front of his brand-new, forest green Chevy Cavalier across the uneven entrance, muttering curses under his breath, cringing at the potential long-term damage he was causing to the suspension.

Shit, I don't get paid enough to cover damn repairs.

He crinkled his nose in disgust, his eyes cast downward at the glint of light hitting his gold wedding band.

Another waste of time. If it weren't for his boys, he would have deemed his fifteen-year marriage a failure. She never appreciated him, nagging him at every turn. It was always about her. *Always.*

The car continued to bounce down the gravel drive of the old colonial estate he'd bought at a discounted price from an extended family member. The house was run-down, the white siding stained a deep yellow-brown, and the concrete porch stained and cracked and chipped. To the casual observer, it appeared to be just another dilapidated, abandoned plantation house, but to him, it was paradise.

He navigated the overgrown bushes, trees and sundry vegetation and parked behind an old-growth magnolia, hiding the car from view. Not that anyone could see much from the road since he'd let it grow until the acreage was little more than a wilderness hiding the house and its surrounds.

"Hey, Pa," his oldest son called out from the front porch, where he was sitting in the shade playing checkers with his younger brother. "You musta had to work late?"

"Yep," he answered. "You been here since school let out, Junior?"

Junior, who was fourteen, nodded. "Yeah, and I brung Bubba with me, just like you said to." Pride etched the boy's expression, but his Pa ignored him. It was a simple task, and there were much more difficult ones yet to come, and he was going to dive right in.

"You check on her?" Pa demanded, slamming the car door and heading up the six concrete steps to the porch. "Or have you two just been out here playing games?"

Both boys' eyes fell to their hands, and their silence was all the answer he needed. Pa's jaw set so hard it ached as he ran up the steps. They were nearly teenagers, and yet they still were having trouble learning his business.

They'll learn to deal with it, he thought to himself as he pushed the heavy front door inward and crossed the threshold into the decrepit, stale manor. It was disgusting the way the place stunk, and he could only imagine if his crabby wife set foot inside. The thought made his lip curl upward as he stomped across the worn, original hardwood floors.

Every impact of his boots raised a small cloud of dust. He

Annie

wore the same pair of service-issued boots and faded coveralls whenever he visited the old house, not wanting any trace of the place on his work attire.

"There's just a bunch of mice in here," Junior called from behind him, offering whatever lame excuse for his lack of diligence he could come up with in the moment.

"You're just scared of a little girl, is what," Pa snarled, pausing at the foot of the stairs to glare at his oldest son. "She's been here for nearly three days without nobody checking on her. I can't have that. Don't want her to die before you boys ever get to—"

"I don't wanna do what you do," Junior interrupted timidly. "I don't think Mama would approve of it."

Anger simmered in his chest. He glared at the boy, shaking his head. "She just wouldn't understand," he said with a growl. "A man wants what a man wants. There's no shame in that."

Junior's face scrunched up in an exaggerated frown, and his thin, chapped lips parted as if he was going to say something more, but he didn't. He stayed silent, falling back and slipping out onto the front porch. Pa watched him go, and for a moment, he considered following him out and teaching him a lesson. But he needed to check on the girl first.

She hadn't been an intentional target, but his trip to the elementary school had dangled the dark-headed fifth grader in front of him like a carrot in front of a hungry horse. He'd spent the next two weeks stalking her, learning her schedule, her habits. She was from a good family on the north side of Chattanooga, and that had complicated things. It was easier to go for the poor, less likely to be watched girls. But this one? He was certain she was worth the risk.

His hunger to lay his eyes on the child drove him forward. He turned again and continued up the stairs.

He'd locked the girl in a small bedroom on the second floor

where he knew she'd be safe. There was a window, but he'd paid it no mind, knowing she'd sustain a severe injury if she tried to jump. The room contained no furniture, nothing other than a stained mattress on the floor. Yeah, she was safe enough; of that, he was sure.

He stopped at the top of the stairs, took a deep breath, and then made his way along the hallway, listening for the muffled sobs. They always cried nonstop for the first couple of weeks, and some never stopped. Those never lasted as long, usually falling victim to his impatience. Maybe this one just wasn't a crier.

What a relief that would be.

He chuckled to himself as he stopped in front of the old oak door, took a plastic Halloween mask from a hook on the wall, put it on, and took the key from his pocket. Involuntarily, he glanced back along the dark hallway. And it was dark. When he'd first bought the place, he'd intended to have the electricity turned on, but when the time came, he didn't have the money. Not only that, but his wife had taken to watching his seemingly every move. *Bitch!* he thought as he inserted the key into the lock and turned it, turning the knob with his other hand as the lock clicked.

He pushed the door open and stepped inside, his eyes focused on the mattress in the corner... And his heart jumped to his throat.

The girl wasn't there. He flung the door the rest of the way open and gasped as he took in the empty room. *Where the hell is she?*

His long, slender legs covered the distance to the window in a flash. The glass was broken. There was dried blood on the sill and on the remaining glass shards.

"You stupid, stupid girl," he growled to himself as he

Annie

peered downward at the patch of flattened knee-high native grass.

"Damn, damn, damn!" he shouted.

The girl could've escaped at any point over the last two days, days he hadn't had the time to visit due to work-related restrictions.

"Damn it all to hell!" he shouted, shoving back from the window, then turned and stormed out of the room, his footsteps echoing along the hallway like thunder as he ran to the stairs.

"Get the hounds, boys! She's gone!"

As he ran down the stairs, he could hear the ruckus on the front porch as his sons jumped up from their chairs. He ran out to the front door, where they met him at the threshold, their faces drained of color.

"Well? Are you both plumb deaf?" Pa roared, throwing his hands in the air. "I said, go get the dogs!"

Without a word, Junior and Bubba turned and ran down the concrete steps and dashed away, their thin arms flailing in rhythm with their skinny legs. They were both showing signs of being built just like their father: tall, muscular, with a shock of dark brown hair. Whether or not they had the same urges, Pa still wasn't sure about.

Without giving the boys a second glance, he ran down the steps, made a left and circled around to the back of the house and the spot where the girl made her escape.

He could hear the dogs baying as he stared at the broken stems of the Johnson grass and the spatters of dried blood, and he smiled, nodding to himself. The dogs should have no problem tracking her, and, more than likely, a twelve-year-old girl would have no chance of outrunning his prized trio of bloodhounds. They were often loaned to the city for search-

and-rescue duty or, on rare occasions, to track down escaped criminals. But no one knew why he *really* owned them.

"Over here, boys," he called, listening to the dogs whining as they strained at their leashes. "C'mon. Let's get them on the trail. The blood looks... kinda old. I don't know how long it's been since she jumped."

"Why the hell would she jump?" Junior gasped, looking up at the broken window. "She probably got hurt an'..."

The look of concern on his son's face bothered Pa, but he didn't say anything. It would take time to drain the empathy from his son, but he would do it. Just as it had been done to him.

"Get the dogs on the scent," Pa instructed, grabbing his youngest son's shoulders and guiding him and the dog he was trying hard to control to a splash of dried blood. "Now, go find 'em," he snapped. The bloodhound whipped around and took off, almost jerking the lad off his feet.

A minute later, his oldest son, two in hand, was racing along behind his brother, the dogs straining at the leash, with Pa following, nervously raking his fingers through his hair. He'd had plenty of kids try to escape, but he'd never had one get a head start, and it worried him. Would the girl remember anything? He didn't think so; he sure as hell hoped not. He always wore a mask, but now he wasn't sure how effective that had been.

And now she was on the run. "Shit!" he muttered to himself as he followed his sons. "She could lead 'em right back here, and if she does..." He trailed off, unable or unwilling to contemplate the consequences of that scenario. That would put all eyes on him. Yes, he had connections, and he would exercise them if he had to, but... He couldn't afford to get caught. That would ruin everything. And he couldn't have that. He had to find her, and quickly.

Annie

Not quite an hour later, three-fourths of a mile west along the roadside that bounded the property, the trail went cold. The girl, by some miracle, had escaped.

"What do we do now, Pa?" Junior asked as they stood in the ditch at the side of the road, wondering what had happened to her.

"Nothing," he answered, taking a pack of Marlboros from his shirt pocket and shaking one loose. "Can't do anything except wait and hope her memory ain't so good. She didn't see much, so..." *Shit, shit, shit!*

Chapter Two

7 years later...
July 10, 2023
11:35AM

"It's about time we made a start on some of these old case files," Chief Johnston said as he slapped a stack of dusty files on my desk, ignoring Samson's loud huff from behind me. "Ever since we disbanded the cold case unit, I've been getting pressure from the families and press and podcasters to do something."

"Thomas Drews?" I asked, frowning.

"No." Johnston shook his head. "Not your boyfriend. The victims' relatives and yuppy college students at UTC. They keep calling and asking about some of the old cases, and they are still technically active... You know the drill, Kate."

"Figures," I said with a sigh, ignoring the comment about Thomas Drews being my boyfriend. A handful of dates didn't make a boyfriend, not yet anyway. "Everyone is getting more and more interested in true crime, especially with the podcasts and documentaries and... geez, whatever the media fixates on on any given day."

Chief Johnston nodded and then tapped the top file. "This one," he said. "Emma Jacobs in particular. It's long gone cold, but her father still calls every few months or so to ask if there have been any developments. I want you to start with that one. Maybe a pair of fresh eyes will see something we missed." He stared down at the file and shook his head. "You know," he continued, "I don't think anyone's looked at it since Floyd retired."

"I'll take a look at it," I said.

"You do that, Kate, and soon," he said as he turned away. "And let me know," he called over his shoulder as he headed out of my office, leaving the door cracked open.

"Well, this is going to be interesting," I muttered under my breath as I looked at the stack of dusty files. I swiped my hand across the top and then coughed as I inhaled a lungful. "We need better housekeeping around here."

Samson snorted, and I wasn't sure if it was just a coincidence or if he actually thought what I said was funny. I was going with the latter. However, all jokes ceased when I flipped open the top file; it was pretty damn thin.

Emma Jacobs, I thought, *geez, another missing child. Will it never end?*

My heart sank. In all of my time on the force, of all the cases I'd handled, it was still the missing children that upset me most. And to make it worse, Emma Jacobs, a ten-year-old little girl, had been missing for almost four decades.

"July 25, 1986," I said aloud. "She'd be forty-seven now. A lifetime missing." The thought was sobering, and I distracted myself from it by flipping through the contents of the file,

Annie

including a witness account, several photographs of the child, and a half-dozen yellowed missing persons' flyers. But really... There wasn't much.

I read the notes of the detective in charge, Floyd Harrison. *Assumed abducted on her way home from school.* I also noted that the girl's bicycle had been found. *Two blocks from her home. Hmm.*

I pursed my lips, mulling over the amount of work reopening the case would entail, not to mention the witness who may or may not remember or may not even be still alive. "And that," I told myself, "means time is probably of the essence." But I also knew the statistics of solving a case like this, and they weren't good, especially when the only person of interest listed was the girl's father. Clearly, that hadn't panned out.

Just out of curiosity, I closed the file and pushed it off to the side in favor of the next two files in the stack. They were somewhat thicker, which meant they contained more substance, or so I hoped.

The first was a case of a murdered middle-aged woman. She'd been shot in the head while sleeping in her bed. It didn't take me fifteen minutes to decide the husband had done it... Unfortunately, there'd been no proof, and he was now deceased, so the case remained open, consigned to the morgue in the basement of the Chattanooga PD.

"Hmm," was all I had to say about that one as I set it aside, opened file number three, and flipped through the pages. *Geez, another missing girl.*

My gut clenched at the similar lack of information in this file, too. There were only *three* pages. *Damn! Who the hell...? Oh, I see. Floyd Harrison and Bruce Watson, again. Hmm.*

This girl, Louise Hackett, did not go to the same school—

or even live in the same town—as Emma Jacobs. However, they were both ten years old... And they were both abducted on the way home from school. *Well, well, well.* I checked the date. My stomach flipped. The same year, 1986. "That can't be a coincidence," I muttered, ignoring a huff from Samson. "And there's no mention of a connection to the Emma Jacobs' case." I frowned, half closed my eyes and shook my head. "What the hell?" I continued, barely hearing Samson sit up. "Surely *someone* must have explored that option?" I blew out a long breath, fluttering my lips like a horse; not the most ladylike thing to do, I know, but who says I'm a lady anyway? And I was stunned by the total lack of information in the Hackett file.

I drummed my fingers on the desk as I stared at the flimsy file. After heaving a deep breath, I leaned back in my chair and mulled it over. I didn't like the way either of the missing children's cases had been handled. To me, it seemed there'd been little work done on either case other than the initial missing person report and a couple of interviews, in both cases with the parents. Where were the coordinated searches? Interviews with the people in the surrounding area? It seemed as though no one had done anything beyond take the report and make a simple canvas of the area.

"I don't like the way this is shaping up," I muttered, "or the way it's making me feel."

I spun my chair around to face Samson, who peered up at me with an inquisitive expression. "There's nothing to go on, Sammy."

Samson shook his head violently, rattling the metal tags on his collar. Was that a shake of disagreement, or was he just being a dog? The latter, I think.

I stared at him. He stared back at me, then settled down in

Annie

his bed and closed his eyes. Clearly, he didn't feel the conflict I did.

I blew a frustrated raspberry, causing him to instantly go on the alert and raise his head, then lower it again after giving me a reproachful look.

I smiled, turned again to my desk and closed the Hackett file. I'd made up my mind. I would at least go check the evidence locker and see what was there for these cases. With the advances in DNA technology, it might be a good place to begin—if we were indeed to begin.

Oh, we're to begin, Kate, I thought. *Johnston's got his teeth into the Emma Watson case, and knowing him as I do, he isn't going to let go until I close it, one way or the other.*

I stood, grabbed the two missing girls' case files and tucked them under my arm, then said to Samson, "You coming? Or are you going to stay and nap?"

He lifted his head, then dropped it down again, resting it on his paws and looking up at me with furrowed brows. I chuckled and then headed down to the evidence locker. I wasn't sure what I would find there, but I was hoping it was more than I held beneath my arm.

I made my way across the situation room to the elevator, avoiding conversations along the way, and then down to the basement where the evidence locker was located.

"Hey, Bandy," I greeted Officer Bando by his sobriquet. An overweight, underworked uniform delegated to the nether world where very little ever happened. "I'm looking for boxes connected to these files."

He peered at the labels and raised his brow. "These are nearly forty years old," he said.

"And unsolved," I said.

Nodding, he pushed back from the desk. "Well, let's go see

what we can find. Hopefully, there's something," he said, buzzing me through.

Hopefully, I thought as I followed him into the dimly lit depths through the narrow gaps between the rows of shelves that towered twelve feet high. It was rare that I paid Evidence a visit, but I needed to see for myself if there was anything that needed to be sent off for testing. If so, I figured we might have a place to start.

"Okay, well, here's the box for the Hackett case." Harrison Bando reached up and pulled down a banker's box labeled *Hackett, Louise, November 14, 1986.* "Kinda light, ain't it?" he said as he handed it to me.

My heart sank as I flipped the lid open.

"This is it?" I said, staring balefully down at a handful of missing persons' flyers. "How can this even be evidence?"

"Uh." He squinted down at the label. "Looks like they were found in a dumpster. Like someone took 'em down and threw 'em away... I assume."

I took a deep breath, shaking my head. "You'd think there'd be more."

Bando—who, with his smooth complexion, looked to be in his early twenties, though I knew him to be in his late thirties — shrugged. "I don't know. All I can do is help you find the stuff."

I nodded. "Right. Let's move on to the Jacobs' case."

Bando took the case number and began searching. "Not seeing anything."

My shoulders fell, frustration filling my chest. "Nothing?"

"No. But let me check the system. These old cases were supposed to be logged, but there's no guarantee." Bando left me standing there, holding the box containing the flyers and nothing more, and made his way back to the computer at the front.

Annie

No wonder nothing's been solved, I thought. *There's nothing here to work with.*

At that point, I really wasn't sure what I was going to tell Johnston. Best case scenario, we *might* be able to pull some DNA from the flyers, *but why bother? Whoever put them up—probably the parents—were hardly likely to have abducted the girl... though stranger things, right?*

"It's not showing anything." Bando's voice jerked me out of my thoughts. "It doesn't show there's any evidence at all."

"Did it show this?" I held up the box of flyers.

"Yeah, that was shown, and since that case happened after Jacobs', my guess is that there either never was one, or it was lost."

"Lost," I said snarkily. "How the hell could it have gotten lost? And even if it had, it should be there in the computer, right?"

"Not hardly, Captain," he replied easily. "We didn't have computers in eighty-six, so if it got lost..." He trailed off.

"All right, I get it," I said. "So I'm screwed, then."

He slowly rolled his shoulders in an exaggerated shrug but didn't reply.

I trudged back up to the second floor without thinking about anything other than the two case files. They were awfully light, and if we *did* take it on, there would be hours of work just trying to figure out where to begin.

"Hey, Captain," a voice called just as I reached my office door.

I turned to see Anne Robar standing a few feet away.

"Anne," I greeted her, taking in the frown on her face, her eyes dropping to the files under my arm. "I was going to call you," I lied. "The chief wants us to take a look at some cold cases." I held the files out to her. "Why don't you do a little digging and see what you can find? There's not much here and nothing downstairs in evidence, either. Let me know what you think. Do we take them on or not?"

Anne took the files from me and said, "Do we even have the resources to take on cold cases?"

I shrugged. "You know the chief," I replied. "Whatever Lola wants, Lola gets. I'm sure you'll figure it out."

Chapter Three

July 10, 2023
6:30PM

After an otherwise uneventful day, I headed home, changed into my running gear, and Samson and I went for a run. Then I cleaned up, having promised to meet Harry and Amanda for dinner. It had been a while since we'd caught up, everyone being busy with their own lives and such. So, I showered, put my hair up in a ponytail, dressed in a brand new pair of black pants and a white blouse, and put on some heels. Then I settled Samson in after having fed him a heaping plate of home-made dog food—a recipe I found on Pinterest—and headed out, hating to leave him by himself, though I supposed that for one night, I could abide by the fine dining rule of no animals allowed.

My destination was Alleia, an Italian restaurant in the Southside Historic District. I was lucky enough to find a parking spot on the street less than a block away, where I pulled into the space and put the car in park.

The Emma Jacobs case still hung like a rancorous bat in the murky depths at the back of my mind. I just hadn't been able to push it away, and I intended to ask Harry if he remembered it. Granted, he wouldn't have been there at the time, but he was there before me, and maybe he knew the two detectives.

"I thought that was you," a familiar voice called out as I slammed the car door shut.

I grinned as I turned to see Harry and Amanda, arm-in-arm, walking toward me.

"Wow, you two clean up nice," I said as I took in Harry's dress jeans, white shirt, dark blue suit jacket and Amanda's knee-length black dress.

"Thank you," Harry muttered. "I prefer a more casual gig, but Amanda loves this place."

His wife nudged him playfully and then turned to me. "You look great, Kate. I was disappointed to hear that Thomas wasn't joining us."

I smoothed out my blouse and joined them on the walk to the restaurant. "He's in California on official *podcast* business," I replied.

"Sounds serious." Harry chuckled. "What's he into this time?"

"Remember the girl who disappeared on the Golden Gate Bridge about a decade ago?" I answered. "The camera footage showed her walking onto the bridge, but she disappeared."

"So maybe she fell in," Amanda said, the reporter in her activating. "Or maybe she jumped. I mean, wouldn't that be the obvious answer?"

"That *would* be," I agreed as we neared the entrance. "But apparently, the way the current was flowing the day she went

Annie

missing, her body should've washed up on the shore. Not to mention, the security footage has a gap in the timeline." I listed off the facts that Thomas had given me before he left.

Harry grabbed the front door handle, pulled it open, and stepped back for Amanda and me. "Sounds like one hell of a mystery."

"Isn't it always?" Amanda laughed as she stepped inside.

I followed behind her and let Harry take care of the reservations. Me? I was just along for the ride, and as the hostess led us to the table, I checked my phone, just in case Thomas had reached out. He hadn't.

Relationships at my age always seemed complicated, and while we were working toward something serious, we both still had our own lives to live, and meshing them together wasn't always easy.

"Here we are," the hostess said, gesturing to a corner table at the back of the room.

We thanked her and took our seats, and I peered out the window, looking out onto Main Street.

"So, how's work, Kate?" Amanda asked as she sipped on her water, and Harry perused the menu. "Busy as usual?"

"Not too bad, really," I said. "It's been fairly slow so far this summer. Well, as slow as it can be. There's always something going on, and in, I guess, some ways, we're always overloaded—but we're just not *over* overloaded right now."

"Sounds like a vacation to me." Harry laughed.

"I suppose." I chuckled, picking up my glass of water and taking a sip.

When our waiter, a young man in his twenties, appeared, I ordered a Wanderlust cocktail while Harry and Amanda chose a Pinot Noir wine. As we waited for our drinks, I took my shot to find out what Harry knew about my cold cases.

"Harry, I know you weren't working at the PD back in

1986, but do you remember hearing anything about Emma Jacobs or Louise Hackett?"

Harry's brow furrowed. "Who?"

I frowned, the question already answered by his reaction. "Two missing kids," I said. "Johnston's back on his cold case high horse and wants answers."

"They should never have disbanded the cold case unit," Harry muttered, shaking his head.

"Lack of funding, I guess," I said. "I think maybe someone's pressuring him. He mentioned the Jacobs girl's father."

Harry nodded. "When did you say they went missing?"

"1986. Both girls went missing in the same year," I replied. "The case files are thin, and..." The waiter set my drink down in front of me. I swooped it up, took a sip of the sweet drink, and wondered if I should've just gone with the wine. "Jacobs went missing on her way home from school, and the single witness made it sound like it *might* have been an abduction, but the only person of interest listed was the father."

Harry took in a long, drawn-out breath. "And there was *nothing* else? Did you check the evidence locker?"

I nodded. "I did. There was nothing. Same for the other girl, Louise Hackett, just a few missing persons' flyers. Their cases are similar, too. Louise went missing on November 14, 1986, almost five months after Jacobs."

Harry shrugged. "That doesn't necessarily mean anything. One could've been a runaway. They both could've. Maybe they just didn't list it in the file."

"Ten-year-olds?" I said, cocking my head. "Two of them?" I shook my head. "I can't see an elementary-aged child pulling off the kind of runaway that ends with them missing for nearly forty years."

"I have to agree with Kate," Amanda said. "Even in the early eighties, a missing ten-year-old should've gotten major

Annie

news coverage; two, even more so. And there was a witness?" she asked.

"Maybe the witness wasn't reliable," Harry reasoned. "There are plenty of times people just *want* it to be something dramatic. They could have ruled out abduction."

"It wasn't noted." I sighed, already thinking of the amount of work that would be involved in trying to rule it out. "If it was, it's not in the file."

"Who were the detectives assigned to the case?"

"Floyd Harrison and Bruce Watson," I answered. "They handled both cases."

Harry frowned, then nodded. "Yes, I remember them. I didn't know either all that well, but I do know that they both had good reputations. Eighty-six... whew, that was a long time ago. Before my time, and Johnston's. I think Milton was the chief back then. Oh well. I'd start by talking to the two detectives. They were closest to it. If anybody knows anything, they will."

"I think it's intriguing, the lack of information," Amanda said thoughtfully. "When a child that age goes missing, everything usually stops. How come the local media didn't get hold of it, I wonder. And the families... I can't imagine a child going missing and having no answers after forty years. That would be devastating."

I nodded as the waiter arrived to take our order. I ordered the gnocchi and then declined the offer for a second drink. I wasn't in the mood to have more than one.

"So," Amanda said and looked at Harry, who gave her a funny look, and then looked back at me. "I'm dying to know how you and Thomas are doing. I hear you've been seeing a lot of each other, right?"

I chuckled at the question. "Yes, I suppose we have, but

before you ask any more questions, we're both very busy. He travels a lot, and I work a weird schedule."

Harry nodded. "I've listened to all his podcasts. He's quite an investigator. From what I hear, he's solved quite a few cases."

"It's... impressive," I agreed.

"Oh, don't be so modest," Amanda said, laughing. "I think it's wonderful that you're seeing someone, Kate. You deserve it."

"You think?" I said, quickly changing the subject to their daughter, Jade. Harry and Amanda happily fell for the trick and talked extensively about her starting school in the fall, as well as her new hobbies and that she was already reading quite well for a five-year-old. And I listened, relieved to have the focus off of me. However, I had to admit that while they talked about their daughter, I couldn't push the two missing girls out of my mind.

Jade was five years younger than Emma Jacobs had been at the time she went missing, and I could imagine that her parents must have loved her just as much as Harry and Amanda loved Jade. And that was the most sobering moment of my evening. Her parents had been forced to deal with almost a lifetime of questions about what had happened to their child.

And all I had to work with was a few pages from an investigation that went cold thirty-seven years ago.

I excused myself early, thanking them and wishing them good night. It had been a nice evening, but not one I wanted to remember.

Chapter Four

July 11, 2023
5:45 AM

I awoke the following morning to the sound of my alarm and almost hit the snooze button, but I didn't because Samson was already up, sitting beside the bed, his tail slapping the floor. He was now considered a senior dog—I didn't know how old he was, but given the slight graying around his muzzle, I figured he must be about seven, maybe even eight—but you wouldn't know it. He still had the energy of a puppy.

"Fine," I said groggily as I flipped back the covers. "We'll go for a run."

His tongue lolled out of the side of his mouth, and I patted his head as I slid out of bed. I went to the bathroom, splashed some cold water on my face, put my hair up in a ponytail, and slipped into a pair of black Nike running shorts and a white tank top.

Even in the early morning hours, the July heat was still

oppressive, and I would be more than happy when summer turned to fall.

I downed a bottle of water from the fridge and strapped my phone to my waistband before leading Samson to the front door. I stepped out onto the front porch and looked around. It was nice living in a house in a neighborhood instead of my old apartment. The street was almost always quiet in the morning, save for a few other early-morning runners like me.

I did some stretches, took a few deep breaths, and then we headed out, down the porch steps and across the front yard to merge onto the sidewalk heading north. Samson loped along beside me, his energy at a much higher level than mine. I laughed as I shook my head at him.

I wish I had that kind of energy, I thought as my sneakers pounded the pavement. I adjusted my left earbud and pressed it once, allowing a stream of classic rock to flood in along with the rest of the sounds of the morning. I wasn't one to always listen to music on my runs, oftentimes preferring the quiet of the early morning, but occasionally, it was nice to have one earbud in and give myself a little rhythm to run to.

As we jogged, I checked the GPS, intending to clock four miles, a medium run for me because I intended to hit the gym later that day, a new habit for me. Since the owner was nice enough to allow Samson to come along while I trained, it made a lot of sense. I wasn't getting any younger, and I needed to stay in shape.

As we rounded the end of the street, coming up on the wooded area at the turnaround point, my heart skipped a beat. I took a deep breath and shook it off, reminding myself that there was no one lurking among the trees. The cyanide-wielding woman had long been put away for the murders of three lawyers, and while it wasn't impossible for someone else to be creeping around, I deemed it unlikely.

Annie

"I don't know why it still gets to me," I said to Samson as I made a sharp U-turn and headed back to the house.

He looked up at me, panting, with that goofy look on his face. Was he smiling? I like to think so. But whatever it was, it was reassuring. I picked up my pace, almost to a sprint, racing him to the front porch. It was an exercise in futility. I arrived sweating, and he arrived looking ready for more of the same.

I mounted the steps to the front porch, breathing hard. I linked my fingers at the back of my neck—which opened up my lungs—and breathed deeply for a few moments. Then I looked at Samson and said, "Well, big fella, I guess we should go get ready for work, huh?" He gave me that lopsided look and shook his head, and I grinned at him.

"I know how you feel, Sammy," I said. "I feel the same, but I'm going to have to have an answer for Johnston, and soon. He's not one to let things go."

Samson looked up at me and then huffed. Even he knew how tenacious Johnston could be, but there were, I'm sure, worse chiefs to work for. Johnston was a straight shooter, not one to be swayed by the wealthy and powerful in the city. So, while he could be an ass, as could I, we held a mutual respect for one another, and, in general, we got along. Though there had been times in the past... But I digress. I needed to get to work and see if Anne had figured anything out.

"Let's go, Samson," I called to him as I stepped up to the front door and punched in the code. I wasn't a huge fan of the keypad lock I'd had installed only a few days prior, but it was convenient. I never had to worry about making sure I carried a house key with me.

As soon as we were back inside, I fixed Samson a bowl of kibble for breakfast, started my coffee, and then headed upstairs to take a quick shower. I turned the water on and adjusted it so that it was barely warm, stepped inside, waited for my body to acclimatize, and then slowly turned it colder.

Five minutes later, refreshed and invigorated, I stepped out of the shower and dried myself off with a rough, sun-dried towel. I dressed in a pair of blue jeans and a white blouse, fashioned my hair into a ponytail, clipped my badge and Glock to my belt, and then slung my lightweight blue leather jacket over my shoulder; it was already too warm to wear it, but once I arrived at the department—someone, I'm assuming it was the chief, had the AC set at a balmy sixty-eight—I'd put it on.

"You finished up with breakfast?" I asked Samson as I entered the kitchen, noting his almost empty bowl.

He looked up at me, then turned and trotted to the back door. I smiled and followed him and let him out into the backyard to do whatever he needed to do before we left for the day. While I waited, I made myself a cup of coffee and popped a piece of wheat bread into the toaster, opting for a low-maintenance breakfast. Before it had finished, Samson was already scratching to come in.

I let him in, took my toast from the machine and slathered it with homemade apple butter, and then stood at the bar to eat it. I glanced at the clock. It was seven-thirty. I finished up my toast, tossed the paper plate into the trash, and washed my hands.

"We need to get a move on," I told my canine partner as I dumped my coffee into a to-go mug and then topped it off. After one last look around, I grabbed Samson's leash, and together we went to the garage.

Two minutes later, I backed out onto the street with Samson secured on the passenger seat beside me.

"I wonder if Anne will have figured anything out," I thought aloud as I put the unmarked cruiser into drive.

In the past, I would've stopped in at Starbucks or McDonald's, but lately, I'd been trying to cut down on my calorie intake, and every time I thought about it, I wondered why. Was it because of Thomas, or was it the fact that I was about to turn forty-five? Whatever it was, I usually shrugged it off, as I did that day.

As I neared the halfway mark of my drive, my cell phone began to buzz in my pocket. I fished it out at a red light and was surprised to see Thomas's name.

"This is Kate."

"And this is Thomas." He laughed, causing me to smile. "You do have caller ID, you know."

"It's a habit," I answered him, making a left at the light. I glanced at the clock. "Isn't it pretty early there? What, four-forty-five?"

"Yeah, but I figured I'd get an early start at the bridge. I wanted to hit it at the same time they said the girl was spotted there. And, well... to wish you good morning, of course."

I smiled. "Well, good morning to you, too."

"Still thinking about the cold cases they've thrown at you?" he asked.

"Not so much," I admitted. "There's not enough substance to either of them for me to think about, just the bare bones. I don't know if I'll be able to justify the resources."

"Fair enough. What about a private investigator? Did either of the parents go that route, I wonder?"

"I don't know. Hard to say. There's nothing in the files about any such thing. But I don't know," I said, repeating myself. "The files are so thin. I have to wonder if... I don't know, Thomas, and I won't until I dig in and look deeper."

"Files get lost, Kate," he replied, "and they get taken home, especially back in those days when police procedure wasn't what it is today. I never know what to expect when I go deep diving into an old case. Sometimes I'm pleasantly surprised, and others... Well, not so much."

"I wish I could say I was pleasantly surprised when the chief handed me this one," I said. "But anyway, I'm here now, so I need to go. Best of luck with your case. You'll fill me in when you get a chance?"

"Always. Have a great day, yourself, Captain." With that, we hung up and I put the car in park in the lot at the rear of the rather dour-looking two-story building on Amnicola Highway.

I peered into the rearview mirror and straightened out my already-frizzing hair. Then I sat for a moment, thinking.

"Damn humidity," I muttered, then turned to look at Samson. "Oh, how I wish you could talk," I said, reaching over and patting his head. He looked stoically back at me.

"Fat lot of help you are," I said. "Well, never mind. Let's go and see what they have in store for us today." And with that, I climbed out and went around to let Samson out. I clipped the leash to his official K-9 harness, and together we walked slowly to the rear entrance. Me? I was hoping for an uneventful day, which was something I always hoped for but rarely received. A captain's life is not a happy one, to paraphrase the line from *The Pirates of Penzance*. And as I headed inside that morning, my gut was already telling me that it was *not* going to be an easy day. And I didn't like that one bit.

"Captain," Anne Robar greeted me as soon as I stepped out through the elevator doors. "I think..." Her voice trailed off, and I took in my detective's disheveled look, her hair pulled up in a messy bun and the dark circles under her eyes, making me think she hadn't had much sleep.

Detective Anne Robar was four years older than me, and I'd known her almost as long as I'd been on the force. I'd requested her, along with her partner, Hawk, when I first

Annie

made lieutenant and was told to form a special major crimes unit. She was an attractive woman, not quite a beauty but... well, attractive. She wore her slightly graying hair closely cropped, emphasizing her heart-shaped face. Her hazel eyes were clear and intense, and she had the skin of one who'd spent far too long in the sun without protection. At five-ten, she was two inches shorter than me, but she carried herself well. She was short on patience and didn't take any crap from anyone. She was married with two teenage boys; one had graduated that year and was headed to UT, and the other would graduate in 2025. She was a senior detective and a good one. How she'd never made sergeant was beyond me. Maybe it was her FU attitude... who knows? Maybe it was the way she dressed: T-shirts and jeans, always. I don't think I'd ever seen her wear anything else, certainly never in a skirt. One thing I did know was that Hawk loved her like a brother.

"What is it?" I asked, noting the two files clasped firmly in her hands.

She looked me in the eye and said, "I think we need to talk. In private."

Chapter Five

July 11, 2023
8:05 AM

Anne Robar was silent as we walked across the situation room to my office, and something about that bothered me, though I couldn't put my finger on why. Maybe she'd found something. What I did know was that silence wasn't something she was known for, and that alone bothered me.

I unclipped Samson's leash and sat down at my desk.

She shut the door behind her, walked over and stood in front of my desk, sighed, shook her head, and then her shoulders drooped.

"I really think we should take on the Jacobs' case, and... and maybe Louise Hackett's as well. Both of them. I think they're connected."

I nodded slowly, taking a sip of my coffee. "Okay, I can see how you could make that assumption, given how close they are in time."

"Well, yeah, that, and I think there's a third case. Maybe more."

My gaze narrowed. "And what case would that be?"

Robar took a seat in one of the chairs across from me. "Mine."

I almost thought I heard her wrong, and so I stared at her for several seconds, trying to process what she'd just said. "You're going to have to expand on that," I finally said, shaking my head as Samson went round and sat down beside her and rested his head in her lap.

She stroked his head, staring soulfully down at him, then she began, "When I was a young girl—twelve, actually—something... *really*... bad happened to me."

My heart sank as she stumbled over her words. "Take your time, Anne," I said softly, already able to tell that the story she was about to tell was going to be monumental.

"I don't remember all that much," she continued, her eyes still on Samson's head. "I was lured into a car one day after summer school. I was on my bike, actually. Usually, I rode home with my sister, but she had practice that day, so I rode home alone. A man in a light green car pulled up alongside me. I don't remember much about the encounter." She stopped, shaking her head. "It's as if it's just blocked right out of my memory."

I knew where it was going, and I braced myself as a tear rolled down Robar's cheek. "You got in the car with him, right?"

She looked up then. "I did. I don't know why I did, but I did. He took me somewhere... to... a house... an old house. I remember spending what felt like forever trapped in a small, empty room. There was a mattress on the floor. That's all there was, nothing else. I remember it was filthy, stained. And

Annie

it's strange, Kate." Anne sighed. "I remember more about that damn mattress than I remember about anything else."

"It's a common phenomenon," I reassured her. "It's not that uncommon for children to grasp onto the finer details while blocking everything else out."

Anne nodded. "Well, that must've been what I did. Anyway, I was able to escape. I smashed the window. I had a jacket with me, and I covered the shards of glass as best I could, and I climbed through the opening. I remember it was a long way down. The jacket came loose, and I fell. I broke my arm, and I cut myself on the window glass. I don't remember much else other than running through the woods for what felt like forever."

She glanced down at Samson as if she was gathering the courage to continue. "I made it to a fence, and it took everything I had to climb over it. I don't remember someone picking me up, but I know they did. They took me straight to a hospital here in the city. My parents and the police came. I had been missing for nearly four days."

"What became of the case?" I asked, already knowing the answer.

She frowned and then snapped, "Not a damn thing, Kate. It was like once I was better, I was returned home to *heal* physically, and then the rest of it was just swept right under the rug. I remember two detectives came around asking questions, but that was it. Nothing. My family never talked about it."

"And where did this happen?" I felt as if I was interrogating her and made a mental note to ask my questions as gently as possible. "I'm so sorry, Anne."

She dismissed me with a wave of her hand. "It was nearly forty years ago, Kate. I'm fairly certain I've moved past it. In fact, I must be honest, I've never thought much about it at all...

not until you handed me these two cases." She set the two files on my desk. "They're like... They're... It's what happened to me, Kate. Especially that witness report about seeing the man in the light green car. I *know* that's the color of the car that took me. I lived on the other side of town, of course, but it's still within Chattanooga."

I nodded, taking a deep breath. "So your case file...?"

"I don't know," Anne said, shrugging her shoulders. "I came in early this morning to look for it. It should've been uploaded into the system, but it's not there."

"Have you ever looked for it before?" I asked, thinking that maybe sometime in the past she must have.

She shook her head. "I haven't. I couldn't... I just... couldn't. The nightmares stopped when I was... I dunno, sixteen or so, I guess. But..." She paused. "I really want to take on this case, Kate. I want some closure."

I was silent for a moment, mulling it over. As much as I understood where Anne was coming from—and hurt for her—I also knew there was a chance her case wasn't related, just as the two cases I'd been handed weren't connected. However...

Damn, the similarities.

"When was this?" I asked, flipping open the two files side by side so I could see the dates.

"July 10, 1986," Anne said.

"Humm, same month as the Jacobs girl," I said, what we were both thinking aloud. "And then Louise Hackett goes missing five months later... That's almost... That's..."

"Not a coincidence," Anne said, completing the thought. "There's no way that *three* girls were abducted within five months of each other and them not be connected."

"It should've been *all* over the news," I said, frowning.

"There was some coverage, but..." She trailed off and took

Annie

her phone out of her pocket. "I was able to dig up some old articles and news footage, but it's not much. It's almost as if.... Maybe they didn't want to panic the public. You know how these things can get out of hand."

I pinched the bridge of my nose, trying to ward off the impending headache. "Maybe," I said. "But surely the children's safety would have been more of the first priority."

"Maybe they didn't want the guy to run?" Anne said. "Scare him off."

"What about your parents?" I asked. "What did they do about it?"

"They reported me missing, of course, but then, when I was found, nothing. Well, we moved to South Pittsburg. But I don't remember anything else. As I said, they never would talk about it."

I looked at Samson. He was still resting his head on Anne's lap. "Are there any more cases similar to this?" I asked. "If these three cases are connected... there are probably more."

"I've yet to do any serious digging, but from what I've found so far, no."

I nodded. "Anne, you're all we've got," I said, locking eyes with her, "other than a single witness."

Anne sighed and nodded. "And that witness is in a nursing home for Alzheimer's patients," she replied. "I checked."

Almost a worst-case scenario, I thought, my gut sinking. "Which means that whatever we learn from that source won't be admissible in court, if we even get that far."

"I know," she said quietly. "But there's bound to be more people who know something, and you know..." Anne paused. "As years pass, sometimes the fear of speaking up passes as well. People... *die.* So, then, coming forward with information isn't as intimidating as it once was."

"That is true." I drummed my fingers on the desk, picked up my coffee, took a sip, and then said, "But I have to know, Anne, are you *sure* you want us to take this on? I don't want to put you through something that might traumatize you."

She nodded. "I understand, Kate, but I need this. I *know* these two cases are connected to what happened to me. It can't be a coincidence. Reading the witness report and what little there is in Emma Jacobs' file... It was like reading my own story all over again."

"We need to find your file."

"I'll start digging for it," Anne said quickly. "And I can do all the legwork myself if I need to. I know we have limited resources, but..." Again, she trailed off, and I continued to stare at her, wondering if she was too close to it and what Johnston would say when he found out that Anne had also been abducted.

"You're right," I said, breaking eye contact. "I learned a long time ago that when it comes to crime, there's no such thing as coincidence." I paused for a moment, then continued, "I do think we should brief the rest of the team, though."

I glanced at the clock. It was eight thirty-five. "Everyone should be here by now," I said, "and there is no better time than the present."

I took a deep breath, knowing I was about to commit to... what? I wasn't sure if we'd be able to find anything, but I figured it would probably make Chief Johnston happy that we were taking it on—albeit reluctantly. And now, with the trauma of one of our own. Well, I probably wouldn't mention that part to him right now.

Anne stood up with an eager look in her eyes. "So we're taking it? Right?" She brushed off her slacks, her eyes locked onto mine. "I *really* want to work on this, Kate. I want answers for the families of these girls... and for myself."

Annie

I stood up, took a deep breath, stepped around my desk and hugged her. "Gather up the team, Anne," I whispered in her ear. "Bring them in. I can't promise the whole team's devotion to it, but... well, we'll do what we can do. I'll tell the chief we're moving forward."

And hope for the best.

Chapter Six

July 11, 2023
9 AM

Anne, still clutching the two files, watched as the rest of the team trailed into my office, some looking more awake than others as they pulled out their chairs and sat down. Jack, in particular, looked bleary-eyed, and I decided to have a quiet word with him later. He looked like he needed a vacation.

I continued to watch Anne, wondering how she would be able to handle a case that was potentially dynamically intermingled with her own dark past.

I had no idea, Anne, I thought as I took my seat at the table and cocked my head to one side.

"What's up, Cap?" Hawk asked, frowning.

Arthur "Hawk" Hawkins was now almost sixty-five years old and only months from retirement. He'd been a detective for more than thirty years. He was a good-looking man: five-ten, with white hair, blue eyes, an aquiline nose, clean-shaven, and tanned face and arms. He was just a little overweight at one hundred ninety-five pounds and was wearing his signature suspenders and white shirt with the sleeves rolled up. I'd known Hawk almost from the day I joined the force, and I regarded him and his wife, Jenny, as two of my closest friends. He was a tough old curmudgeon with a big soft heart, and I was going to miss him.

"I'm not really sure," I admitted quietly. I was still trying to process what had happened to one of my own all those years ago and the gravity of not having any answers, though it wasn't unusual at the beginning of a new case. It was, after all, our job to find those answers.

"You okay, Captain?" Corbin, my partner, asked me as he took a seat next to me. "You look a little weathered this morning."

"Are you saying I'm looking old?" I said, frowning at him. "Because if you are, I *don't* appreciate that."

He laughed, shaking his head. "No, of course not, but you do look a little... *bothered*."

"Well, you're about to find out why," I told him, turning my attention to Anne. I didn't want to tell her story for her, and I figured she may or may not be ready to share her personal connection with these cases. I figured I'd leave that up to her.

Tony Cooper, Tracy Ramirez, Jack and Corbin were all looking at Anne. She was still on her feet, rocking back and forth from toe to heel. Hawk was leaning back in his chair, his arms folded across his chest, staring stoically at me.

"Would you like for me to debrief?" I asked Anne.

"No, I think I have a handle on it," she said, then turned to look at the rest of the team and began. She gave them a relatively short explanation of the two cases, focusing mostly on the witness account from the Jacobs' case.

"So, someone saw a man in a light green car lure a young girl into his car, and no one called the police?" Corbin said when she'd finished. "When did this happen?"

"1986," Anne answered. "In July of that year, and then Louise Hackett went missing in November."

"Geez, Annie," Hawk said, scratching his ear. "Really?" Hawk and Anne were partners, a team all by themselves. Their friendship went way back to a time even before I was a cop.

"Yeah, I know," she said, looking at him with a shrug.

"This is a really old case," Cooper said with a dour expression on his face. "And all we have is a single witness who saw a green car. Do we even have time for this? I mean, I definitely agree that it needs to be looked into, but... Well, we all have active cases right now."

"I know," I said. "Which is why I'm not putting the entire team on it... Not right now, anyway. We can't afford to put that kind of effort into a case that's nearly four decades old. We all know the outcome for the missing girls is grim, but I think we can agree that the families still deserve justice, or at least the closure of knowing what happened to their children."

"I agree," Ramirez said, brushing her dark hair from her face with her hand. "But it's not going to be a simple task to dig up new information on any of this. It could take months."

"Another valid point," I said as I leaned back in my chair and folded my arms. "But again, Chief Johnston wants it done, so it is what it is."

Anne cleared her throat. "And I'm already knee-deep in it, so I figure I can take it on," she said, glancing at me. "And Kate can work it with me... since the pressure is coming from the chief."

Okay, well, that's not necessarily true, I thought, feeling the urge to argue with her. But I didn't, realizing she was trying to avoid having to tell them what happened to her.

"She's right," I said. "I intend to work on it with Anne."

"Seems to me like you have your work cut out for you," Corbin said. "And you said the witness is in the nursing home with Alzheimer's?"

Anne sighed. "Yes."

Corbin shook his head but said nothing more, instead blowing out a quick "Whew."

"Tell me about it," I said. "We know it's not going to be an easy start, but we also know that all it takes to break a case wide open is a single break, and then it can go from cold to hot pretty damn quick." *And what you don't yet know,* I thought, *is that we have what may be a third victim, Anne, who also saw the green car but survived.*

"And I'm willing to chase it until I find one of those," Anne added. "I figured we could start by interviewing the two detectives who worked both cases. It's my opinion that neither case was worked properly, just some rudimentary legwork and a couple of interviews. Nothing more than that, and both cases quickly went cold."

"That's odd," Ramirez said, leaning forward and clasping her hands together on the tabletop. "Since when does a case die like that? Even the coldest cases are usually assigned to a new detective every two or three years or so. Rookies get handed cold cases all the time, and I would have thought two missing ten-year-olds would be a top priority."

"You're right, Tracy," I said, uncrossing my arms, "and that's something we intend to pursue, but right now we have a lot more questions than answers." I reached for my coffee and looked down into the cup. There wasn't much left, and the

Annie

bitter liquid had shifted from lukewarm to cold; I downed it anyway.

"I see one of the detectives is Bruce Watson," Cooper said, looking at one of the case files. "I know him. He's still fairly involved in the city. His wife attends my wife's book club."

"Then I think we'll begin with him," I said, looking up to Anne, who was scribbling something down on a notepad. The end of the pen dug deep into the paper, and her knuckles were white. That worried me, and I wondered, not for the first time, if allowing Anne to work the case was a good idea.

"Well, you'll have to keep us updated," Corbin said, breaking into my thoughts. "It's a really interesting pair of cases with so little information available. But then again, back in those days, they didn't have the technology we do. Still, there should be more, so yes, I'd say the best place to begin is with the two detectives."

"And at the time of the alleged abduction, most people would've been at work," Hawk added. "I can do a search of the archives and see if anything has been digitally uploaded. I mean, surely there must be some media files, and in a case like this, news articles may have just as much, or even more, information than the case files."

"Thanks, Hawk," Anne said and then sighed.

"You okay? Hawk asked, giving her an inquisitive look. "You look... Not good."

"I'm fine," Anne replied, "just a little tired, is all."

"Very well, then," I said, pushing back from the table. "Other than Anne, the rest of you can get back to your current caseload. I'll let the chief know what we've decided, and we'll see where it goes. If things pick up, I may request some assistance from you all, but until then, we need to keep working on the active, present-day workload."

Everyone nodded and pushed back from the table. I

glanced at Anne. She was focused on her phone. There were so many questions I wanted to ask her about what had happened to her in her past—and why the hell I had no idea she'd kept such a traumatic secret from me.

"I think we should begin with Bruce Watson," Anne said, looking up at me. "He's retired and should be home. Cooper was right. He is still very active in the community, and I don't know why he wouldn't be willing to talk about it."

"What about your family?" I asked. "Would they be willing to talk to me?"

Anne looked... sad. "My sister might," she said. "I don't know about my parents, though. No one ever talks about what happened. Like I said, it's like they swept it under the rug and forgot about it."

"Did you ever speak with a therapist?" I asked, thinking there might be some long-lost information in the doctor's file—which Anne should be able to access.

"I don't remember..." Anne answered, trailing off. "I'll ask my sister, though. She would know."

I nodded, taking her word for what it was. "Well then," I said, "for now, we'll focus on Bruce Watson. He should be able to fill in some of the gaps on the Emma Jacobs case, as well as Louise Hackett. From there... Well, let's see what happens."

Anne nodded, turned away and left my office to schedule the meeting, I supposed.

Me? I gave myself a mindless task and straightened up the chairs. It was *not* the way I had expected the day to go, and I still had to consider whether or not Anne should be persuaded to tell Chief Johnston what happened to her. My gut, however, was telling me that now was not the time. Though I was pretty damn sure he'd be totally pissed that I hadn't told him, and I knew he would find out eventually.

"I have no idea what the hell I'm doing, Sammy," I said as I

Annie

set my empty coffee mug down on the credenza behind my desk. "I just hope Anne can handle it. If it goes sideways..."

Samson lifted his head, cocked it to one side, looked up at me and huffed as if to say, *Trust her, Kate. She can handle it.* At least that's what I wanted him to be thinking.

I sighed and then whispered, "I sure hope so."

Chapter Seven

July 11, 2023
11 AM

It was a little before eleven that morning when Anne and I, along with Samson, climbed into my unmarked cruiser to go talk to Bruce Watson. I was feeling a little lethargic after a morning of paperwork and explanations to seemingly every high-ranking officer in the building, but especially the chief who, though pleased to hear I was taking the Emma Jacobs case, immediately began to pressure me as to when, what and how.

I needed a decent cup of coffee, so we decided to stop and grab some lunch along the way for two reasons: one, I needed to clear my head, and two, it would give us a chance to discuss what Anne had discovered about Bruce Watson and for me to observe her. Not that I didn't think she could handle it. As an officer, I knew she could. But this was personal, and from personal experience, I knew it could become a serious problem; lines became blurred and protocol was thrown out the window.

I parked outside of Hardee's and killed the engine. "You hungry, Samson?" I asked my canine partner as I slid out into the Tennessee summer heat and opened the rear door for him.

"I think Samson is always hungry." Anne laughed, shaking her head. "I know my dog, Tate, is always up for a snack."

I chuckled and clipped the leash onto his harness. Though his status as a K-9 officer was officially honorary, he was allowed to wear an official harness and a badge attached to his collar. "I'm sure Samson could be stuffed to the gills, but if he gets a chance to nab some human food, he's going to do it."

"That's how I feel about brownies," Anne joked, patting Samson's head before opening the door.

Once inside, I ordered a mushroom and Swiss meal with fries and a large coffee for me, and a burger for Samson. Anne ordered a cheeseburger, and I paid for everything while Anne found us a booth in the back corner. It was early and there was only a handful of other patrons, most of them getting orders to go.

I dropped Samson's sandwich to him, which he engulfed in just a handful of seconds, and I laughed at him as he sat watching my every bite.

"So, Bruce Watson," Anne began and took a sip of her Dr. Pepper. "He retired in '98, a couple of years before you joined the force. That would've meant that he worked with Harry, right?"

I shook my head, hesitated, and then shrugged. "Ninety-eight? Harry was still a rookie on the beat then. He told me he didn't know either of them all that well."

"Hmm, I see," Anne said and took a bite of her burger. "Well, there goes that."

We ate in silence for a few minutes, and I discreetly

Annie

watched her. I could see the wheels were turning in her head, and while it was common for Anne to be meticulously detailed and thoughtful, I had a gut feeling that this one was going to consume her. I don't know if she noticed or not, but she rolled up her partially eaten burger and said, "You know..." Then she paused and let out a sigh before continuing, "I was doing some research about recovering memories, like after trauma..."

"Okay..." I said, shifting in my seat to give her my full attention. "And?"

"And there's a doctor here in Chattanooga, Doctor Angelica Webber. She's supposedly really good, though from what I hear, her methods aren't... well... *conventional*. And she does past life regressions."

"Ah," I said, taking the last bite of my burger, much to Samson's obvious consternation, so I handed him a fry and told him that was it. Then I waited for Anne to continue, but she seemed to zone out, lost in her own thoughts. "Have you spoken with her?" I finally prodded her.

"Not yet," Anne answered. "I don't know how I feel about hypnosis and all that. It seems..." Her voice trailed off. "Well, it's inadmissible in court."

"That would be true," I said, leaning back in the booth. "But it's not about that, is it? It's about you and your healing process."

"I'm thinking about giving it a try," she replied and then took a sip of her drink. "I'm not sure... We'll see."

I nodded, knowing where she was coming from. "I understand," I said. "You done? If so, let's go talk to Watson."

"Trauma-induced amnesia is what I think I am dealing with," Anne said as she pulled the car door closed. "And I'm not sure if it was the blood loss or the trauma of what happened to me in that house... I wish I could remember where it was. When I jumped from that second-floor window, I broke my arm in two places and cut my other arm on the broken glass in the window frame."

"You were a tough kid," I said as I started the car. "Not many kids would've kept going after sustaining injuries like that."

Anne shrugged. "Survival kicks in."

"Sure, but I don't think that's all it is," I mused as I headed across the Market Street bridge and turned left onto Cherokee Boulevard. Bruce Watson had retired to a nice-looking two-story house on West Bell Avenue, not a particularly upscale area, but nice enough.

"While I was doing my research," Anne continued, "I found that Robert Milton, the chief at the time, was the reason that Sam Nunez, the serial killer who targeted teenage boys, was caught. That being so, I don't understand why these two missing girls didn't get the same amount of attention."

I sighed, recalling the case. I wasn't there at the time of that one either, nor was Harry. "I don't know either," I replied. "Sometimes the evidence is so sparse a case goes nowhere. Sometimes the opposite is true. This could be one of those cases. There's little enough in the two case files, but that doesn't mean that a solid effort wasn't put forth. And, of course, they didn't have the technology we have today."

"True, but anytime children go missing, I feel like it should be a priority," Anne said as her gaze drifted to the window. I understood her frustrations.

"So this doctor," I said, changing the subject. "Does she have a good reputation?"

Anne nodded, looking back at me, and said, "Oh, yeah. Apparently, her patients come from all over, which is why I think I'd like to give her a try. Just to see, you know? I mean, I don't know how I feel about hypnosis or if I'm even suscepti-

Annie

ble, but... Well, I can't remember anything anyway, so what have I got to lose?"

I nodded. "Good point," I said rather mindlessly. The wheels in my head were turning, wondering what would happen *if* Anne remembered what had happened to her. I mean, there was a chance that Anne's abduction wasn't connected to the cases we'd been handed, but from the outside looking in, it seemed to me that all three cases had to be connected. Had the detectives simply missed the connections, or had they, for some reason known only to themselves, been less than diligent in their handling of the two cases? As to Anne's case, the file appeared to be missing, so we had yet to learn who handled her case. *Maybe her parents will remember*, I thought. *But she's correct; something's not right about it, and I have no idea what it is.*

I glanced back at Samson in the rearview mirror. He looked up at me, tilting his head as if to ask me what I was thinking. Under normal circumstances, had I been alone, I would've bounced my thoughts off him. Not that he would answer, of course, but simply voicing my thoughts, even to him, seemed to give that sense of someone listening.

"This is... quite nice," Anne said as I turned onto Bell. "Not quite what I expected, but nice enough, I suppose."

"Well, retired detectives aren't exactly rich," I pointed out with a laugh.

Anne nodded but didn't seem to find it nearly as comedic as I did. "Hmm," was all she said as I drove slowly along the street, counting the house numbers.

"Here we go," I said as I pulled up in front of the two-story and obviously well-kept home. From my guess, it was about twenty-two hundred square feet, and the older gentleman mowing the front yard confirmed we were at the right place. I recognized Bruce Watson immediately, having seen his photo multiple times.

Watson didn't seem to notice us at all at first, with his red baseball cap pulled down over his eyes as he pushed the lawn mower across the yard. He made the turn, spotted the car, stopped, turned off the mower and stood, feet apart, fists on his hips, and he did *not* look happy to see the unmarked police car.

"Maybe he's just old and grumpy," Anne said, having picked up on the man's seemingly aggravated expression.

I turned to look at her. "I don't know," I muttered, my gut already sending me a warning. "Let's go find out."

Chapter Eight

July 11, 2023
12:30PM

I stepped out of the car and into the midday July heat, instantly questioning why the hell Bruce Watson was mowing the yard on such a hot afternoon. It seemed to me that it was a good way to get heat stroke, but who was I to judge? Maybe the old detective had more grit than me. Or maybe he was used to the heat. It was forecast to rise into the mid-nineties that afternoon, as I recall.

"What can I do for you?" Bruce greeted us, if you could even call it a greeting. He sounded as irritated as he looked, and I inwardly cringed at the cruelty in his tone. Normally, retired detectives didn't mind chatting with law enforcement. He'd been one of us for more than thirty years... So why act so put off by our arrival?

"I'm Captain Kate Gazzara, and this is Detective Robar," I introduced us, plastering a pleasant smile on my face. "We were hoping we could speak with you about an old case you worked on in the eighties."

"I worked a lot of cases in the eighties," he grunted, letting out a sharp sigh. "No way I can remember them all. You're better off just to use what you got in the file."

I raised my brows as he turned his back to us and rolled the lawn mower into the garage. Anne and I exchanged glances and then followed him.

"So, you don't remember the Emma Jacobs case, then?" I asked, a hard edge to my voice.

He hesitated, his back still turned to us. Just by his body language, I knew I'd struck a nerve.

He spun around, his face reddened and glistening with sweat. "Why the hell are you digging into that old case? I swear, this new era of detectives has gone downhill, always trying to solve these old cases for the fame and glory." He shook his head and shoved the mower toward the back of the garage. The front of it collided with a wall of pegboard, and Anne jumped.

What is wrong with this guy? I thought, as Samson emitted a low growl. I nudged him with my leg, a signal for him to hush. I didn't need him giving Watson a reason to kick us out. After all, he didn't *have* to talk to us if he didn't want to.

"We've been tasked to—"

"It's Greg, isn't it?" Watson cut off Anne and turned to face us, his eyes narrowed. "Greg Jacobs was always real annoying, always calling in, bugging us nonstop."

"Well, it *was* his daughter," I reasoned. "I'm sure he just wanted to know if there'd been any developments; that's reasonable enough, I would have thought."

Watson glared at me. "You oughta just let it go. We all know how this kind of case ends up. If she ain't off living her life under a different name, there's only one alternative."

Annie

I sighed. "Either way, her family still deserves the closure, don't you think?"

He didn't look the least bit convinced. "You gotta detach yourself from that train of thought. If you don't, every case that doesn't get solved will drive you batshit crazy."

"I've been working in law enforcement for more than twenty years now," I replied. By then, I was becoming irritated. Despite the respect I had for all retired officers, this one was beginning to rub me the wrong way. "We're working the case because the chief handed it to us, and we're going to do our best to solve it."

"Right; good luck with that," he grunted, wiping his hands on his T-shirt, leaving two damp smears across it. "Well, all I can tell you is to look in the case file. I don't remember a thing about that case—other than the annoying father. Kids go missing all the time. Most of them are just out playing runaway and then turn up back home. At least, that's the way it was back then."

I nodded, wondering if I should mention the other missing girl, Louise Hackett, but I didn't. He was beginning to loosen up, albeit just a little bit. "I would agree with that," I said, "but the case file is... There's nothing much there."

"One witness statement and the missing person report, to be exact," Anne added, her voice neutral.

For a split second, Watson's expression changed, then changed back again. "Why am I not surprised?" he said with a shrug. "Stuff gets lost all the time. You know that. The file gets moved a hundred times. Things fall out and get lost."

I folded my arms. "The evidence box is missing from the locker."

He shrugged again. "No idea, Captain."

Samson sat down on my left foot and stared at the retired detective. There was something about the way he was scrutinizing him. Clearly, he was picking up something I wasn't, and it bothered me. He obviously didn't like Watson, and neither did I.

"Okay, so the contents of the file are lost," Anne said, her voice flat. "The evidence is lost, and you don't remember anything about the case other than the annoying father?"

Bruce looked her dead in the face. "That's right. That's all I got. You two are wasting your time."

"How about we give you some of the details?" she said. "D'you think you might be able to remember anything then?"

Watson looked agitated, on edge. "I told you, *no*," he snarled.

"You're not even willing to try?" Anne pressed him.

"Nope!" he snapped and turned and walked away toward the garage. "I told you. I don't remember anything. Now clear off and leave me alone."

"Wait," I called after him. "One more thing."

Watson stopped, shook his head, then turned to face us.

"What?" he snapped.

"What can you tell us about Floyd Harrison?" I asked. "He was your partner, wasn't he?"

Watson burst into a fit of stilted laughter. "He was an odd fella, Floyd. He damn near went crazy trying to play detective. He was better off working somewhere else. He quit in '87. It wasn't working out for him."

"I see," I said. "And d'you know what happened to him?"

"Yeah," Watson replied. "The guy threw away all his benefits, bounced around from job to job. He works at some little hole-in-the-wall grocery store out in Spencer, so I heard. Never could understand his reasoning. Guess he had a weak mind."

"You don't know why he quit?" I asked. "He was your

partner, after all, for six years, right?" I couldn't imagine not knowing why your partner of six years would quit like that.

"Floyd Harrison had a great track record at the force," Anne added. "He solved multiple cases—"

"Just because he was a good detective didn't mean he had a good attitude," Watson snapped. "He couldn't handle the work we were doing. You don't know what you're talking about. You didn't know him. All you got to go on is his damn record. I knew him. He was a frickin' head case, is what he was."

"Okay, Mr. Watson," I said, figuring it was time to quit before it got hostile, and, by the look on Anne's face, it was headed that way sooner rather than later. "Thank you for your time." I stepped forward and handed him my card. "If you think of anything that might be helpful, please give me a call."

He looked at it but said nothing, then turned and strode away into the garage, leaving us standing there. He took one last look at us, shook his head, and walked into the house, slamming the door behind him.

"Well, that went well," I muttered caustically as I turned away and led Samson back to the car. Bruce Watson wasn't what I'd expected, and with every minute that passed during that short, volatile interview, the more I realized we needed to talk to Floyd Harrison sooner rather than later.

"D'you think Watson's still in contact with Harrison?" Anne asked as she pulled the car door shut. "Maybe he's still talking to him, keeping tabs on him."

I was thinking the same thing. "Well, here's my take on it," I said as I started the engine. "I find it strange that Harrison is long gone from the force, but Watson still knows where he is. Why wouldn't he have lost touch with him after all these years if he really thought that poorly of him?"

"You'd think," Anne said, snapping her seat belt. "But I

think we need to take a ride to Spencer sooner rather than later. It's a small town. Shouldn't be too hard to find him, and if all else fails, we can stop in at the local PD. They'll know."

"Right," I said as I pulled away from the curb and headed to Highway 111. "Let's do it and hope that Watson hasn't warned him we're coming."

"Don't you think there's something fishy going on?" Anne asked as the GPS chimed. It was a one-hour and three-minute drive north of the city.

I looked at her and raised my brows.

"I do," she said with a shrug.

"All I can say is this," I said. "I have never met a retired detective quite so abrasive. He sure as hell didn't want to talk to us, did he? And you know damn well he knows more about the case than he's letting on—has to—and I have to wonder what he's hiding—and why."

Chapter Nine

July 11, 2023
2:15PM

It took a little over an hour to drive to the small town of Spencer, some sixty-five miles to the north of the city. We drove for the most part in silence. I was, as usual, lost in thought, and I could tell Anne was, too. Watson's reaction to our visit was unexpected, and because of that, I had to wonder if we'd get the same reception from Harrison.

I pulled into the lot outside Lyle's One Stop and parked right out front. "Ready?" I asked, turning to look at Anne.

She nodded but didn't say anything. She unbuckled and opened her door. I grabbed Samson from the back seat, eyed the *Absolutely No Pets* sign, and shook my head. We entered the store and looked around. It was welcoming, and I immediately noticed how clean and tidy it was. The produce section was filled with what was purported to be locally produced vegetables, the aisles were neat and clean, and the shelves were fully stocked. *Nice,* I thought as we stepped up to the counter.

"I'm Captain Gazzara, Chattanooga Police Department, and this is Detective Robar," I said to the young woman behind the counter. "Does Floyd Harrison work here? Is he available?"

"Floyd?" The young girl's dark brows shot up in surprise. "Why? Has he done something wrong?" She appeared to be genuinely concerned. And then I noticed the employee of the month awards on the wall behind her. Floyd Harrison was recognizable only by his name.

"No, he hasn't done anything," Anne answered. "We just wanted to talk to him. Is he around?"

"Oh?" She looked genuinely confused. "Um, yes, he's around back. There's a truck supposed to be here in about thirty minutes. He's just getting things ready for it."

"Is it all right if we go and chat with him?" I asked.

She nodded. "I'm sure it's fine. It's that way, through the double door. You'll see."

"Thank you," Anne said, nodding to her, and we headed to the rear of the store and through the doors into a large storage area. It was hot out there. I looked around, taking in the rural setting, noting the farm just beyond and behind the store.

"Interesting place to work," I commented mostly to myself as Samson and I followed Anne. She walked with determination, and I let her lead, curious about the approach she was going to take with Harrison.

We knew Floyd Harrison was quite a bit younger than Bruce Watson, and I tried to do the math in my head. Watson had to have been pushing eighty. *He'd said Harrison quit the force in 1987. Thirty-six years ago. So, how the hell old was this ex-cop who was now working at a gas station? He looked to be*

Annie

in his mid-sixties. That would have made him no more than twenty-nine when he quit. How quickly had he been promoted to detective?

"Floyd Harrison?" Anne called out.

The salt and pepper-haired man turned to her, a confused look on his face. "Yes?" He was tall and slim, with a lean face and a scar under his left eye. He was wearing a T-shirt with Lyle's One Stop emblazoned across the front and a pair of worn jeans. He looked at Samson, then at me, then at Anne.

"Cops?" he said. "What can I do for you?"

I introduced us and watched as the color left his face. He glanced around as if he was looking for someplace to run, but he didn't. He looked as guilty as hell. *What is it with these guys?*

He cleared his throat, sighed, rolled his shoulders, and then said, "Okay, what do you want?"

Anne glanced at me. I nodded. She looked back at Harrison and said, "We're looking into one of your old cases. Emma Jacobs. Remember that one?"

He nodded, but instead of becoming belligerent like Bruce Watson had, his expression morphed into one of somber resignation.

"Sorry," he said quietly, looking down at the floor. "I can't help you. I don't know anything other than what's in the file."

"There are only three pages in the file, including the missing person report," Anne replied through gritted teeth. "There has to be more to it than that."

He didn't look up but said, "Yep."

"We talked to Bruce Watson," I said. "He wasn't too forthcoming. He said there might've been more, but it probably got lost. What d'you think?"

"I'm not surprised," Harrison muttered, shaking his head. "I can't tell you anything you don't already know... Look, take my advice; you'd be better off steering clear of that whole damn mess."

"Why's that?" I asked, noting the way Harrison appeared to be visibly folding in front of us. He *knew* something, and I knew it.

Floyd finally looked up at me. "I can't help you, Captain Gazzara. I got people I care about. I can't—" He paused, looked around, then said, "I can't talk about it, okay?" He turned around and went back to moving a stack of flattened cardboard boxes. "Y'all ought to let it go, too."

Nope, not happening, I thought to myself. *Definitely not, now.*

"Were there any suspects, persons of interest?" Anne asked, pushing him. "Anything at all?"

Floyd continued to shake his head, moving more stacks. "I don't think y'all understand what you're getting into. There's a reason I quit, and I don't want no part in that mess."

"You keep calling it a mess," I said. "Why?"

He slammed the stack of boxes down and then turned and glared at me. "Let me tell you something, *ma'am*; it *is* a mess. You went and talked to Bruce, huh?" Harrison was growing agitated, his jaw nervously ticking. "I'll bet he told ya to get the hell away from him. Well, there's a reason."

"But were there ever any suspects?" Anne insisted, her frustration mounting. "There had to be rumors. Something?"

Floyd threw up his hands. "Of course, there was! There was tons of rumors. We thought ole Greg Jacobs himself did it. He was a strange cat, always poking around and acting suspicious."

"Did you clear him?"

"No idea," Floyd snapped. "No idea, no idea, no idea." He went back to stacking the boxes, and I started to wonder if his mind was all there. Had he seen something that caused

Annie

PTSD? I knew a mental tick when I saw one, and I was aware that's what was going on with Harrison. The man was trembling as he worked, and I was beginning to worry he was about to have a breakdown.

Anne opened her mouth to say something, but I held up a hand and stopped her. "It's okay, Mr. Harrison," I said gently. "I won't ask you any more questions. Thank you for your time. I'm sorry we bothered you." I handed him one of my cards. He took it and stared at it for a moment, then shoved it in his pants pocket and went back to work without looking up.

I nodded to Anne and then gestured back to the car. "If you think of anything or remember something you think might be important, please let us know."

He didn't say anything. I turned away, but Samson wouldn't move. I tugged at his leash. The dog pulled me toward Floyd.

"Come on," I muttered under my breath. "Let's go, boy."

Floyd looked at Samson and his face softened. "Always did like the canines." Something in his voice triggered me to release Samson, and he went barreling over toward Harrison. Floyd knelt down and bearhugged Samson, rubbing his face into the long fur around his neck, almost like he was cuddling a child.

"Good boy," I heard him whisper in Samson's ear.

Anne and I exchanged glances, both of us surprised by what we were seeing.

"I hope you find her," Harrison said as Samson came back to me a few moments later. "And bring hell down on who did it." He stood up, turned away and went back to work.

I stood watching him for a moment, but he didn't look at me. I considered having another go at him, but then I thought better of it. If Floyd wanted to talk, he could come to us when he was ready. "Thank you for your time," I said, retrieving the leash and then turning to go back into the store.

"I worked as a detective for six years," Harrison said as I turned away. I stopped and turned to face him.

"I put in the hours in uniform," he said bitterly. "I made detective by the time I was twenty-five. Can you believe that? Young, ambitious. That's what I was. I thought I was gonna save the world, solve every case that came across my desk."

I nodded, walking slowly back toward him. "I think that's what we all want," I said quietly.

He nodded, a somber expression on his face. "Yeah, well, it didn't work out that way for me. Them little girls, they just kept going missing, and no one wanted to do a damn thing about it, Captain. I had the answers..." His voice trailed off, and all the alarms went off in my head.

"What do you mean?" Anne jumped forward. "You had the answers?"

He instantly shook his head. "Nope. I just mean, I thought I had the answers. Sorry." He shook his head again and then turned away. "I don't know what the hell I was saying. Sorry."

Something is wrong with this guy, I thought, breathing out. "Look, Floyd," I said. "I understand how you feel. It's hard to take when little kids are involved. Just take it easy, okay? You have my number. If you want to talk about it, you can give me a call, anytime, night or day."

"Okie doke," Floyd mumbled under his breath. "Best be on your way now."

This time, Samson started dragging me toward the car, and I followed his instigation, though my brain was hanging on the last words of Floyd's mumbled and jumbled diatribe.

I had the answers...

Did he really have the answers? Or was he just stumbling and mumbling? I couldn't be sure, but the way he referred to

Annie

the girls in plural made me think *someone* had connected the cases—and that *someone* was Floyd Harrison.

So why quit? I asked myself, glancing back at the mumbling, twitching man as we made our way back into the store. *Why give up if you "had" all the answers? Is he just full of shit, or?*

Something in my gut was telling me he wasn't, that he did, indeed, have the answers.

Chapter Ten

July 11, 2023
3:30PM

"That was weird," Anne said as soon as we were back in the car. "That was *so* weird."

I nodded, still trying to process it. "It was... different, that's for sure."

"You think maybe he's losing it, or d'you think there's some credibility to what he was mumbling about?"

"I'm not sure," I said as I pulled out onto the main road. "I'm not even sure I can even make an educated guess."

"I'm thinking he was run off," Anne said thoughtfully. "I think he knows something, and I think there's a reason why no one wants to talk about it. And did you hear him, Kate? Did you hear what he said? He was talking about missing *girls*, not just one, and he knows they're all connected. I'm telling you, Kate, he *knows*."

I didn't answer. I just looked at her. I could tell she was

now heavily invested in the case and that, for her, it was personal, and I didn't like the way it was going.

My silence must've made her aware of what I was thinking because she sighed, shook her head in what appeared to be frustration, and said, "Sorry, Kate. It's just that I have a feeling someone knows more than they're telling, and it's frustrating. I find it intriguing that Detective Harrison was once so eager and ambitious, and then his career tanked so precipitously. Don't you find that a little strange?"

"This case is starting to feel that way," I admitted, unable to shake off the feeling. Floyd Harrison's interview left me feeling decidedly uneasy, and I couldn't figure out if it was just the way he appeared so troubled or if it was more than that. "I don't know what I think about it," I said, "but I do know we have a lot more digging to do, and I think we can write off the two detectives. We're not going to get anything more out of either of them."

"No kidding," Anne muttered. "But maybe Floyd will come around. He seemed like he wanted to talk, but something was clearly holding him back."

"I don't think he was all the way there," I said. "It seemed to me he was exhibiting signs of mental stress, maybe even PTSD."

"Yeah, PTSD," Anne agreed. "I thought that, too. And what about the way he connected with Samson? You know how Samson is; he either likes you or, well, you know better than I do. He took to him immediately, and that, to me, means he can't be all bad, right?"

"That was strange," I said, glancing up at the rearview mirror. "I've never seen him do anything like that before. Hah, maybe he was a service dog. Give me a minute, will you? I need to think."

She nodded, and we drove the rest of the way in silence.

Annie

Me? I tried to get a handle on the two detectives. I couldn't. All I could think of was that they were both hiding something, something to do with the two missing girls and possibly Anne's abduction, too.

"I think I'm going to call Doctor Webber," Anne said as we stood outside my office a little while later.

I sighed. "Okay. If you want to give it a try, go for it."

"I know it's a bit unusual," she said, "but I think it's worth a shot. If I could recover my memory, I could be a key player in solving the case."

"If they're related."

"Oh, come on, Kate," Anne said. "We know they are."

"Well, we're assuming they are," I said. "We have to be careful. Tunnel vision could lead us down the wrong rabbit hole, and we both know that's happened more often than we'd like to admit, and it's not somewhere I want to go, capiche?"

"I know, I know," Anne said. "I'll figure it out. See you tomorrow, Kate." And with that, we parted ways, and I led Samson into my office to gather the rest of my things to head home for the day. I knew Anne wasn't going to let up. And I knew that if I was in her shoes, I wouldn't either. But why after all these years?

It must be because the Emma Jacobs case hit a raw nerve with her, I thought, *brought it back to the forefront of her mind.*

I shut down my computer, and as the screen went black, I happened to catch sight of a file on my desk I hadn't seen before. The label on the front read, *Smithson, Anne, "Annie."*

I straightened up, frowned, and grabbed it. There was a blue sticky note attached to the front of the folder, and I recognized Chief Johnston's handwriting.

Thought you might be interested in this.

"Smithson is Anne's maiden name," I mumbled to myself, tucking the file under my arm. "He knows. Let's go, Samson."

I made a beeline straight to the chief's office, but when I got there, the door was already locked and the lights off.

Damn it, I thought. *I'll have to catch him tomorrow.*

"Well, let's just go home then," I said to Samson. He looked up at me and showed his teeth in that signature smile of his. I never knew a dog could smile until Samson came along, and while his origin would always be a mystery to me, there was never a question that he was one of a kind.

And so we headed home, leaving the PD and making the twenty-five-minute drive through the late afternoon traffic to my house. I skipped the heat by pulling straight into the garage and closing the door as soon as I had cut the engine, then I climbed out and let Samson out before I picked up the file I had left on the console. I still hadn't opened it; I was nervous about what I would find inside.

"I'll look after we clean up and eat," I told Samson. I really needed to either hit the gym or go for a run, but I wasn't feeling it. Instead, I checked my phone to see if I'd missed anything from Thomas, but I hadn't. I set it aside, feeling a little disappointed.

I filled Samson's bowl with kibble and gave him fresh water, and while he ate his dinner, I took a shower and then opted to Door Dash some Chinese food, shrimp in garlic sauce, to be precise. Once Samson was done, I cleaned up after him and let him out into the backyard to do his thing, and then I settled down to wait for my food. It arrived some fifteen minutes later, by which time I'd realized I was close to starving.

After my food arrived, I set it down on the kitchen table where I'd left Robar's file.

"Well... I guess we should take a peek," I said to myself, feeling as if I was about to invade her privacy, though I knew

Annie

that Johnston wouldn't have set it on my desk had he not thought it was something I should see.

I opened the box of shrimp in garlic sauce first and then the fried rice, and I built myself a plate. Then I sat down, and before I even took the first bite, I flipped the file open. My heart sank at the sight of a young Anne Robar, though back then her name was Anne Smithson, Robar being her married name. And, apparently, she was affectionately called Annie.

I unclipped the initial missing person's report and took it out of the folder. Unlike Emma Jacobs' file, there was a lot more content in this report.

Well, sort of.

Anne had told me she'd been riding her bike and never made it home, and that's what I read. The report continued onto a second page, on which was affixed a 5x7 picture of her in the hospital. The fall she had taken had broken her arm in multiple locations, and when she was picked up by a Good Samaritan, she had been in rough condition.

Who was the Good Samaritan? I wondered as I dug through the pictures and papers, desperate to find the location where they'd picked her up. But there was nothing. "What in the world?" I said aloud, my frustration growing. *Why the hell would they not have taken this information?*

I read over the notes and saw the two detectives assigned to the case were, of course, Bruce Watson and Floyd Harrison. Were these two just *that* bad at their job? Where was the oversight? What? The more I flipped through the folder, the angrier I grew. There was no location for her pickup, and there was no name given for the person who found her.

"This is absolutely ridiculous," I groused, slamming the folder shut so hard Samson jumped up from where he was sitting beside the table.

"I have to talk to Chief Johnston about this tomorrow," I

muttered. "This is an absolute disgrace to the department and to the families of these girls. How could we not have cared what happened to them?"

Samson whined loudly, then put his head on my thigh. I stroked the fur on top of his head, calming myself down as I pushed the folder away with my other hand. I heaved a deep breath and turned my attention to my dinner, but by then my appetite had failed me. I wasn't hungry anymore.

I took another deep breath, then forced myself to lean forward and smell the contents of my plate. The food smelled amazing, and the lure of the sweet sauce caused my stomach to growl. "Maybe I am hungry after all." I chuckled down at Samson, who by then was drooling on my black knit shorts. I curled my nose up at him but gave in and scraped a little of the rice and sauce onto a side plate and gave it to him.

"That's it," I said. "No more, though. You don't need to eat this stuff." And with that, I dug into my dinner, though every so often, I glanced over at the file. I had so many questions, and while I knew Chief Johnston wouldn't have the answers, at least he could back me up if I ended up on a war path of my own making. And that's exactly what I planned to do. Someone was hiding something, and I planned to find out who and what, no matter what it took or whose toes I trod on.

Chapter Eleven

11:43PM
July 11, 2023

I hadn't been in my bed for more than an hour when I was awakened by my phone ringing. I reached out and grabbed it from the nightstand. "Gazzara," I grumbled groggily.

"There's been a car wreck at Frazier and Forest Avenue, Captain," an unknown voice said crisply. "They need you there ASAP."

"Who is this?" I gasped, sitting up in bed.

"Lieutenant Harper, Traffic," the voice replied.

I rubbed my eyes with the back of my hand. "Car crash?" I asked. "Why d'you need me for a car crash?" I still flipped back the covers, swung my legs out of bed, turned on the bedside lamp and looked at the clock. It was 11:43. *What the hell?* I thought as I sat there on the edge of the bed for a moment, looking around, disoriented.

"It's a homicide," Harper said. "And the Chief said you'll want to see it."

I heaved a sigh, stared at the floor for a moment, then gathered myself together and said, "Okay. I'm on my way. Don't let anyone touch anything. I'll be there as soon as I can." Then I hung up the phone.

I could've asked for details, but what was the point? I'd learn soon enough, and the fact that Chief Johnston was involved had me feeling decidedly uneasy. It was almost midnight, and the chief should be at home sleeping. Someone must've called him because... Hell, I didn't know, but it had to have been an emergency, and that made me pick up the pace.

I let Samson out into the backyard while I finished getting dressed. I threw on a pair of jeans and a T-shirt, made coffee, and some fifteen minutes later we were on our way.

It had been quite a while since I'd been called out in the middle of the night, but as usual, one of my team members had also been alerted, and again, I had to wonder what the hell was going on.

I drove across the Market Street Bridge, lights flashing, and turned right onto Frazier and immediately saw what appeared to be a half-a-hundred red and blue lights flashing a couple of blocks away. It was, in fact, only a half-dozen blue and white cruisers, two fire trucks, an ambulance and several unmarked cruisers.

I pulled up behind one of the unmarked, put Samson on his leash and let him out. We walked the short distance to the wreck site at the corner of the two streets. An old nineties model Ford F150 was crunched on the front end, where it had struck an iron light pole, and its passenger side front fender crumpled.

Well, now, what have we here? I wondered as we made our

Annie

way to the taped-off area. *It's not much of a wreck. He couldn't have been doing more than ten or fifteen miles an hour.*

I didn't recognize any of the night shift faces, but they knew me.

"You're gonna wanna see this, Captain," one of them said as I ducked under the yellow tape. I eyed the small crowd of onlookers and followed him to the wrecked truck.

"This is the wildest crash I've ever seen," the officer said. "I thought the ole boy must've been drunk, but then I got a closer look..." His voice trailed off, probably because he caught the look on my face when I saw the driver.

You have to be kidding me, I thought.

"Captain?" the officer said. "You know this guy?"

I sighed, wiping a bead of sweat from my forehead. "Yeah, I know him," I replied. "His name's Floyd Harrison. He's a retired cop."

"Yeah, that's right," the cop said. "I ran the plate, and that's the name that came up."

And that's why Chief Johnston told them to call me, I thought.

"Give me a rundown," I said as I approached the faded red and white truck. I wasn't asking for much; the driver's side window was rolled down, and I could see the gunshot wound to the side of his head.

"Uh, we got the call at seven minutes after eleven, anonymous," he said. I checked his name tag. It read K. Jolly. "I was first on the scene. There's not much more to tell. We canvased the area, but no one saw anything. Looks to me like someone pulled up alongside and shot him, right?"

"Did you check the cameras?" I asked, walking around to the front of the truck.

"There are no cameras," Jolly said.

"Story of my life," I grumbled. "They never are when you need them... So this is it, then? You have a victim with a gunshot wound to the side of the head, no witnesses, and no cameras?"

He gave me a sheepish look. "Yeah... But we're going to keep looking."

"Hah!" I said. "You called CSI, right?" I asked, more for something to say than to question the officer. I already knew Mike Willis and his team would be on the way. Doc Sheddon, too.

The officer nodded, possibly too afraid to answer me.

"Right," I said. "I need you guys to keep everyone back. This is going to be a tough enough scene to process without a crowd of looky-loos getting in the way. Back 'em off a block in every direction."

He nodded again, turned and walked away.

Me? I stood there staring at the murdered ex-detective, wondering what the hell was going on, and I didn't like the look of anything I was seeing. I was certain it was no coincidence that less than twenty-four hours after my visiting Floyd Harrison, he'd turned up dead.

What were you doing in Chattanooga, anyway? I wondered. *I wish you would have answered my questions. If you had, maybe you'd still be alive.* And then I regretted not having pressed him harder, but hindsight is always twenty-twenty. And then my phone began to ring in my pocket. I fished it out and answered it.

"Chief," I greeted Chief Johnston. "What are you doing up at this time of night?"

"Yeah, well," he muttered. "I assume you've made it to the wreck off Forest."

"Yep," I answered him, stepping away from the group of officers. "I take it you heard who the victim is."

Annie

"Couldn't sleep," he said. "Had the scanner on. Kate, did you speak to him today?"

"I did. Yesterday, actually," I replied, glancing at my watch. "Anne and I drove to Spencer. He didn't have much to say. It's odd he's here in Chattanooga."

"I find it odd that he ended up dead right after you interviewed him," Johnston said. "Look, I rarely get into your business, Kate, but I know Anne's history. I knew it when she was hired."

"Are you trying to say—"

"*No,*" he cut me off. "I'm not saying Anne's implicated in anything. What I'm saying is that if someone is willing to cut out an ex-detective, a detective who was involved in these cases, then they might be willing to cut out the one surviving victim."

"So you think Anne's abduction is connected to the Jacobs case, too?"

He was silent for a moment, then I heard him sigh. "We can't go jumping to conclusions, but, as you know, the most obvious answer is usually the correct one. Get to the bottom of it, Kate, and keep your head down. I have a bad feeling about this one."

"Will do," I said and disconnected the call. I was about to stuff the phone back into my pocket when I received a text from Tracy Ramirez to let me know she was on her way.

Maybe I should've sent a message to Anne, but I needed some time to digest what had happened. It could wait until morning.

"Well, it looks like I beat Doc Sheddon this time," Mike Willis said, smiling, as he watched his team begin to unload their equipment. "What a rarity."

"Oh, I'm sure he's on his way." I chuckled, lightening up a little. While Johnston's bad gut feeling seemed to hang over my head like a thunderhead, I did my best to shake it off. It wasn't all that uncommon for drive-by shootings to happen, so this one *could* be random. But no, it was too much of a coincidence. Someone wanted to shut Floyd Harrison up.

"Looks cut-and-dried," Willis commented as we made our way over to the truck. "I figure someone pulled alongside and shot him, and he rolled into the pole. It's not the first time I've seen something like this. Probably road rage. It's becoming more and more prevalent these days. Someone cuts someone off. He gets angry, pulls a gun, and bammo."

"Bammo?" I said, grinning. I shook my head. "Maybe, but I don't think so. I talked to the guy only yesterday. He's an ex-cop, a detective."

"No shit?" Willis said, his eyes wide.

"Yeah, no shit," I replied. "I'll let you get on with it." And I stood back, watching as Mike's team began to work. I looked back along the street. There were no skid marks, and judging by the lack of serious damage and the downward slope toward Frazier, I figured Harrison must have taken his foot off the gas and was slowing as he approached the traffic lights. That being so, it would have been easy for the killer to pull up alongside and shoot through the open driver's side window. *Poor guy probably didn't know what hit him,* I thought. *Hmm, so you were coming south on Forest. Where the hell had you been, I wonder?*

I looked north, in the direction from which Harrison had come, then nodded. *West Bell Avenue?* I thought. *Could be. Did you go to see Bruce Watson? That would make sense. Hah!*

I sighed, bent down and stroked Samson's head.

"What a mess," I muttered as Doc Sheddon pulled up and got out of his big black SUV, babying a cup of coffee in his hand.

Annie

"Kate Gazzara," he called as soon as he saw me. "I wasn't expecting to see you here."

"Well, here I am," I said, walking across to him. I reached out and took the huge Styrofoam cup from him and sipped on it.

"That's enough, Kate," he said, snatching it back, chuckling.

"Fun change for me to grab your coffee," I said, smiling at him. "It's usually the other way round."

"As you say," he said dryly. "Hey, Sammy." He reached down and patted his head. Sam managed to get a lick in on his hand before he snatched it away.

"So," he said and took a sip. "Let's go take a look at this fella. I heard he was once a detective. Name of Harrison, I believe."

"Did you know him?" I didn't know why I even asked. Doc shook his head.

"No, sure didn't. I might be ancient, but I'm not *that* old." He laughed in his own stilted way and then ducked under the tape, leading the way to the truck. He greeted Mike Willis, and the two exchanged some sort of pleasantries—or maybe not-so-pleasant pleasantries—and then Doc got to work. He snapped on a pair of latex gloves and jerked the driver's side door open.

"Gunshot wound to the left temple," he stated, leaning in, squinting at the body. "Clean shot. Probably a 9mm. Time of death? Not more than an hour or so. You should be able to figure it out for yourself. It was probably only minutes before it was called in."

"Eleven-oh-seven," I said. "That would put the time of death right around eleven?" I asked.

"Probably," Doc said as he grasped Harrison's jaw and turned his face toward him.

I sighed, took out my phone and glanced at the screen, knowing it was time to bring in my entire team—something I really hadn't wanted to do. But Harrison's death, if it was connected, and I was now almost certain it was, was an escalation, and our cold case was suddenly feeling very warm.

Chapter Twelve

July 12, 2023
7:15 AM

After a long, grueling night of working the crime scene, Ramirez, Samson, and I made it back to the office—Ramirez was in her car and I was in mine. I handed her a twenty and asked her to stop at Hardee's along the way and get breakfast for both of us. I'd already texted my team and asked them to assemble in my office at eight that morning.

It was seven-fifteen when I stepped into my office. Samson went straight to his bed and settled in. I started the coffee, already battling fatigue from lack of sleep. Ramirez arrived ten minutes later, set my breakfast down on the desk, and dropped down into the chair in front of my desk.

"What a mess," she commented as she unwrapped her sausage biscuit from McDonald's. "I've never heard of a detective being murdered like that."

"Me either," I admitted, hesitating to say anything more. Anne still hadn't told the rest of the team what had happened to her and how there was a chance she was closely connected to the case. I figured it was probably best if it came from her, and I wasn't yet absolutely sure that Anne's abduction was connected, and if it wasn't, it was irrelevant. And if it was, her case file contained a lot of photos but little more information than the other two files, and her lack of memory was a real problem.

I wonder if there's an evidence box, I thought as I took a sip of my coffee.

"You're quiet, Kate." Ramirez gave me one of those looks. "Not feeling well?"

"No, I'm fine," I told her, shaking my head. "Just a long night, I guess. And I was thinking that Floyd Harrison knew a lot more about the case than he said he did."

"Yeah, you mentioned that," she said. She took another bite of her breakfast sandwich, eyeing Samson, who was still noisily chowing on his own sausage biscuit. "How could anyone have known that you were talking to him, though?"

I pondered the question. "You can count the ways," I said. "He could have called Bruce Watson, or Watson could have called him, or, after we talked to him, he could've assumed we'd hunt Floyd down? After all, Watson was the one who told us where Harrison worked. And, finally, I have a feeling there's someone here in the department with an axe to grind."

"No kidding," she said, nodding. "What makes you think that?"

"Just a gut feeling," I replied and leaned back in my chair, coffee in hand.

"Should we pay Watson a visit?" she asked.

I shook my head. "Not yet," I said. "There's more to do

Annie

here yet, and I want to bring the rest of the team up to speed. They should be here soon."

"But if Watson did have something to do with the abductions," she said, "then... it would mean..."

"At this point, we can't make any assumptions," I said. "Assumptions are dangerous. You know that, Tracy. We need evidence, and that means we have to go to work, all of us."

She nodded thoughtfully, but I could see by the look on her face that she'd already made up her mind about Watson.

We finished our breakfast just as the rest of the team began to file in, all of them giving me wary looks as they took their seats. None of them knew what had happened, including Anne, and I didn't like the idea of dropping it on her out of the blue. But, given the events of the last nine hours, I didn't have much of a choice. All I wanted at that point was to get the rest of the team up to speed and moving in the same direction.

"You two look like you've been up all night," Corbin said as he sat down. "And that's never a good sign."

"No, it's not, especially in this instance," I replied as I grabbed a napkin and wiped the corners of my mouth.

"What happened?" Anne asked, giving me a curious look as she settled into her chair.

I sighed. "Floyd Harrison was murdered last night, shot to death in his car at the corner of Frazier and Forest." Anne's mouth dropped open. She was speechless.

I gave them the short version of the events of the evening and of the day before. They remained quiet throughout. I finished my precis, then looked at each one of them in turn.

"Any comments?" I asked.

"You think someone knew?" Cooper asked.

"I think so," Ramirez said. "And I think we need to go take a look for security footage. I know they say there is none, but there are a lot of doorbell cams out there. I think we should canvass the streets in both directions. We're looking for a red 1998 F150 and a second vehicle following close behind."

"Good idea," I agreed. "You and Cooper can handle that."

"We need to find more witnesses, or just any witness," Hawk added. "We need to go talk to people, check out the bars. I don't mind picking that up."

"Why don't you take Corbin with you?" I suggested, eyeing Anne. I could see something in her expression, and I wanted to speak with her in private.

Corbin nodded.

"Anne and I need to dig into the notes we took yesterday," I said. "And then we'll figure out where to go from there. We'll meet back here at five."

Corbin nodded and said, "Sounds good to me."

"Great." I clapped my hands together. "Let me know what you find out, and try to have reports on my desk by the end of the day. The chief has his hooks into this one, for whatever reason, so we need to show him we're on top of it."

They all nodded, rising to their feet and talking amongst themselves as they exited my office. Anne, however, sat silently in her chair, waiting.

"He was... *shot?*" she asked.

I nodded. "I have no idea if it's connected to our case or the fact that we talked to him yesterday, but it looks—"

"*Bad,*" she finished for me. "I don't know what to think, Kate."

I stared at her. Her face was pale, and her hands were shaking, and then I got it: she was scared, and I knew why, and I understood. If Harrison's murder was connected to the abduction cases, she was a likely target. "Why don't you take a personal day?" I said quietly, taking a seat beside her. "You don't have to put yourself through this."

Annie

She shook her head as she looked down at her hands, clutched tightly together in her lap. "No! I think if I go home, I might just pace myself right into the ground. I need to be part of this."

"I understand," I reassured her. "But you know as well as I do that things aren't always cut and dried. Floyd Harrison's death may or may not be connected."

"It is," Anne said blankly. "I just know it is."

She sounds like Chief Johnston, I thought, my own gut feeling telling me she was right. But it wasn't enough, and I refused to let my gut feelings guide my investigation. That was never a good idea, though in Harry Starke's case... Well, I'm not Harry Starke.

"We're going to follow leads as they come," I said. "Just as we always do. But again, why don't you take that personal day? There's nothing wrong with taking a mental break."

"No," she said adamantly. "I just need to stay here and keep working on it. I'm beginning to have nightmares." Anne turned to me. "And I think they're repressed memories being stirred up by the investigation."

I hesitated. "Even more of a reason to—"

"Keep working on it," she cut me off. "If I regain those memories, it might mean I gain answers to questions. Just think, Kate, I could lead us right to the guy who did this if I can just remember what he looked like."

"He?"

"Yeah, I know it's a he," she said quietly. "From the dreams."

"What else did you get?" I asked, my curiosity piqued.

"Not much," she said. "Just the room I was being held in. I know it was the second story—and the mattress—but that's about it. I just heard his voice."

"Okay, well, that's a step in the right direction. Do you think if you heard his voice, you'd recognize it?" I asked.

She nodded. "Absolutely. I know I would, and I'd like to meet with Emma Jacobs' father, just to see... Well, you know, Harrison mentioned him as a person of interest."

I took a deep breath, deciding to go with her gut. "I'll arrange it right now," I said.

Chapter Thirteen

July 13, 2023
9:45 AM

It took more time than I expected to track down Greg Jacobs. His current address wasn't listed anywhere and hadn't been for over fifteen years since he'd left the home where he lived when Emma had gone missing. However, thanks to some contacts in property management, I was able to locate him as the tenant of a single-wide in a trailer park off Airport Road.

"Seems like a bit of a downgrade from his upper-middle-class home," I told Samson as I pushed back from my desk. "I wonder what happened."

My canine partner eyed me, then rose to his feet as I grabbed the leash. I also needed to speak with Anne's family, but for that, I'd need to take Corbin with me or just go it alone since no one on the team knew about her abduction yet. I really didn't like that aspect. It wasn't a good idea to hide things from the team, and now that we were all working on it together, I was going to have to talk to Anne about bringing them up to speed.

I led Samson out into the incident room and looked around. The only member of my team present was Anne, and she was bent over her desk, staring at her computer screen.

"I've located Greg Jacobs," I said as I stepped up behind her.

She nodded, leaned back in her chair, tapped the keyboard and closed her browser. "Are we going now?" she asked, swiveling around to look up at me.

"I figured we would," I replied. "The man's almost eighty, so I highly doubt he's working. I don't know that for sure, of course, but it's an educated guess."

"Well, let's go find out," she said, smiling at me. She stood up, stretched her arms up over her head as if reaching to touch the ceiling, then she let them fall to her side and continued, "I've just been doing more research into Doctor Webber... You know, the psychiatrist. I think I am going to schedule an appointment."

I nodded. "I think that's a good idea," I replied, looking down at Samson. He was pulling gently on his leash, looking toward the elevators. "How about you tell me all about it on the way?"

She nodded, reached down beside her desk, picked up her shoulder bag, and then followed me to the elevator.

It was almost ten o'clock that morning when we stepped out into the parking lot at the rear of the Police Service Center into a blast of warm air. I held Samson back for a moment, clicked the button on my key fob to unlock the car doors, ran him to the car, then wrenched the rear door open and he hopped inside, off the already blistering concrete. It was going to be another hot summer day with temperatures reaching into the mid-90s, and while I much prefer the heat rather than the

Annie

cold, dreary days of winter, I was ready for some cool autumn days. It seemed to me this summer was warmer than usual, but maybe that was just me.

"It's the dreams that get me," Anne said as I buckled Samson's harness to the restraint. He cocked his head and seemed to frown. I grinned at him and said over my shoulder, "What dreams?" Then I stepped back, closed the door, went around to the driver's side and climbed in.

"So," I said. "What dreams?"

I started the engine, waiting for her to continue.

"I don't know why I've started dreaming about it so much," she said, folding her arms as I pulled out of the parking lot. "You know, this is not the first time I've looked into it. I did a lot of digging on my own time when I was a rookie detective. I tried to find my case file, but it was missing."

I glanced sideways at her, frowning. "You couldn't find it?" I repeated, wondering what the hell was going on.

"It wasn't there," Anne said, her brows creasing. "I admit I didn't want to go poking around too much. I was a rookie and... well, you know what I mean. What happened to me was disclosed when I was hired, but since I was a minor when it happened, it was... sealed or something? I do know it wasn't made public knowledge. But what happened to the file—"

"Anne," I said, cutting her off. "I have your file."

"You do?" She swiveled in her seat to look at me.

"Johnston put it on my desk yesterday while we were out," I said, staring straight ahead through the windshield. "It's not much different from the others. There's not much in it. Mostly photos, the missing person's report, some canvassing reports, but not much else."

Anne pursed her lips, then took a deep breath and said, "That's so strange. I wonder where he found it?"

"I don't know," I admitted. "That's a question for him,

though. I should probably talk to him about it. I'll go see him at the end of the day... if he's still around."

"There's something so wrong about this case," Anne whispered. "Maybe there's some—"

"Let's not jump to any conspiracy theories," I said, cutting her off, shaking my head. "I've already been down that road. There's so little in any of the files, but we have to remember there's a significant gap in technology between now and the eighties." But even as I said it, I was telling myself I was just trying to avoid the obvious. I mean, what was it Sherlock Holmes said? *When you have eliminated the impossible, whatever remains, however improbable, must be the truth.* I had a deep-seated feeling that was going to be the case, but I also knew I had to keep an open mind.

"Or mishandled," Anne added. "I think it's probably safe to say it was mishandled. I remember little about those days, but I don't think I was ever interviewed."

"There's no record of an interview in the file," I said. And, on thinking about it, it was inconceivable, and I couldn't come up with a viable reason why she wasn't interviewed. *Then again,* I thought, *maybe she was, and maybe the report was...* I shook my head. Reports don't get lost, *ever!* Unless...

"You know," she continued. "The other strange thing is that when you introduced me to the two detectives—Watson and Harrison—they didn't seem to know who I was."

"Well, you are about thirty-seven years older," I reasoned. "And it's hard to keep up with all the names over the years."

She nodded and then scrunched up her nose as I turned off Airport Road into the Whispering Pines Trailer Park. "This... This is where Greg Jacobs lives?"

"It is," I replied. "Not quite what you'd expect, is it?"

"No, it's not," she said as I pulled in and parked in front of the office. "They were a wealthy family back in the day."

Annie

"Times change," I remarked as I looked around. It was a nice, clean, mobile home neighborhood, but vastly different from the five-bedroom, two-story home where the family had lived at the time of Emma Jacobs' disappearance.

"You stay here," I said. "I'm going to step inside and find out which one is his."

"Wait, you don't know?" Anne asked as I pushed open my door.

"Nope." I chuckled. "The best I have is that he lives here somewhere."

I left the car running with Samson and Anne inside and headed into the single-wide office.

As hot as it was, I was wearing just a pair of jeans and a white blouse. Thus, my weapon and badge were on my belt for all to see.

"What can I help you with?" the woman sitting behind a small desk asked, peering at me from over the top of her pink plastic-rimmed glasses. Her tone was as cold as her stare, and I could tell she wasn't surprised to see law enforcement at her door.

"I'm looking for Greg Jacobs," I said, smiling at her. "I'm Captain Gazzara, Chattanooga Police."

Her expression changed to a frown. "What could you possibly need to talk to him about?" she asked. "That old man hasn't left his trailer in more'n ten years."

"I just need to talk to him, is all," I said, still smiling.

She pursed her thin lips and then nodded and said, "This about his daughter?"

I stared at her for a moment, then said, "Yes."

"About frickin' time," she muttered. "It's about time someone gave a damn about those girls. I swear it was a crime how they just kept lettin' all those girls go missing and no one ever did a damn thing about it. Hell, I bet they're still happening."

"Not that I've heard of," I said, and I hadn't. "So, where can I find him?"

"Oh, right." She sighed. "Sorry. Um..." and she gave me the number of his trailer. "As I said," she continued, "he doesn't get out much, but he sometimes visits old Juno Vasquero, a gentleman who lives across the street." She looked at the clock on the wall and continued. "He'll be at home now. Juno works down at the gas station and probably isn't home yet."

"Thank you," I said and paused, then continued, "Did you know any of the girls or their families that went missing?" It was worth a shot. You never can tell when a lead might be sitting there right in front of you.

She shook her head. "I only know what Greg Jacobs has told me. He don't talk about it much anymore, though. What I know is what I've heard from the people around the trailer park. It's quite a pleasant community, you know? Once he moved in, they all started talking. You know how it is."

I nodded. "Yes, unfortunately, I do," I said. With that, I thanked her and then headed back out to the car, smiling to myself. I had a feeling the interview with Greg Jacobs was going to be interesting.

Chapter Fourteen

July 13, 2023
10:30AM

"Here we are," I said as I noted the house number, crookedly attached to the top of a once snowy white, now slightly yellowed single wide. It was set on a nicely manicured lot, though it was my guess that the mowing was done by the park staff, not the tenant.

"Yikes," Anne muttered, just as two mutts dragging chains began to bark at us as I pulled in behind a late nineties model pickup truck.

Samson let out a low growl as one of the dogs came barreling toward the car, only to be jerked to a stop when he reached the limit of his chain.

"Maybe Samson should stay in the car today," Anne said.

I shook my head. "Absolutely not!" I said. "It's already almost ninety degrees. He's coming with us." I killed the engine and climbed out, eyeing the two pit bull mixes jerking at the end of their steel ties. I frowned, figuring I should probably call animal control. It's a crime to leave animals out like that.

"Be on your best behavior," I warned Samson as I let him out. "We don't have time for any fights."

He growled around the front of the car in response, and inwardly I braced myself for what was to come. There was no way we'd make it to the front porch without crossing the reach of the two black and white dogs. I gritted my teeth as Anne fell in step beside me.

"Maybe they gave us the wrong address," Anne said, her voice barely audible over the incessant barking.

"I don't think so..." I replied as I shortened Samson's leash even further. He was about to tear my arm out of its socket.

But then, the metal door flew open and out stepped a man, tall, gaunt, with white hair and a heavily lined face.

"What do you want?" he griped from the rail around the tiny porch, eyeing Samson as we continued toward the porch. I kept Samson on my left side, away from the two dogs. By then, he'd fallen into step beside me.

"Are you Greg Jacobs, sir?" Anne asked.

"What of it?" he snapped.

"I'm Detective Robar, Chattanooga PD, and this is Captain Gazzara."

The man's face flashed with a hint of curiosity. "That's me," he said, squinting and frowning at the same time. "You say you're *Anne Robar?*" His beady brown eyes bored into Anne, and an uneasy feeling washed over me. I didn't like the way he was staring at her. For that reason, I put a hand on her arm, and we stopped just out of reach of the two dogs.

"That would be correct," Anne said tersely.

"Then you're Annie Smithson, the little girl who went missing and then turned back up? That's you, huh?" He took a

Annie

few gimpy, weak steps toward the end of the front porch, his white T-shirt gleaming in the sunlight. "You know, my Emma would've maybe never been taken had you not escaped."

Anne's face flickered with a pained emotion, but I jumped in before she could respond.

"That's quite an assumption," I snapped, "and it's inappropriate. We're here to talk to you about your daughter. Now call off your dogs so we can talk."

He stared at me, then nodded.

"Castor. Apollo," he said in a low, crusty voice. "Kennel!" and the two dogs backed away around the end of the trailer and disappeared into what looked like some sort of wooden dog house under the trailer.

"All right. I'll hear you out, lady, but after all these years, it better be damn good. Come on up."

"Thank you," I said, nudging Samson forward and up the four wooden steps.

"I don't normally let visitors come in the house, but I don't want the neighbors asking questions," Jacobs said with a grunt as he held the door open. "I like my privacy."

"We understand," Anne said as she followed me up onto the porch.

We stepped across the threshold into the home, and I was taken quite by surprise: there was hardly any furniture. The only place to sit in the living room was a large but well-worn couch. There was a flat-screen TV and a couple of side tables, and that was about it, but that wasn't what really caught my attention.

It was the writings. All over the walls. And the photographs. There weren't many of those, and they were small, too small to identify without stepping up close. I couldn't make them out or the writings, but I intended to peruse the strange red marker mumbo jumbo once the interview was done or I'd gotten rid of the sick, uneasy feeling in my stomach.

"You know, they thought it was me who did it," Jacobs said loudly from behind us as he closed the door and the room went dark. The drapes were closed, and what little light there was emanated from a flickering fluorescent lamp in the kitchen. I had to stand for a minute while my eyes adjusted.

I don't like this one bit, I thought to myself as Jacobs limped around us, pulled out a bar stool and sat down on it.

"Sit yourself down," he said, gesturing with a nod of his head at the couch, and we did. Samson parked himself between my knees and sat there staring at the man, who didn't seem to bother him one bit.

"They came knocking on my door that night, and then they started questioning me like I had been the one who took her, all because I didn't have a good alibi."

"You had an alibi?" I asked and watched him tense.

"It's in the file," he said, "if you bother to read it."

"There's nothing in the file," I said.

He popped his jaw audibly, then looked at Anne and said, "No shit? Now why doesn't that surprise me? If there's nothing in the file, it's because the cops didn't give a rat's ass about those girls going missing. I'll bet you and your folks remember that, don't you?" He was still staring at Anne. "Remember how they'd come around, ask a few questions, and then tell ya they'd get back with you... You know what? They never did. We had to go knocking down the damn police department door to try to get them idiots to do anything."

"I understand your frustration," I said as I watched Anne shift uncomfortably. It wasn't like her to be unnerved, and I knew it was best if I drove the interview, at least for the time being. "So, your alibi?" I asked again.

"Well, that's the thing, isn't it, lady?" he scoffed. "I lied,

Annie

and because I lied, I failed the polygraph. But it wasn't because I had anything to do with my daughter disappearing." His voice caught in his throat. "It was because I was seeing a lady outside of my marriage, and I didn't want my wife to know or cause the lady grief. I came clean about it in the end though, and it all checked out."

"Who were you seeing?" I asked, standing up to take my notepad from my pocket. I sat down again and looked at him, my eyebrows raised.

"Patricia Gillian," he answered. "I stopped seeing her as soon as it came to light. Losing your daughter will put things into perspective real quick. I miss my wife." He nodded over to a mantle, and as I squinted into the darkness, I realized it was a makeshift shrine. "Lost her about ten years after Emma disappeared. She forgave me for the affair, but she never was able to handle our daughter's disappearance. She needed answers. And she never got them."

"I understand that," Anne said, her voice softening. "I never got any answers, either."

He pursed his lips, rolling them against each other, then he licked them and said, "You know there were more of 'em, right? It wasn't just you and Emma that got nabbed. There was more, and the damn cops just kept writing them off like they meant nothing. How could they do that?" His voice went up an octave as he grew angry. "How could they not be all hands on deck when a little girl vanishes out of thin air? And what about you? You came back clinging to life, and they *still* didn't do a damn thing. There you were. Real evidence that something bad was going on."

"I don't remember," Anne replied, shaking her head. "But we're trying to make up for it now. Is there anything you can tell us? We don't have much."

He laughed, his voice stilted and awkward. "I gave them

cops so many statements that you should have my whole life story in your file."

"Well, we don't," I said. "So, why don't you tell us what you can remember?"

"My little girl was picked up by someone in a green car. I don't know the make and model," he said, frowning. "My memory just ain't what it used to be. I know that there was a cop who responded; he lived a couple streets over. Always thought there was something strange about him."

"Do you know his name?" I asked, noting the distant look in his eye.

"Uh, maybe. Let me think." He tapped his forehead with his index finger, the tapping noise the only sound in the dimly lit trailer.

Anne and I exchanged a glance, and then she stood up and stepped over to the wall to look at the writing. I could see she was frowning as she read.

"Victor? Vinny," Jacobs said, breaking the silence. "It was Vinny. Romano? Something like that. I know the first name was Vinny, though."

I jotted it down. "And what was it about him you thought was strange?" I asked.

Jacobs took a deep breath, his eyes fixated on Anne. "I guess it was just the way he acted real gung-ho at first. You'd have thought he was gonna find her right away, and he was always around... But then..." He trailed off. "He just kinda disappeared. He wasn't even a cop for much longer after that, I don't think. I don't know for sure. I tried to ask him about it one night when I ran into him in a bar downtown, but you know what? He just looked right through me. He was too drunk to know what was going on."

I nodded, making a note to check Vinny Romano out.

Annie

"You interested in that?" Jacobs asked, directing his question to Anne.

"What is it?" she asked. "It looks like scripture?" She turned back around to face Jacobs, a perplexed expression etched on her face.

"It is scripture and my mottos. It's how I live these days. I found God in the walls of this house, and he talks to me and I write what he says."

"I see..." Anne said, her voice trailing off a little. "And when did you start this?" she asked.

"I ain't crazy," he snapped, sliding off the bar stool. "And I started it after my wife died, leaving me alone in this putrid world."

Anne nodded. "That must have been really hard."

"Yeah, and you two can see yourselves out," he grunted in response and then disappeared down the hallway into the darkness. "I'm done talking."

"That's that," I said, gesturing toward the front door. "I think we have enough here to keep moving forward."

"I agree." She led the way to the front door, grabbed the knob and pulled it open, and the dim light gave way to bright sunlight. I lowered my eyes, squinting, waiting for them to become acclimated, and then I followed Anne down the steps and back to the car. The two dogs were standing together at the end of the trailer, watching us warily, but they made no move toward us.

Once I had Sammy safely in the back, with the door closed and the air conditioner blasting to cool down the car, I turned to Anne and asked the burning question. "So, what was written on the walls?"

Anne shuddered. "Nothing I could make any sense of, just a lot of expletives about cops and quotes from the Bible. I think the poor guy has lost most of his marbles. Did you notice how he said there are more missing girls, though?"

"I did," I replied thoughtfully.

Chapter Fifteen

July 13, 2023
12:15PM

We rode back toward the police department, for the most part, in silence. My mind was in a whirl of activity. Why were the detectives back in 1986 so lax in their investigation? Because lax, they surely were. There was no telling, so I gave it up in disgust, pulled into a Subway and put the car in park.

"Hungry?" I asked.

"Sure," she said, shrugging her shoulders. I could tell she was out of it, and I wasn't sure why. She hadn't gone into detail about what she'd seen written on the walls of Jacobs' trailer, and I had to wonder why. And I was worried about her. The deeper we delved into the case, the more I couldn't figure out where her head was.

"Come on," I said as I opened the car door. "We can take a few minutes."

"Do you think it's true?" Anne blurted before I could slide out. "Do you think Emma Jacobs would still be alive if I hadn't escaped?"

I let go of the door and turned a little toward her, hesitated for a second, then shook my head and said, "I think that idea is nothing more than the ramblings of a bitter old man. Of course I don't. It doesn't matter what would've happened had you not escaped. You did, and you're a survivor, Anne. You can't let what Jacobs said guilt you into thinking it could've turned out any other way."

"Maybe so," Anne said as she opened her door and stepped out. She turned to look at me, her expression still difficult to read. "I just wonder—"

"Stop it, Anne," I said. "That kind of thinking isn't going to do anybody any good, especially you. Whoever did this is a crazy son of a bitch. If it hadn't been you, it would have been someone else, so quit trying to blame yourself for what happened to Emma Jacobs."

I got out of the car, slammed the door, let Samson out, and together we walked into the Subway.

"I think sometimes crazy is engrained in someone's DNA," I said as we stood waiting to be served. "Tragedy tears some apart and fortifies others. You don't know what the outcome would've been for Greg Jacobs had it not happened to Emma. Blame it on fate if you like. Had you been just a couple of minutes later on that street, the green car would have been and gone; same for Emma. It's all just a quirk of fate."

She nodded, still distracted. She ordered. I ordered and paid for both. She didn't seem to notice.

She's lost in her head again, I thought, and once again I was concerned about her state of mind, and I wondered if it was time I took her off the case. I knew it was probably the

Annie

right thing to do, but I also knew that if I did, she would be devastated, so I decided I'd continue to let things ride, at least for a while.

We got our lunch and took a seat at one of the booths. I faced the door and Samson took a seat at the end, patiently waiting for his lunch. I unwrapped his plain turkey sandwich and gave it to him.

"You think the cop had anything to do with it?" Anne asked, peeling back the paper around her sandwich. "I mean, it seems like a stretch since he was the responding officer."

"You mean this Vinny Romano?" I asked. "We need to talk to him," I said and took a bite of my sandwich. I chewed for a moment, swallowed and then said, "And I also think I should sit down with your parents and your sister. There are no formal interviews with either of them in the file."

"I don't understand that." She shook her head, setting her sandwich down. "I know the police talked to them. Why would they not file the interviews?"

"Maybe they did," I replied. "Maybe the report got lost," I reasoned. "It has, after all, been thirty-seven years, and who knows how many hands have gone through the file?" It was a stretch; I knew it. And then there was Floyd Harrison. His death was no coincidence. I knew that, too.

"You and I both know there's more to this," Anne said. "And yes, you need to interview my parents and my sister... I think I'd rather not be there."

"I understand," I said. I'd had no intention of including her in that interview, but I kept that to myself.

"I need to tell the team about what happened to me," she said with a deep sigh. "And I think I should do it today, don't you? Now that we're all working together, it seems like the right thing to do."

I nodded. "Yes, I do," I said. "The sooner, the better. There are potential leads with your case."

"Yeah, *me*," she said and laughed bitterly. She picked up her sandwich and took a bite. "What d'you think about my seeing that doctor? Who knows what memories I have repressed somewhere deep in the back of my mind?"

"It's worth a try," I said, "but I wouldn't expect too much. There have been cases of so-called memories being unlocked and innocent people convicted of crimes they didn't commit. There's no guarantee that repressed memories will lead us to the perp."

"That's true," she muttered, staring down at her half-eaten sandwich.

She pushed what was left of her sandwich aside and picked up her coffee, held it in both hands, and stared down at the inky liquid. Me? I took another bite, then set my sandwich aside, too. I'd suddenly lost my appetite. Little more was said as we sat there for a moment sipping our drinks. I was wondering what the team would think when they heard Anne's story. It was going to be one hell of a punch in the gut; I was sure. I wished I could debrief them first. I knew she didn't want their sympathy, and I wanted to make sure that didn't happen. But then again, they were professionals.

They can handle it, I thought as I took a last sip of my coffee.

As I crumpled up the sandwich paper, my phone buzzed in my pocket. I took it out and saw I had a message from Thomas.

How're things going with the cold case?

I smiled, happy he'd reached out, but I wasn't sure how to answer it. Was it going well? Hell, no. I had a little cluster of information and a whole bunch of unknowns. I sighed, and I

Annie

texted, *Hard to say. It's still early days. How are things going with your case?*

I hit send, put the phone away, looked up at Anne, and said, "Ready to head back to the office? My guess is most of the team will be back by now. We can reconvene and see what they've found out, if anything."

"I guess," she said.

We slid out of the booth, threw our trash away, and then walked out into the heat of the summer afternoon. I grimaced as sweat beaded up across my forehead but continued onward.

"One of these days it won't be ninety-something degrees outside," I told Samsom as he panted. I got him situated, climbed in, started the car, and waited for the cool air.

"There was something I wanted to ask you," Anne said as I pulled out onto the street.

"What's that?" I asked, glancing at her.

"I emailed Doctor Webber this morning, and she reached out to me just now. She said she can see me this evening after work."

"I see..." I said and waited for her to continue.

She hesitated and then spoke, "I was thinking it might be beneficial if you went with me. I thought about taking my sister along, but you know, she was also subjected to trauma, in her own way, of course. So I think it might be better for me if someone... someone who's supportive went with me."

I blew out a breath, mulling it over. "What time's your appointment?"

"It's at seven. I'm sure you could bring Samson along. He's great at feeling people out, too."

I laughed. "He *is* good at that. But yeah, sure, we can go along with you if that's what you want."

She smiled. "Thank you, Kate."

"No problem." I pulled into my spot, turned off the engine and applied the parking brake—something I rarely do—but I was preoccupied by the thought of what Anne had just asked. I wasn't a big fan of what we used to call shrinks when I was a lot younger, but I was hoping this Dr. Webber would at least be able to help her and maybe even provide us with a lead that would help solve the case, rather than send us down a rabbit hole of misinformation.

Chapter Sixteen

July 13, 2023
3PM

It was mid-afternoon by the time I was able to get my team together. I sent them a text, telling them to join me in my office as soon as they returned.

In the meantime, Anne went back to her desk, and I sat down at mine and stared at the two whiteboards on the far side of the room. They were depressingly bare: just a few photographs and a long list of questions that needed to be answered. We needed to get a grip. This had become more than just Emma Jacobs. It was Louise Hackett, Anne Robar, and now Floyd Harrison, and maybe a whole lot more.

We needed to get our information straight and get a game plan as the present clashed with the past. I needed to interview Anne's family. We needed to double-check Greg Jacobs' alibi—his lover Patrice Gillian—and talk to ex-cop Vinny

Romano. I also had it in mind that maybe I should talk to Greg Jacobs again.

I also need to ask Chief Johnston about the whereabouts of Anne's file. Why couldn't she find it previously? I hadn't been able to let that go. I shook my head, frustrated. I looked across to where Samson was napping peacefully in his bed.

"What do you think about all this?" I asked.

He opened his eyes but didn't even lift his head.

"Fat lot of good you are," I muttered.

He closed his eyes again.

I leaned back in my chair, clasped my hands together behind my neck, and closed my eyes, but not for long.

There was a tap on my door. I sat upright and leaned forward. The door opened and in walked Corbin, followed by the rest of the team, who were looking decidedly the worse for wear.

Must not be great news.

They filed in and took their seats at the table. I rose to my feet and stepped around the desk, catching Anne's gaze as she, too, took a seat at the table. She'd disappeared to the incident room when we'd gotten back, saying she wanted to look deeper into the Jacobs as a family unit, given the affair he was having. I didn't think Greg Jacobs had anything to do with the missing children. It made no sense. Why would he abduct his own daughter?

"Hey, Kate," Hawk said as he leaned back in his chair. "It's been one hell of a long day." He had that look of failure on his face. "I don't know about the others, but I got nothing."

"Nothing?" I said as I sat down at the table. "Seriously?"

"Nothing," Hawk said. "I mean, there was some video footage from a camera some two hundred yards away that caught the tail end of what happened—a black truck pulled up

Annie

alongside Harrison's truck, then drove away. But it was too far away to make out any details."

"It was late," Ramirez said, sounding defeated.

"True," I admitted.

"We didn't do any better," Cooper added. "But we did manage to talk to Watson. His wife was his alibi, along with two of her friends. It checked out."

I frowned at that, thinking he was now the only lead we had, the only connection between the cases. "What about Harrison himself? Anything come from digging into his background?"

"There's a lot," Corbin began, leaning back in the chair. "He doesn't have any family... well, none that he's close to, and it didn't take us long to figure out why. It seems he had some sort of mental breakdown years ago. His daughter was only a few years old at the time. We interviewed her, but she knew nothing. She said she hadn't spoken to him in years."

"Any details about the mental health issues?" I asked.

"She didn't know, but she said it was explosive and that he was paranoid," Corbin said. "That's all I have. I was going to see if I could get the details now that he's passed away. There's a chance I might be able to pick that apart further."

"What did he do in his spare time?" Anne asked. "Do you think there's any way he could've been involved in something else?"

"Who knows what someone does in their spare time?" Ramirez said. "He could've been dealing drugs, for all we know, or involved in the darker party scene. But we've found no evidence of that. According to the family that owns the grocery store, it appears he spent most of his free time at home. He worked all the time, putting in long hours, and seemed happy to stay whether or not he got paid."

"Then what was he doing in the city at that time of night?"

I said, thinking about it. The question had so many potential answers.

"We're still waiting on his cell phone records," Hawk said. "Hopefully, that'll give us an idea."

"What about his cell phone, Jack?" I asked.

He shook his head and said, "It's locked."

"What about your interview today, Captain?" Corbin asked. "You interviewed Greg Jacobs, right?"

I nodded. "It wasn't a bust, but I don't think he's responsible for Emma's disappearance. He doesn't get around all that well anymore, and he doesn't have a driver's license."

"I called Juno Vasquero, his alibi, when we got back," Anne said. "He confirmed he was at his house. I think Jacobs is a troubled guy but not a suspect. He did give us some insight, though. He mentioned that he'd given multiple statements... But none of them are in the file."

"Lost?" Ramirez's dark brows rose. "Seems like a lot to lose."

"Yeah," I said. "It's pretty damn thin. Look, I don't know what we're dealing with here. We don't know if Jacobs is a reliable source. He mentioned a patrol officer, the responding officer when Emma was reported missing. Vinny Romano. He said he thought there was something off about the guy, that he was upbeat when he interviewed him, but then went downhill fast from there. He left the force soon after. The last Jacobs saw of him was in a downtown bar, and he was dead drunk. One has to wonder why."

"Can't hurt," Cooper said. "He might know something."

"It feels like we've hit a brick wall," Ramirez said. "We have no leads, not even for the Harrison homicide."

"There is one more lead," Anne said and sat up straighter in her chair. She looked over to me, and I gave her a reassuring smile. "D'you have my file, Kate?"

Annie

I pushed back from the table, went to my desk and picked up the file. Then I paused for a moment and stared at it. I looked across my desk at Anne, my lips pursed. She nodded, and I returned to the table and set it down in front of her. I knew she hadn't seen it before, much less gone through it, and I was a little nervous about her seeing it right there and then.

But she didn't open it. Instead, she passed it to her left, to Corbin. He took it from her, read the tab, saw the name on it, and looked at her. Again, she nodded. He nodded back and then flipped it open.

"I was ten years old when I was abducted," Anne said.

"What—" Hawk said, but she cut him off.

"Shush," she said, smiling at him.

"I remember little, but I'm hoping that I can change that."

Everyone was quiet, and I could see by the looks on their faces—especially Hawk's—that they were struggling to process what they were hearing. It wasn't an easy story to hear and learn about the trauma she must have endured. It was a short story that ended with her hospital stay, and when she was done, Ramirez batted a tear away from her eye.

"We're thinking it's more than likely related to the Emma Jacobs case," I said when Anne had finished. "And probably the Louise Hackett case as well. They all happened within the same year, in the same local area, and we have the green car."

"Wow..." Cooper shook his head. "What the hell happened here? How did all this get swept under the rug? This means we have a serial killer abducting children, and we have *nothing*? It makes no sense. It's un-frickin' thinkable."

"I agree," I said. "And I don't know what to make of it. I think I need to talk to the chief."

"What about the chief at the time?" Corbin said. "Robert Milton, I think it was? And wasn't he the one who caught that serial killer who was targeting young boys?"

I nodded. "I'm trying to avoid going that far up the chain, not without knowing exactly *what* our questions are. He was overseeing a lot of cases. I'd be more interested in talking to the captains or detectives."

"How about Finkle?" Cooper asked. "He was around at that time, I think. He was, wasn't he?"

I inwardly cringed at the thought. Captain Henry Finkle and I had a history—and not one I wished to resurrect.

"Yeah, possibly," I said. *Hmm, was he?* I wondered. Even if he was, I didn't want to be the one who interviewed him. *He would have been twenty-four or five,* I thought. *He might remember something.*

"Now that you've all been briefed," I said, "I think we should take some time to think it through. Jack, we need to get into that phone. See what you can do." He nodded, and I continued, "We'll reconvene in the morning." I eyed the clock on the wall. "It's been a long day, and tomorrow morning, we'll assign tasks. We'll meet again tomorrow here in my office. I'll let you know when."

They all nodded and pushed back from the table. I was exhausted and ready for a solid night's sleep. But I'd told Anne I would accompany her that evening and was hoping I could go home first and get in a quick run and shower.

I caught Anne's arm as she headed for the door and said, "Send me the address, and I'll meet you there. I need to go home first."

She nodded. "Thank you, Kate."

And, with that, I parted ways with my team, sending them off for the evening while I packed up my things. I grabbed the leash and connected it to Samson's harness. "I'm so ready to go home," I chuckled to him as we headed for the door and almost bumped right into Chief Johnston.

Annie

"Let's chat, Kate," he said gruffly, nodding over my shoulder into my office.

I nodded, inwardly annoyed. I knew this was coming, and I had questions for him, too. I was just hoping they could wait a day. "What can I do for you, Chief?" I asked as he closed the door behind himself.

"I need you to tell me why you're harassing retired detectives," he began, folding his arms across his chest. "I get that you have to do your job, Kate, but that shouldn't include harassment."

"What?" I couldn't hide my surprise. "I'm not harassing anyone. Where did you get that from?" *Oh, wait a doggone minute; I know. Bruce Watson.* I had to stop myself from rolling my eyes.

"Bruce Watson was a good detective," he began, "and he put in a lot of good years on the force. There's no need to be bugging the hell out of him. He said you showed up, and then you sent two more detectives to his house afterward."

"That would be correct," I snapped, white-knuckling the leash in my hand. "Anne and I visited with him to talk about the Jacobs' case, and he was less than forthcoming. He was the lead detective on that case, damn it. Of course, I wanted to talk to him; I still do. And yes, I sent them to talk to him about the Floyd Harrison homicide. It needed to be done."

"And accuse him of being connected to the death?"

I sighed. "I highly doubt any member of my team would do such a thing. We ask everyone for alibis. You know that. It's protocol, nothing more. No one is accusing him of anything. And, I might add, he was totally uncooperative when I talked to him about Emma Jacobs. Why was that d'you think, Chief?"

Chief Johnston nodded, ignored the question, showed his teeth and bit down on his upper lip—it looked like a snarl—

grimaced and ran his hand over his jaw. "I don't need to be getting heat from the old guys. I wasn't here when the Jacobs child went missing, and you know how this city works. They still have a lot of pull around here."

"They have no pull as far as my investigation is concerned," I argued. "And if they'd have done their damn job the way they should have—"

"Kate," Johnston cut me off. "I'm well aware of how you feel about this, and I understand that it's a personal matter, given that Robar is involved. If it's too much, let me know, and we can stop it right now. I'll hand it off to someone else."

I could feel the anger bubbling up in my chest. "The hell you will," I said and immediately bit my tongue. No one ever talks to Chief Johnston like that, but he didn't seem to care. "You don't need to hand it off to someone else," I continued. "All I need is to be allowed to conduct the investigation as I see fit. If that means interviewing retired detectives... or active officers, I need the freedom to do that. As it is, I have *nothing* to go on except for Bruce Watson and possibly other officers, active and retired." I took a breath and then continued. "All I have are three files containing only a handful of documents. There's no evidence in storage. There's... *nothing*."

"I *know*," he said. "I know, and because I know, I understand your frustration, Kate. However, it doesn't change the fact that I have to take heat when you go bothering people who retired long ago. They don't want to hear about the cases they failed to solve."

"I think there's more to it than that," I said, knowing it was a mistake to voice my suspicions.

"You make sure you have solid evidence before you throw that concept around. If the media catches wind of corruption... Well, you know what that will do to us. We don't need it."

"I'm aware," I told him, letting out a sigh. "I'll keep my

Annie

theories to myself, but while we're talking about it, where was Anne's file? She said she informed the interview board about her abduction when she applied to join the force. She also told me she looked for it but couldn't find it."

Johnston paused, frowning. "It was in the personnel files. I'm sure it was placed there when she was accepted. You know the drill, Kate. We don't want anyone to be able to access active personnel files without good reason. She could've put in a request for it, and I'm sure it would've been granted."

I nodded. I had no idea if Anne had gone that route or not, but Johnston's explanation made sense.

"Chief, I just can't let go of how weird it is that these three girls were abducted and there's virtually no record of it. If that happened today, the entire city would be up in arms."

"I think they were up in arms then," Johnston replied. "The technology back then wasn't what it is today, and they were understaffed."

"Okay," I said. "I get that, but why won't Bruce Watson talk to us? He obviously knows more than he's letting on. Why is he acting like we're coming after him personally? You say he was a good detective. The stand he's taking makes no sense."

The look on Johnston's face seemed to indicate that he agreed.

"Look, Chief," I continued, "I know you always have the best intentions, but this time... well, I just don't think that's the route to take. Watson needs to talk to me." And then I waited for the ax to fall. Surprisingly, it didn't. Instead, he just stared at me as if he didn't quite know what to say next, so I pressed on.

"And what about Floyd Harrison?" I asked. "D'you think his death is not connected? Of course you don't. I talk to him one day and he's dead the next? That's more than coincidental, which again means we need to talk to Watson, or at least protect him."

"Look..." he said, then pursed his lips and frowned, "I feel the same way you do, but we have to go carefully. We get it wrong, and it will end up burning us both."

I took a deep breath. "You're right. I know that," I said. "And I'm being as careful as I can."

He took a deep breath, shook his head, and said, "How's Anne holding up? This has to be traumatic for her, reliving it over and over."

I answered him honestly, "I'm keeping an eye on her. I offered to let her sit it out, but she wouldn't hear of it. She's going to see Doctor Webber tonight. Apparently, the doctor is renowned for recovering suppressed memories. She asked me to go with her, and I agreed."

"Risky move," he said. "But I get it. The problem is it could create false memories. Sometimes imagination fills in the gaps."

"We're both aware of that, but she's determined to do what she can. I just hope she's not putting too much pressure on herself. I'll try to get a feel for what goes on, if the doctor will let me observe."

Johnston sighed. "Good luck with that. You know how doctors are about privacy, especially psychiatrists. I hope it's successful, but even if it is, it's not admissible in court. But if she could give us a name or location, you'll at least have something to work with." He paused; the look on his face changed, it hardened, and he said, "But unless and until you can give me a damn good reason, you're to stay away from Watson, understand?"

I huffed, then said, "Of course, I won't talk to him again until I have the evidence to support it."

"All right," he said, letting out a sharp breath. "I think you have a handle on it, Kate. If and when you think you need to talk to him, you come to me first. I need to be a part of the process."

"Yes, sir."

"Have a good evening," he said, and with that, he turned and left my office.

I glanced down at Samson and said, "Whew! That was intense. I don't know what we're getting ourselves into, buddy, but I have a feeling we're going to keep on ruffling feathers."

He opened his mouth, panting, then closed it again and showed his teeth in one of his famous smiles.

I shook my head and chuckled as I led him out of my office, locking the door behind me.

I was hoping for an easier evening, one that would allow me to take a break from everything that had been thrown at me the last twenty-four hours, especially my conversation with the chief.

I took the elevator to the ground floor, turned left, and made my way to the rear entrance and from there to my car. I stepped out into the early evening heat, still thinking about what Johnston had said to me, and I couldn't help but wonder why he was so adamant that I stay away from Bruce Watson. *Surely*—I cut the thought off almost before it could begin to form. The chief might be a snarky son of a bitch at times, but he was a straight arrow. *But that doesn't mean there aren't others*—Again, I chopped the thought before it could fully form and take me places I really didn't want to go.

I buckled Samson into the front seat and then stood for a moment beside the open door, thinking. There was something about the evening air that had me feeling antsy, but I chalked it up to the impending appointment I was going to attend with Anne, and I shook my head. I wasn't at all enthusiastic about what she was going to do.

It has happened so many times. The doctor helps the patient conjure up memories that are simply figments of their imagination—or the *doctor's* imagination—and those memories lead to the arrest of an innocent man or woman, but more often than not, it's just another dead end.

And a waste of time, I thought to myself as I opened the car door and climbed inside. I started the engine and sat there for a few moments, zoning out.

Maybe I should call Harry and get his opinion, I thought. *See if he knows anything about this doctor.* There were few people of note in the city that Harry didn't know.

"I'll call him after we eat dinner," I said, glancing at Samson. "It would probably be better to go for a run first, too. I need to clear my head." I put the car in drive and headed home.

Chapter Seventeen

July 13, 2023
5:35PM

It was a little after five-thirty that evening when I parked the car in front of the garage. I turned Samson loose in the backyard while I changed into a pair of white running shorts and a navy tank top. It was still extremely hot and humid outside, but I didn't want to wait until I returned home from Anne's appointment to run. I was hoping for a quiet night and some solid sleep.

I grabbed my earbud and shoved it in my ear, connecting the Bluetooth to my phone so I could listen to some music while I ran. Sometimes I liked the quiet, but that evening, I felt I needed the distraction. I let Samson in and clipped his leash to his collar. It was too hot for a harness.

"Ready?" I said after I downed the rest of my water. "Not too far tonight. It's going to be a hot one. I want you to stay on the grass, okay? Don't want you burning your paws on the hot concrete."

He bounced happily as I closed the garage door.

"Here we go," I said as we stepped out into the heat. I did a few stretches, but I figured I'd keep it short. I still had to get back in time to eat and make it to the appointment. I took off at a jog, and Samson bounded along on the grass verge to my right.

I hadn't gone but a couple of blocks and was wiping the sweat from my forehead with the back of my hand when my smartwatch buzzed with the notification that I was running a little slower than normal, but I didn't worry about it. It was too hot to push myself. The last thing I needed was a heat stroke. I ran three more blocks, about a mile, then turned around and headed back toward the house.

My head was throbbing, and my heart rate was way up as I slowed to a walk once I hit the driveway. I spent the next few minutes resting with my hands on my knees, sucking in oxygen. "That was a mistake," I stuttered. "It's way too hot," I looked at Samson. He was also panting heavily, his tongue lolling out.

"It's okay," I said, straightening up. "Let's get you a drink."

I punched the numbers into the keypad. The lock clicked, and I opened the door. The cool air hit us like a brick wall, one of the most pleasant experiences I'd had that day. It was so refreshing, and all I wanted to do was take a shower, put on some pj's, and relax for the rest of the evening. But that wasn't an option, and not for the first time that day, I regretted agreeing to accompany Anne.

I spent the next few minutes getting Samson some fresh water and his kibble for the evening. While he ate, I headed upstairs to the master bedroom, stripped out of my sweaty shorts and tank top, and took a long, cool shower. Then I

Annie

dressed in a pair of dark blue jeans, a white blouse, and a pair of flats. I blow-dried my hair and pulled it up into a ponytail, resisting the urge to leave it down. With the humidity so high, it would just frizz out in an ugly mess. I applied a little makeup and went down to the kitchen to find Samson whining at the back door, so I let him out, wondering what I was going to eat. I didn't have much time, so I decided on a Cup O' Noodles. It wasn't much, but it was better than nothing. I took it out of the microwave and then let Samson back in while I waited for it to cool.

"You ready to do this?" I asked him after I'd inhaled my makeshift dinner. I guess he was because he took a step forward and sat down at my feet, so I grabbed his leash and clipped it to his collar. "Seems like it's been nonstop for us today, huh?"

He smiled up at me, and it warmed my heart.

"Whatever would I do without you?" I said, ruffling his ears. He stood up, his butt wiggling, and I grabbed his harness, just in case, though I didn't intend to put it on him unless someone gave me trouble.

Two minutes later we were in the car with the engine running and the AC on full, though it was still blowing warm air. I entered the address into the GPS and reached for the radio, and as I did, my phone rang.

Oh geez, I thought, *not another dead body, please.* It wasn't. It was Thomas. I smiled, answered and said, "Hey."

"Kate Gazzara," he greeted me cheerily. "I was just calling to check in on you."

"I'm right as rain." I laughed, feeling a little lighter for hearing his voice. "What about you?" I asked as I backed out onto the street.

"Well, I'm thinking we should have dinner when I get back to town. What do you think?"

I smiled and said, "I like the sound of that."

"Great," he said and chuckled. "It might be a little while, but I promise I'll make good on it. This case is moving along, so hopefully it won't be too much longer. I've located a witness. How's your case going?"

I paused for a moment, then said, "So-so. You know how it is with cold cases. Right now, I'm on my way to see a doctor named Angelica Webber. Have you heard of her?"

"The hypnosis lady, huh?" He burst into laughter. "What're you going to see her about?"

"I have a potential witness who might have some repressed memories." I didn't want to give him all the details, though I have to admit I was tempted. He seemed to have a good grip on cold cases, and his ability to solve them seemed to be second to none.

"I don't know Doctor Webber personally, but she seems to be on the up-and-up. I've heard a few success stories. You never know what might draw out a memory, but then again, who the hell knows? Maybe it's all just mumbo jumbo."

I frowned. "Seriously?" I asked.

"I mean, when you think back to your childhood," he continued, "or even what you did a week ago, sometimes our mind fills in the gaps with things that may or may not be the truth. That's why no two witnesses will have exactly the same recollection of an event they both saw at the same time. If they *are* the same, they're often fabricated."

"That's a point," I agreed. "I'm just hoping it's not too much for her."

"Hopefully not," he said. "But I'm sure the doc is used to handling trauma patients."

"I hope so," I said hesitantly.

"You need to loosen up a little, Gazzara. Go with your gut and ride it out."

Annie

"Well, aren't you the motivational speaker?" I teased.

"Maybe in another life." He laughed. "But listen, I'd better get back to it. I want it done. I'm ready to get back to Chattanooga. I'm looking forward to spending some time with you. Tell Samson hi and bye for me."

I felt my face heat up a little as we said our goodbyes, and I stuck the phone in the console. It was the exact conversation I needed before walking into the evening with Anne. I knew I needed to be there to support her and that I needed to stop worrying about the outcome, but that was easier said than done.

I pulled up in the parking lot of a new single-story office building on the south side of town. The doctor's office—unmarked except for the gold script on the glass door—was next door to a law firm I'd never heard of.

I put the car in park and left the engine running; Anne had not yet arrived, so I took a moment to grab my phone, intending to Google the doctor. But before I could, my phone rang *again*. Only this time, it wasn't Thomas. It was Amanda, Harry's wife.

I frowned. It wasn't uncommon for her to call me, though it was something of a rarity. I answered, hoping everything was okay with Harry.

"Amanda," I said.

"Hey, Kate, I hate to bother you," she said. "But I think I might have some useful information for you. I was doing some research on your cold cases... I... I just couldn't let it go. There was something about those girls going missing and the lack of information that bugged me. Do you have a minute?"

I glanced around the car and looked at the clock on the dash, noting I was ten minutes early. "I... might have a moment," I said hesitantly.

"Okay," she said. "I've found some articles I think you

might find helpful. The media did take the missing girls' cases seriously. In fact, I went through Channel 7's archives and found some of the old news tapes. It's going to take more than ten minutes, though. Are you free anytime soon?"

I sighed, unsure of how to answer that loaded question. "I have an appointment in ten minutes," I said. "But I can probably swing by your place after I finish up here. You've piqued my interest, and if I don't hear you out tonight, I won't be able to sleep."

Amanda laughed, taking my words as a joke rather than the truth, which it was. "Well, that works for us," she said. "I'll be able to put Jade to bed before you get here."

"Perfect. I'll send you a text when I head your way."

"See you then, Kate," she said and hung up.

I shoved my phone in my jeans pocket just as Anne pulled into the parking lot. It was perfect timing. A sign that the experiment was going to go well?

I sure as hell hoped so!

Chapter Eighteen

July 13, 2023
7PM

Anne and I got out of our cars, said our greetings, and then Samson and I followed her into the building. She was surprisingly calm and collected, and I wasn't sure if that was a good or bad sign. She had her hair pulled back in a neat bun, and she was wearing a T-shirt and jeans rather than her work attire.

"I wonder if she forgot," Anne said, breaking the silence as we stood in the dimly lit area.

"No idea," I said as I looked around. It was nothing like the waiting area you'd expect at a regular doctor's office. The typical rows of chairs had been replaced with purple velvet couches, and the walls were covered with matching abstract murals. I couldn't decide if it was a comforting or unnerving experience.

Samson, seemingly as unenthused as ever, seated himself

beside me with his tongue lolling out of the side of his mouth. I checked my watch. It was exactly seven o'clock; and it was at that moment, as if it had been orchestrated, that a tall, blond woman appeared through a door at the rear of the room.

"Hi," she greeted us. "You must be Anne and Kate."

"Kate," I confirmed, giving her a nod as I scrutinized her. If I ran into her out and about around town, I would never have labeled her as a doctor. She was middle-aged and was wearing a pair of enormous, round-rimmed glasses and a floor-length purple and white tie-dye dress.

She matches the walls, I thought to myself, and I half expected her to lead us into a darkened room with a crystal ball.

"This is Samson." Anne gestured to my canine partner.

Dr. Webber smiled and said, "Ah, the more the merrier." But then the corners of her mouth turned downward as she turned back to Anne. "As long as you consent to them being present. You don't need to feel any pressure."

"I want Kate with me," Anne replied confidently.

"Very well, then." Dr. Webber nodded. "Let's get to work. Follow me, please." She turned and stood back to allow Anne to enter. Samson and I followed.

The room was... comfortable, again, unlike any doctor's office I'd ever been in.

"Please," Dr. Webber said, "sit down." She looked at Anne and gestured to a large, comfortable wingback chair. Then she looked at me, raised her eyebrows, and nodded to a chair set back against the wall.

"Now, if we're all comfortable," she continued, taking a seat opposite and some six feet in front of Anne, "before we dive in, I'd like to explain what it is we're about to do."

What are we about to do? I thought. *A séance?* My mind reeled at the possibilities, given Dr. Webber's obviously eccen-

Annie

tric nature and the oddly dark and psychedelically decorated office.

"I focus on comfort," she continued, "and when we're appealing to the repressed memories hidden away in the dark corners of our mind, it's better done in the dark. Now, I know it can be a little unsettling at first, but I promise it's done for no other reason than to help you relax."

Anne nodded, and I was expecting her to say something, but she didn't.

"So, are you ready?" Webber asked, picking up what looked like a TV remote from the small round table to her right.

Anne nodded.

The lights dimmed even further until all that was left was a dimly glowing purple light on the doctor's side table, and I found myself struggling to adjust my eyes.

"Kate and Samson," she turned her attention to us. "You will sit quietly while I conduct the session. At the end of the session, we can all chat about what we've discovered, if Anne is comfortable with our so doing. If not, I request you remain silent throughout. Is that understood?"

"No problem," I said, eyeing Anne. "Are you okay?"

She nodded, shooting me a reassuring smile. "I'll be fine."

"Very well, then. Let us begin." Dr. Webber leaned forward and squeezed Anne's hand.

"I think it's also important for you to know that we might not be able to recover anything," Webber began, her voice soft as the sound of the ocean played through hidden speakers. "And there is also the chance that if we *do* recover partial memories, they may well be figments of your imagination. Let me take a moment to explain. Repressed memories occur as the result of extreme trauma, traumas so severe they are removed from the conscious memory by repression or dissociation. Such memories can sometimes be recalled. False memories occur when a particularly vulnerable or suggestible patient is inadvertently coached by an authority figure—a doctor, perhaps—to create memories of an experience that never actually happened, and in detail."

She paused for a moment, and I couldn't help but think, *Oh great, so anything that happens here is entirely unreliable.* I pursed my lips, wondering how Anne was handling this rather strange interview.

"Bearing that in mind," the doctor said, "are you ready to continue?"

"I'm ready to give it a try," Anne said, her voice low but confident. "Would you like me to tell you what I remember or..." She trailed off.

"It's better if I don't know," Webber replied. "I don't want to do anything other than pave the way for your mind to recover your true memories."

"Okay..." Anne said, sounding a little less sure of herself. "I'm ready."

"Good," Webber said. "Now, I want you to relax completely, starting from the tips of your toes to the top of your head... good... good. Breathe... breathe... breathe... good... good. I'm going to count slowly down from five, and when I get to one, you'll be asleep."

I shifted back in my seat and folded my arms. Samson was lying at my feet, apparently snoozing.

The ambient sounds of the ocean grew louder, and an incessant ticking noise filled the room as Dr. Webber counted down. When she reached one, she paused for a moment, then said, "Anne, can you hear me?"

"Yes."

"Good. I want you to imagine you are on a beach at the edge of an ocean. You take a step forward, and then another,

Annie

into the water. Can you tell me the temperature of the water, Anne?"

"Cold," Anne replied immediately.

"Take another step," was all Dr. Weber said as the sounds of waves lapping on the shore increased slightly. And I have to tell you, it had an eerie effect on me. Samson continued to snooze.

"It's warmer now," Anne said suddenly. Her voice had changed. It sounded an octave higher.

"Good, follow that warmth. One step at a time, slip deeper and deeper. I don't want you to stop until the water is up to your chin."

Anne fell silent for what seemed to be a staggeringly long time, and she gurgled. It was as if she really was in the water. It was startling, and I swear I felt the hair on the back of my neck stand on end.

"Now," Webber said, "I want you to go deeper until you're completely under the water. Hold your breath. I will count to five... four, five... Good. Anne, you are ten years old. Where are you?"

The sound of the ocean faded away to nothing.

I blinked a couple of times, waiting for Anne to answer, but she didn't, and I found myself holding my breath.

"Anne?" Dr. Webber said. "Are you there?"

"Yes," she squeaked. "I... I... I am." She sounded... *scared*.

"Where are you, Anne?"

"I don't know."

"Can you describe your surroundings for me, please?"

"It's dark," Anne whispered. "It's hot... I don't know... I don't know." And she began to cry, softly.

"It's all right, Anne," Webber said gently. "Concentrate. It's hot, and...?"

"It's dark. Stuffy. Can't breathe. I can hear..."

There was a brief pause, and then she continued, "It's so dark... I can hear... I think... I think it's moving. Bumpy. I'm lying down..." and she trailed off again.

"Anne. Where are you?" Webber asked.

"I don't know. I... I... think I'm in... the trunk."

"The trunk?" Webber asked.

"A car," Anne said. "It's so dark," she repeated, "and bumpy."

What the hell? I thought, sitting up straight.

"You're in a car, in the trunk, and the car's moving?" Webber asked quietly. "Go on, Anne."

"Yes," Anne answered. "But it's slowing down..." Again, there was a pause. "It's stopped," she said. More silence, then, "I can hear something... The engine's stopped. It's quiet now." There was another moment of silence, and then, "The car door... it opened. There's... there's someone else in here."

"Someone else?" Dr. Webber asked. She sounded as surprised as I was. "In the trunk?" she asked.

Anne actually nodded, then said, "A girl... There's a girl in here." Anne's voice broke. She sobbed. "There's a girl in here," she repeated. "I can feel her. She's lying next to me. I can feel her dress. I can feel... her dress... and her arm. It's cold. She's... dead!"

I opened my mouth in amazement and... horror. I looked at Webber. I could barely see her in the dim light, but I could see she was looking at me. She held a finger to her lips. I nodded and relaxed a little.

"Can you tell me what's happening now?" Webber asked.

"Someone's opening the trunk. It's dark outside. I can't... I can't see his face," she whispered, and then, silence.

We waited. Webber said nothing. I stared at her, but she was staring intently at Anne.

Annie

"You said *his* face," Webber said finally. "Are you sure it's a man?"

Again, we waited for her to answer, then she said, "Yes!"

"Where are you, Anne?" she said, breaking the silence.

Anne didn't reply.

"Anne?" Webber said.

"I'm in the trunk," Anne repeated. "It's dark. I can see trees. I think we're in the woods. It's dark. I don't know where we are. I want to go home. Oh, please," she cried. "I'm scared. I want to go home."

And then she screamed, an ear-piercing, high-pitched shriek.

I almost leaped out of my skin. Samson jumped to his feet. Webber sat back in her chair, startled.

"It's all right, Anne," Webber said quietly, leaning forward again.

Anne was sobbing. I started to get to my feet, but Webber held up her hand, so I sat back down and put my hand on the top of Samson's head. He sat down again.

"Yes, we can go home now, Anne," Webber said, and with that, the sound of the ocean slowly increased again. "I want you to swim to the surface, one stroke at a time. The water is warm, remember?"

"Yes," Anne replied meekly. "It's warm."

"I'm going to count from one to five, and when I get to five, you'll wake up," Webber said. "Do you understand, Anne?"

"Yes," Anne whispered.

"One, two, three, four, five!"

The lights came up a little. I scooted to the edge of my seat, and Anne sighed and opened her eyes.

"How are you feeling, Anne?" Dr. Webber asked quietly.

Anne looked at her, shifted slightly in her chair so that she could look at me, and said, "I think I know where to find the body, Kate."

I swallowed hard, unsure of how to feel or what to say, so I said nothing.

Webber looked at me, then said to Anne, "Would you like to tell us about it?"

Anne shook her head. "There's nothing to tell. It's just a feeling I have, but I think I know where to look for her."

Chapter Nineteen

July 13, 2023
8:15PM

"It's too dark now," Anne said, looking up at the overcast sky as we stepped out of Dr. Webber's office. "But maybe tomorrow morning we can go look, drive around. I'm sure it's close. I'm going home to think about it some more. I'm pretty sure I know where to find it."

I put a hand on her arm, and we stopped walking. "Of course," I said, giving her a reassuring smile, though I couldn't help but wonder if what she remembered wasn't just her imagination. "We'll talk about it tomorrow. In the meantime, I want you to go home and get some sleep. Okay?"

"I will," she replied and reached out, squeezed my shoulder, and then turned and went to her car, leaving me to wonder about what had happened. Anne seemed different somehow. Her voice seemed... softer, her demeanor calmer, and I wasn't sure I liked it.

I watched her open her car door, then she paused for a moment, looked back at me, smiled, and damned if she didn't wink.

I led Samson to my car, opened the back door for him to climb in, and buckled his restraint.

It was getting late—later than what I wanted to be out—but I'd told Amanda I'd come by, so I took out my phone, started the car, and sent her a text to let her know I was on my way.

"I wonder what information she has for us," I thought aloud, meeting Samson's eyes in the rearview. "Hopefully, it'll be something more believable than whatever it was we just experienced." I said the words with a laugh, but it quickly faded as I pondered the encounter.

What if it is true? I thought. *What if ten-year-old Anne really did ride in the trunk of a car next to the dead body of a young girl?* I shuddered to think about how terrifying that must've been. *No wonder she blocked it out.* I shook my head as I drove west on Broad toward Lookout Mountain, a dark silhouette against a moonless sky.

I glanced at the rearview mirror. Samson had called it a day and was already asleep, and I couldn't help but wish I was too.

Some twenty minutes after I'd left Dr. Webber's parking lot, I pulled into Harry's driveway just as Maria stepped out of the front door and headed to her car.

I exited my car and waved at her.

"Kate. How've you been?" she asked, pausing beside the SUV's open door. "I haven't seen you much. I figure maybe that's a good thing. Maybe things are slowing down for you at work, huh?"

I laughed. "Every time things slow down, they make up for it when they pick back up."

Annie

"Ah, yes." Amanda's nanny-cum-bodyguard nodded. "There's a reason I retired from the ATF, you know. It's much easier to take care of Jade than to chase bad guys, though I have to admit the *niñita* has given me a run for my money at times."

"Well, she is Harry's daughter," I joked as I let Samson out of the car.

"You have a good night, you hear?" Maria said as she climbed into her car.

"You, too, Maria," I said as I headed for the front door, where Amanda was already waiting for me.

"I thought you'd never get here," she greeted me as she ushered us inside. "Jade's in bed, and I have us set up in the living room."

"Okay?" I said, raising my eyebrows. "That sounds exciting."

"Well, perhaps," she replied. "Can I get you something to drink?"

"Sure. Red wine?" I said as I followed her into the living room, where Harry was already seated on the couch. I took a seat on the other end.

"Ah, there you are," Harry said. "How's the frigid case coming along? I can't believe you've gotten yourself sucked into another one." Harry chuckled, shaking his head. "But then again, I know you do love a challenge, don't you?"

"Something like that." I sighed, getting settled on the couch while Samson laid down at my feet.

I leaned back against the cushions and closed my eyes. "I just had the weirdest experience," I said, my eyes still closed. "I've just come from attending one of Doctor Webber's sessions." I turned my head to look at him, unsure of how much I wanted to share. "It was surreal, to say the least, though not nearly as out there as I'd expected."

He nodded. "I know little about her," he said. "I've heard of her; nothing untoward, but in my opinion, these doctors who practice hypnosis are a different breed. The good ones, those who know what they're doing, I think they have their place. Those that don't..." He shook his head and then continued. "They can do more harm than good. From what I've heard, I think maybe Doctor Webber might be one of the good ones."

"So," Amanda said, handing me the glass of wine, "if you'll direct your attention to the TV, I've mirrored my computer screen."

I nodded, watching as she navigated her laptop. She clicked on a file and opened an MP4 video file.

"This is an old interview from Channel 7's archives," she began. "All of our previous segments are now digitized. Which is good, right?"

The video file was an interview with Greg Jacobs and his late wife, standing amongst a crowd of reporters and police officers.

"This is the video that led me down the rabbit hole," Amanda said as she clicked play.

"We just, uh," Greg Jacobs said as he pushed his glasses up his nose. *"We just want our daughter to come home, so if anyone knows anything—"*

"Please," his wife cut him off, her voice cracking with emotion. *"We just want Emma home. If you have her, please let her go. We just want our little girl back."*

And so it went on for several minutes, Mrs. Jacobs sobbing loudly throughout. As it is with all missing child cases, the video was hard to watch. However, from the way Greg Jacobs' eyes darted around and his skin appeared peaked and clammy, I could understand why everyone said he'd acted strangely. I mean, hell, he was acting strangely right there on live TV. I

Annie

could only imagine what he must have been like in the interview room.

A plain-clothed police officer I didn't recognize stepped up to the microphone. *"Emma Jacobs went missing on her way home from school on Friday afternoon,"* he said, leaning in close to the bank of microphones. *"If anyone saw anything suspicious that afternoon, anything at all, or has any information, please call the Chattanooga Police Department now on the tip line at the bottom of the screen."* With that, the officer stepped back, and the video ended.

"Who was that?" I asked, turning to Amanda.

"Um, not sure," she said. "Police information officer, probably." She shrugged. "Milton was the chief at the time, but he wasn't there. That appeal seems to me to have been thrown together at the last minute."

I furrowed my brow, staring at the blank screen. "What makes you think that?" I asked.

"Well, for starters, the chief *isn't* present, which is unusual. And... well, having done my share of such interviews, it just doesn't feel right."

Interesting, I thought as I stroked the top of Samson's head. "What I can't get over is why they didn't turn the world upside down trying to find these kids. Did they interview any of the other parents?"

"Yes," Amanda said quietly. "Just one other. It seems the other families didn't want to be interviewed."

"And the one that did?" I asked.

Amanda glanced at Harry, then at me. "Anne Robar. Anne Smithson back then. Her parents spoke to the media the night that she arrived back home. They bombarded them. They wanted to get the survival story. You know the hype."

"Right," I said with a nod. "Do you have that?"

She nodded, exited out of the video, and then opened another.

"This is the Smithsons' interview," Amanda said and hit the play button.

I watched as the video came up on the screen. Anne's folks were standing in what I assumed was their front yard. Anne's mother, Anita, looked strikingly similar to Anne; her father was tall, almost painfully thin, his dark hair combed over a receding hairline, his expression daunting.

"What can you tell us about your daughter's escape?" one of the reporters called from somewhere off-camera.

"We don't know anything yet," her mother answered. She sounded tired. *"She's doing well, given what she's gone through. We'd really appreciate some privacy right now. She's gone through a lot, and she needs time to recover."*

"Of course," the reporter said, but then continued. *"How's her morale?"*

"As good as can be expected after what she's gone through," Anne's father snapped. *"And your presence sure as hell isn't making things any better. My daughter just survived everyone's worst nightmare, and you all just want to broadcast it for all the world to see. If you want to do someone some good, get yourselves down to the police department and hound them. They aren't doing a damn thing to find my daughter's—"*

The video ended at that.

"Where's the rest of it?" I asked, turning to Amanda.

"I don't know," she said with a shrug. "This interview was never used. It was never broadcast. It was scrapped."

"So Anne's family was never on the news then?" I asked.

"Not other than just general reporting that she had been found and was safe, and even then, it was just a brief mention. That could've been because of the blowback from the parents, though."

Annie

"Everyone sure seemed to have had a problem with the police," I thought aloud, my stomach tightening as I thought of the thin files sitting on my desk and Bruce Watson's hateful reaction. *Corruption?* I wondered silently. *Surely not...*

"There's one more video I think you should see," Amanda's voice quieted as she took a sip of her drink. "It's not entirely connected, but I'll show you what I found and tell you why I'm showing it to you."

"Okay," I said, watching as she exited the video and opened another.

"I'll explain afterward," Amanda said and clicked play.

A police officer's face filled the screen, and my jaw dropped as I read the name across the bottom: *Officer Vincent Romano, Chattanooga Police Department.*

"Tonight, former police officer Vincent 'Vinny' Romano was charged with aggravated sexual assault and battery in the commission of a traffic stop. An unnamed woman claimed Romano assaulted her near her home in Walden Heights."

The screen flashed to a modest neighborhood, and I recognized it immediately as Anne's neighborhood.

"The unnamed woman alleges Romano pulled her over, forced her into his car, and then brutally assaulted her. Romano denies the allegations but remains in custody pending arraignment."

I rubbed my forehead, trying to wrap my head around what I was watching. "When did this happen?" I asked.

"Less than six months after Anne returned home and a month after another girl went missing," Amanda said. She paused for a second, then continued, carefully, "After Romano's arrest, there were no more missing girls... It just... stopped."

"As I recall, he was the responding officer for one of the

cases," I said, pinching the bridge of my nose. "I guess he needs to be moved up my list."

"It could be unrelated," Amanda spoke up. "I just thought the location was rather interesting."

"Interesting it is," Harry said thoughtfully. "Though I'm not sure if any of it helps."

"It all helps," I said, downing the rest of my wine. "Thank you for showing me these, Amanda. Would you mind emailing the videos to me? I'd like to have my team watch them to see if they see anything of substance we might've missed."

"Of course." Amanda nodded.

At that, I spent the next thirty minutes chatting about nonrelated things, more to give my brain a break than anything else, and then I headed home, hoping to get a good night's rest before... I really didn't know what, but one thing I was sure of: things were about to get a lot more interesting.

Chapter Twenty

July 14, 2023
6:15 AM

I got little sleep that night. I tossed and turned most of it, my head full of images of terrified young girls, grisly murders, and shadowy figures until my alarm rang, rescuing me from the eight-hour nightmare. It was fifteen after six, and I felt as though I'd been put through the proverbial wringer. My head was aching. I had a painful crick in my neck; even my bones hurt.

I groaned and fell out of bed, wondering what the hell had happened. My mind had felt clear when I'd gone to bed, and I really hadn't been that tired. Now, I felt like I hadn't slept at all.

I got up off my hands and knees, staggered to the bathroom, turned on the shower and stepped in, opting to wake up under a stream of warm water rather than pounding the pavement with Samson. He seemed to like the idea because he barely raised his head until I had climbed out of the shower.

I dried myself off, put on a lightweight robe and went down to the kitchen to start the coffee machine. Then I went back upstairs, sat down on the edge of the bed and stared at Samson.

"Geez," I said. "You really do have it easy, don't you?"

He raised his head, looked up and drew back his lips to show his teeth in that classic grin of his and then laid his head back down on his front paws.

Me? I shook my head and said, "Where the hell did you come from?"

He merely blinked.

I sighed, stood up, went to the bathroom, plugged in the hair dryer and blew out my hair before combing it back into a ponytail.

I dressed simply in a pair of lightweight black pants and a sky-blue blouse. It was forecast to be another scorcher, but according to the Channel 7 weatherman, there was a cold front on the way, which meant the temperature would drop into the high eighties.

What a pleasant reprieve that'll be, I thought sarcastically to myself as I slipped into my shoes.

"Come on, boy," I called to Samson. "We might be taking it easy this morning, but we still have to get up and around, and you need to go outside."

Samson rose to his feet and stretched, first his front legs and then his back legs, and stalked stiffly across the bedroom and down the stairs to the back door, where he sat patiently waiting for me to let him out.

I followed him down, smiling to myself, unlocked the door, opened it and let him out.

I closed the door and watched him amble down the steps

Annie

into the yard. Then I poured myself a large mug of coffee, got Samson fresh water and a bowl of kibble, and then popped a bagel into the toaster.

I still didn't feel right. My brain was lagging behind my body by a good half second; every movement I made seemed slow and sticky.

I smeared some cream cheese on the bagel, sat down at the table, and...

Geez, I thought, *do I ever need some caffeine?* I took a deep breath, blew it out through my lips, fluttering them like a horse, and took a sip of the scalding hot coffee. Nothing.

I got up from the table, went to the fridge and added a little icy water to the coffee, then I took a long, slow draft of the inky black liquid, sat down again and waited for the caffeine to kick in. Five minutes later, I was still waiting, and my mug was empty. So was my plate.

I scratched my head with a fingernail, sighed, got up and let Samson in. Then I took out my phone and checked to see if there were any missed calls or texts from Thomas. There were none.

I sighed. I was disappointed but shook it off. There was no reason to be put off by his lack of communication. Due to the three-hour time difference, he probably wasn't even up yet.

Besides, we're adults. Not lovesick teenagers. I pursed my lips and then opened our message thread and typed a quick "good morning" and "hope you have a great day." As much of my life as I had spent alone, I had to admit I liked the idea of having someone to keep up with me on a daily basis.

I poured myself another mug of coffee and sat back down at the table to ponder what the day might bring. I knew Anne would want to go exploring, and the more I thought about that, the more I wondered if it was why I'd had a rough night. After all, I was worried about her, and I didn't want her to run herself ragged chasing memories that might not be real.

I watched as Samson finished his breakfast, then stood up, washed my plate and put it on the drying rack. Next, I turned my attention to my coffee. I poured what was left into my insulated cup and topped it up. I had a feeling I was going to need it.

"Shall we head to the office now?" I asked Samson as I swiped his leash off the counter. "We've had a nice slow start to the day. Now it's time to go to work."

Samson smiled at me as if to say, *Yeah, right. Good luck with that. You know that's never the case.*

I nodded. "Good point, Sammyo. I guess we'd best be prepared for a chaotic day then." I chuckled to myself as I led him out to the garage and opened the rear driver's side door for him to jump in, and it was as I did that my mind flashed back to the Vincent Romano clip.

He was really young in that video, I thought as the image of the dark-haired, dark-eyed mug shot popped into my head. I didn't know how old he was, and I wondered how old the woman he assaulted was. The news clip hadn't mentioned her being a minor. *If she was, it would make no sense for them not to mention it. Was he... is he still interested in young girls? And how would that have worked if he was the responding officer?*

I let it swirl around in my head as I climbed into my car and pressed the button of the garage door opener clipped to the visor. The doors rolled up and sunlight filled the garage, shining through the rear window of my car. I had to squint into the rearview mirror as I backed out of the driveway.

The list of people I needed to interview was growing, and I wanted to find Romano as much as I wanted to speak with Anne's parents and sister, *and I don't have time to go chasing*

Annie

Anne's memories—so-called memories. And I immediately felt ashamed at the thought.

Maybe I can convince her to wait until after we talk to her parents, I thought as I headed toward Highway 153. I looked at my watch. It was just after seven-forty-five. *I'm going to be early,* I thought. *I'll have time to dig into Romano and maybe figure out where he's hanging out these days.*

"He might be in prison," I said, making eye contact with Samson in the rearview mirror. "Then again, it's been more than thirty-seven years. A lot can change in that time; people can change."

Chapter Twenty-One

July 14, 2023
7:55 AM

As I pulled into my parking lot at the rear of the Police Service building, applied the parking brake, and stepped out of the car, nursing my insulated coffee container, the first thing I noticed was Anne's SUV.

"Oh, damn," I muttered. "There goes that!" It's not that I didn't want to help her; I did. It was just that I didn't have time for a wild goose chase.

I heaved a sigh, took a sip of coffee, and let Samson out.

"Oh, well," I said. "I guess we just have to get in there and see for ourselves. Come on, buddy."

There was a cool breeze wafting over the lot as we walked to the door, and I wondered if that cold front they were forecasting was going to move through sooner than they'd expected.

We rode the elevator to the second floor and exited into

the situation room, and as we did, I saw Anne rise from her desk to meet me. *This is not good,* I thought.

"Kate!" she said as we approached. "I was hoping to catch you first thing. Can we chat?" she asked as she followed me to my office door.

"Of course," I said to her as I unlocked the door, pushed it open and stepped inside.

I flipped on the lights and waited for Anne to enter so I could close it behind us. "What's up?"

She spun around to face me and said, "Kate, I know what you're thinking. You're not a believer, and neither was I, but I did nothing but dream last night, and I'm pretty sure I can take you to where I was at in the woods that night. I think we should go. Right now! While it's fresh."

I breathed deeply as I looked skeptically at her, noting the dark circles under her eyes. "Are you sure you're up for this?"

"Yes," she assured me. "I know I am. I'm stronger than you think, Kate."

"Oh, I know you are," I said quickly. "It's not that. I just don't want you to get your hopes up and then be disappointed if we can't find anything. We also need to do some digging into Vincent Romano. I received some new information about him last night. And... Well, I need to talk to your folks as well."

She nodded and was silent for a moment. Then she nodded again and said, "I get that, Kate. I really do, but I *really* believe I can lead us to the next break in the case. If the memories I uncovered last night are real, it means there's a chance we could find a body somewhere out there."

I nodded. "I'd like to believe that's true, Anne, but you and I know it was thirty-seven years ago. Finding a buried body after all that time... well, it's like winning the lottery."

She narrowed her eyes and frowned. "You're doubting my memories, aren't you?" she said.

Annie

"No, not at all," I lied. "It's just that we can't afford to lose sight of reality. We'll chase your memories, but all in good time. I promise." I gave her a smile and took another sip of my coffee, and as I did, my office door swung open, and my partner, Corbin, walked in.

"You two are here early." He grinned. "I guess everyone is in the mood to get up and around today. I thought it was just me."

"Nope," I muttered, plopping down in my desk chair. "It's not just you."

"I wonder if..." Corbin began, but then he caught sight of Anne's drawn face. "Anne. Are you all right?" he asked.

"I really wish people would stop asking me that," she snapped, shaking her head. "I am just fine. All of this might be recent news to you all, but I've been living with it for thirty-seven years. I'm just fine," she repeated. "Like I said, I think I can give us a break in these cases with what I have in my head."

"Oh?" Corbin took the bait. "I take it, then, that you recovered something during your session with Doctor Webber?"

"How did you know about that?" I asked, frowning.

"Anne told us all about it yesterday before she took off," he answered me, rubbing the stubble on his jaw. Corbin was usually clean-shaven and well put together, and I wondered why he hadn't shaved that morning... Was he worried about Anne, too?

Hell, I knew he was. We all were.

"I think so," Anne said. "It wasn't much, but it was enough that once I got home and went to bed... well, that's when it came flooding back. I mean, I *know* where we need to go, Corbin."

Corbin wasn't following, but he nodded and said, "Okay... Go... where?"

Anne quickly retold him what had happened during the session, openly talking about the fact that she was certain she rode in a trunk next to a body. He seemed as horrified by the idea as I had been the previous night, and I could tell he was battling sympathy and skepticism as she wrapped up her statement.

"Wow," he said, seriously. "That's a lot for a ten-year-old to go through." He shook his head. "It's hard to believe. Your resilience is... amazing."

"Thank you," Anne said as she turned back to me. "So, what was the new information?" she asked.

"It's about Officer Vincent Romano."

"Isn't that the officer Jacobs mentioned?" Anne said, frowning. "Didn't he say there was something fishy about him?"

"Oh, he's more than just fishy," I replied. "I saw a news clip last night. Not long after you were abducted, he was charged with sexual assault and battery."

Anne's mouth dropped open. "Wait, what?"

"It's true," I said. "Apparently, he made a traffic stop and then assaulted the woman driver... in your neighborhood."

Corbin shrugged and said, "I have to admit that's a bit of an eye-opener, but let's not make assumptions. He's not the first sworn officer to be so charged, and he's certainly not the last. The timeline is right, but if he assaulted the driver, that means she was at least old enough to drive. How old was she? Do we know?"

"We don't know," I said, shaking my head, "but we need to find out."

"I wasn't sexually assaulted," Anne said. "At least not that I can remember."

"There's nothing in your file that indicates you were," I agreed. *Hell, there's little enough in it at all,* I thought savagely.

Annie

"Well, if that's the case," Corbin said, "what were the kidnapper's motives? Could he have been abducting kids for fun? Or does he get his kicks from killing them? Either way, it doesn't seem to make much sense."

"No, I'll admit it doesn't," I agreed. "And I agree with you; we can't go making assumptions. We need to know more about Vincent Romano. Damn. Jack's on vacation. Corbin, you check the DMV records. The only witness that day said he saw a green car."

"Then it wasn't a police car," Anne stated, her voice flat.

"It could have been an undercover car," Corbin said as we exchanged glances. I had a feeling he was as worried about her as I was.

"Do you have a picture of Vincent?" Anne asked, breaking the silence once again. "Maybe I'll recognize him."

"Maybe," I said as I went to my desk.

I sat down, logged into my computer and typed in the keywords. It took a minute, but eventually I was able to pull up the mugshot I'd seen in the newscast.

I turned the monitor so they could see it. Corbin, standing in front of the desk, put his hands on the desk and leaned in for a closer look, then straightened up and shook his head.

Anne, who was standing beside him, said, "Was he... ever found guilty of the assault charges?"

"There's nothing to say he was," I said, "but I assume he was. I'll have to look it up."

"He looks familiar, but I'm not feeling anything... negative about him? If anything, I feel warm."

I frowned. "You feel *warm?*" I wasn't sure what to make of that, and I had to wonder if it was a product of too much research into regression psychology.

"I don't know how else to explain it," she said. "It's... well, like sometimes, when I experience things that are associated with what happened to me, I'll either get the chills... or I don't."

"So where does *warm* fall into this?" I asked flatly, ignoring Corbin's warning look.

"I don't know," she replied. "I've never felt anything like it before." She frowned, paused for a moment, staring at the image on the screen, then shrugged, shook her head, and said, "I don't think he's the man that abducted me."

"We need to track him down," I said. "I'd like to talk to him. Even if he had nothing to do with the abductions, he was the responding officer, and his report contained more information than any of the others, though it was sparse, to say the least. It's worth a shot," I continued. "Who knows what might come of it?"

"And we should trust whatever he says?" Corbin said sarcastically, eyeing the mugshot again. "He's hardly the most reliable source."

"Maybe not," I said. "But he has no reason not to tell us the truth. I doubt, even if he was found innocent, that he went back into law enforcement." At that, I paused, thinking how best to put what I was sure would be controversial. "He should not have a problem telling us about anything that might indicate someone on our side might not have been quite so... reliable."

"Are you saying that we might be looking at corruption here?" Corbin asked, his eyes wide. He frowned and rubbed his forehead. "That's heavy, Kate."

"It is," I replied. "And I don't say it lightly. We need to proceed with caution. But here's the thing: I can't understand why there's so little information about these abductions in the official files. It's almost as if the files have been cleaned. And if so, it could only have been done internally."

"You really think that?" Corbin asked doubtfully.

Annie

I shrugged, then said, "All options are on the table. We'll proceed on the—for the lack of a better word—assumption that it's possible there's been some kind of cover-up. I'm not saying there was. I'm just putting it out there."

"Fair enough." Corbin nodded. "I'll get a background check on Vincent while you and Anne go for that drive."

"Perfect," Anne chimed in. "I'll go down and wait for you in the car."

That took me by surprise, but before I could say anything, Anne had turned away and was through the door out of the office.

I turned to Corbin and said, "I'm not sure about her. It's hard to tell how she's handling this mess. She seems pretty sure she can find... I dunno, something, but I'm not sure that her memories are real."

"Maybe not," Corbin replied, "but this might be just what she needs to clear her head. Look, I'll hold the fort while you go with her. *If* she finds nothing, no harm done, but if she does, you're looking at a huge break in the case."

I rose to my feet and called for Samson.

"Touché," I said with a sigh. "I'll be in touch."

Chapter Twenty-Two

July 14, 2023
8:25 AM

When Samson and I stepped out of the building, Anne was already in her car with the engine running. "Okay," I muttered, "I guess we'll go in your car." Then I smiled at her through the open driver's side window and opened the rear door for Samson.

"He might shed on your seats," I said.

"They're leather. It'll be fine," she said with a smile. "Come on. Get in."

I nodded, shut the rear door and then climbed into the passenger seat. "All right, let's go. Are you hungry? Thirsty?"

She shook her head. "Not really, but if you are, we can stop."

"I'm fine." I still had the rest of my coffee from home, and I placed my cup in the cupholder. "Let's do this."

I tried to sound upbeat, but I'm sure she picked up on the doubt in my voice.

But Anne nodded as she pulled away from the curb, saying, "I think it would be best if we start from the neighborhood where we were living at the time."

"That makes sense," I replied and then leaned back in the seat. I wasn't sure if Anne wanted to talk, so I said nothing else. Instead, as we made our way across town to the street where she spent the first decade of her life, I thought again about the news video.

"I saw the interview with your parents after you'd returned home," I said cautiously, not wanting to trigger an adverse reaction.

"Really?" she said. "I'm surprised they gave one. I always thought they swept everything under the rug as if it had never happened."

I pursed my lips, replaying the video in my head. Her parents seemed to be the opposite of indifferent.

"I don't think that's the case," I said. "I think they wanted to protect you and were trying to keep the media away. They were obviously concerned that you'd been through enough."

"Hmm," was all she said.

"But your father did make a comment that caught my attention," I added.

"Oh yes, and what was that?" she asked.

"He intimated that the press should be more worried about the police doing their job." I paused and looked at her, but there was no reaction, so I continued, "Normally, I'd ignore that kind of sentiment coming from an upset family, but... in this case, it seems to be a recurring theme."

"Hah," Anne said, then glanced at me. "Well, he was right, wasn't he? The content of the files, including mine, is pitiful, little more than the initial reports."

Annie

"Exactly," I said. "Which is why I'm beginning to wonder what the hell was going on within the original investigation. Was it just poor management? Understaffing? Or something—"

"Or corruption," Anne said, cutting me off. "Has it crossed your mind that maybe it was a cop?"

"It has," I replied, "but if that's the case, why didn't they at least go through the motions? Wouldn't they have wanted to at least make it look like they were doing their job? I mean, what's with Watson and Harrison? From what I can tell, they made little to no effort at all, and Watson was a vaunted detective with a pretty good closing average."

"I don't know..." Anne trailed off as she slowed to squint at an exit sign. "Man, it's hard to know where to exit."

"You were in the trunk," I said.

"The trunk lid was damaged," she said. "It didn't close properly, and I could see out through the gap."

Now that surprised me; she hadn't mentioned it before.

"There was a McDonald's at the exit, and I was looking back down the road, so it's kind of difficult to flip everything around."

Inwardly, I shook my head. I was feeling more doubtful with each passing mile. But I let her get on with it, lapsing into silence as I looked out through the window and saw we were driving west on I-24 out of Chattanooga...

And in the opposite direction from where she was picked up.

Something about that didn't add up, and the more I thought about it, the more I began to wonder if what we were doing was a total waste of time. I mean, how could the memories of a ten-year-old girl enable the adult to navigate to a spot she visited thirty-seven years later? And in the *opposite* direction from where she was found.

I almost said something, but I didn't. Corbin was right. It was better to let her do what she needed to do to heal. *But we also are trying to solve a case, for heaven's sake.* I could've been hunting down Vincent Romano or interviewing Anne's parents. After all, it was more than likely that their memories were intact, and they would remember everything that had happened.

I was lost in thought when my phone vibrated in my jacket pocket. I took it out and looked at the screen, halfway expecting it to be Corbin with an update on Vincent. Anne and I had been in the car for nearly thirty minutes, and it never took that long to track down someone with a record. But it wasn't Corbin. It was a text from Thomas.

Hi Kate. I hope everything is going as well for you today as it is for me. I should wrap this case up sooner rather than later. On a good lead right now.

I bit back a reply, wishing that I could say the same for my own case. Instead, I was sitting in a car with someone who may or may not be able to remember anything at all. I know. It sounds harsh, but it was the truth, and dancing around someone's feelings didn't change the fact that we were probably wasting precious time.

"This is it," Anne said loudly, breaking into my thoughts.

She was excited. I could tell.

She veered off to the right, up the steep exit ramp, and sure enough, there it was, a McDonald's.

Damn, what are the odds? I thought to myself as I glanced back at Samson. He looked totally unenthused, as per usual, and I smiled at him. *It must be nice to live a life so unbothered.*

Anne took another right at the next stop and headed off into rural Tennessee. I didn't know the area, but what I did know was that we were out of our jurisdiction, and with that might come complications.

Annie

I glanced at Anne. Her face was set; she seemed... painfully focused as she turned onto a narrow two-lane road. Me? I continued to sip my now cold coffee in silence, taking in the surroundings. The buildings and homes were... isolated. She made a left onto an even narrower road, and I inwardly shook my head. We were in the middle of nowhere and going deeper.

"We're getting close," Anne said softly, her voice taut. "I know we are."

"Did you get out of the car when you stopped?" I asked.

She nodded. "I had to. He couldn't get to the spare tire. He had a flat."

"He?" I perked up. "So you're now sure it was a male?"

"I... No, not really," she said, "but it must have been. He was... like... a shadow figure of sorts. I think maybe if I actually saw him, I might recognize him, or maybe his voice? The voice is clearer than the face."

"Was he hiding his face?" I asked.

She shook her head as she slowed the car, peering across an intersection. "No, he didn't hide his face. I just can't remember it. I was never supposed to make it out of there alive, was I? So I don't think he cared if I saw his face."

Her words were sobering—almost as sobering as the hard right she made, fishtailing the SUV as she swerved onto a narrow dirt track.

Anne's face was pale as she white-knuckled the steering wheel, muttering something I couldn't hear under her breath. That and the dirt track made it all a little unnerving.

Unconsciously, I ran my fingers over my seatbelt, wondering where the hell we were going and if we were going to get there in one piece.

I hung onto the handle above the door and continued to watch her as we bumped along the old, rutted track until, finally, she slowed almost to a stop and then pulled off into an open area at the side of the road and stopped in front of an old, rusted gate.

She turned to me, her eyes wide, and said, "This is it, Kate. This is it."

Chapter Twenty-Three

July 14, 2023
9:44AM

I looked at Anne in disbelief. I had no idea where the hell we were, but I dropped a pin on my phone and shared it with Corbin, letting him know where we were. He texted me back that he would get it over to Hawk to look into the ownership of the property.

"I can't believe I found it," Anne said as I looked around, her voice edgy. "I really wasn't sure I was headed to the right place."

Remote was the word I'd have used to describe where we were. The gate... It looked as if it hadn't been opened in a coon's age. The track beyond was overgrown and in deep woodland. It was a frickin' jungle.

"Well," I said, "all we can do now is wait for Hawk to gain access for us, Anne." But she threw her door open and jumped out. "We can't go trespassing—"

But she slammed her door, cutting me off.

"Damnit," I muttered under my breath as I jumped out of the passenger side. Samson bounded over the center console, streaking out over the front seat before I could stop him. "Oh, for Pete's sake," I shouted. "Anne! Stop!"

But by then, Anne was already on the other side of the gate. And I watched as Samson slipped underneath and followed her.

"Anne!" I yelled. "We can't do this. It's trespassing."

I glanced back and forth along the dirt track, my hand on my Glock. There was a dead-end sign just up ahead. We were in a place that you don't want to go unless you're supposed to be there. Folks have gotten shot in such places. We were out of our jurisdiction; we had no probable cause, and I was being led onward by a crazy woman working from a thirty-seven-year-old memory that might or might not have been real. And yes, I was pissed.

I wasn't like Harry. He crossed lines, seemingly with impunity. Me? Anne? We couldn't do that. We operated under a strict set of rules, and we stepped over the line at our peril. Now, here we were. *Geez,* I thought as I ran to the gate.

"Anne, come on back," I shouted, my hands gripping the top of the gate. I was certain it hadn't been opened in years. The chain and padlock were completely rusted out.

"Kate, this is it!" Her voice rang out from somewhere deep in the woods.

"Oh, hell," I said as I ran my hand over my face. "Here we go again." I shook my head in disbelief, and while I wasn't inclined to argue with her, I wasn't inclined to break our own damn rules either.

"Come out of there, damn it," I shouted, once again glancing around. I didn't think there was anyone around, but I didn't like the idea of wandering around in a damn forest,

Annie

either. There's no telling what might be out there... bears, wild boars, bobcats, even moonshiners.

My phone buzzed with a message from Hawk—I couldn't believe we had service—letting me know he was contacting the owner to get permission for us to enter the property.

Too frickin' late, Hawk, I thought as I climbed over the gate, trying to convince myself that his text was a good enough reason for me to go ahead.

"Where are you, Anne?" I yelled as I trudged along the overgrown trail, stopping now and then to listen for any signs of her or my dog. I could hear rustling just up ahead, and it wasn't long before I caught sight of Samson's bushy tail and Anne's white blouse.

"Hey, what's going on?" I shouted.

She looked at me and then shook her head. "I know, right? I can't believe I found it." Anne pointed to the remnants of the road leading onto the property. "We drove right up there. I know we did, because when I got out of the car and looked back toward the road, I remember the hill down to the gravel—and I also remember how dark it was and how far away from town we were."

I nodded, seeing the slope down to the gate. I gazed up at the trees. The cover was complete. The day was warm, but there was a cool breeze blowing through the leaves.

"Isn't it supposed to rain today?" Anne said absentmindedly. "It rained that night. I remember getting mud all over my shoes, and..." she faltered. Her voice broke, and a tear rolled down her cheek. "I can't believe I forgot about her."

"You can't be upset about that," I said as I put my hand on her shoulder. "You were just a kid, and you're remembering now, so that's all that matters."

She shrugged. "I don't know why he made me ride in the trunk like that, next to her body. I got to ride in the backseat when we left. He told me I'd been a good girl for being so helpful."

I gritted my teeth as I pictured the sick moment. "You were strong," I said gently, "and you're still strong."

Anne looked down and shook her head. "It's not the same. I don't know where to go now that we're here. It looks so different than it did that night. It was such a long time ago."

"I know," I said softly, looking around at the towering pines. "But we can still look. We might even be able to get some help up here and do a full sweep, but I have to get permission first. Otherwise, we'll be in all kinds of trouble."

"I don't even know where we are." Anne laughed, shaking her head. "This is just crazy. If you asked me to backtrack, I'm not sure I could."

I took a deep breath, trying to think of what to say to her, but before I could my phone rang. I fished it out, hoping it would be Hawk, and much to my relief, it was.

"Hey," I answered. "Were you able to get in touch with the owner?"

"Yeah, I was," he said. "It's a hunting property. They lease it to hunting parties. I wasn't able to get much information beyond that. I have the GPS coordinates. And the guy said to go ahead and do whatever you need to do. It's not hunting season."

"Okay, that's good news," I said as I watched Samson. He had his nose to the ground. "What about the lessees? Can we get a list? How long have they owned the property?"

"I still need to find that out," Hawk said. "The guy said he was busy and that he'd call me back in a little bit. But yes, he agreed to provide the list of people who've leased it. But that's for later. The most important thing right now is that you have permission to be there."

"You are correct," I said with a chuckle. I walked a little

way out of earshot from Anne and said, "I dunno, Hawk. It's a wilderness out here, and she doesn't have any idea where to look. It's going to take a full sweep, and God only knows whose jurisdiction this is. We'll do a little more digging, but I'm not holding my breath. I'll let you know if we find anything."

"Oh, Kate," Hawk said before hanging up. "One thing to remember is that you're looking for bones, scattered bones, most likely. The owner said there's a large coyote population. That might make things difficult."

"Got it," I replied and hung up. Hawk was right. Even if we were in the right place, there was no guarantee that we'd find anything.

I turned and looked at Anne. She was kicking at leaves on the forest floor. *How's she going to handle it if we don't find anything?*

"He buried her," Anne said as I approached. "He said he had to bury her so the animals wouldn't get her. He had to make sure she couldn't be found...." She trailed off and looked up at me. "But he didn't bury her very deep. I remember thinking that, Kate. I remember thinking that my dad had buried our hamster deeper than he buried her. What a horrible thing to think."

"It's okay, Anne," I reassured her. "We can't control our thoughts, and you were coping with a traumatic situation at just ten years old. Kids tend to think like that. You were just trying to make sense of a complex and terrifying situation."

She stared at me, her eyes glistening.

"If he didn't bury her very deep," I said, "we have more of a chance of stumbling upon the remains."

"But the animals?" she said.

"Yeah, I know," I said, "they scatter—We might still find something... What the hell?"

Samson was about ten feet away, yipping, pawing madly at the ground.

"What is it, Sammy?" I said as I ran to him.

He stopped digging, looked up at me panting, then took a couple of steps back and stood still, staring at the ground where he'd been digging.

Suddenly, Anne was at my side, her hand on my arm, staring down at the dirt where Samson had been digging.

"I think he's found something..." she whispered.

I swallowed hard as I stepped forward and crouched down. She was right. Samson had found something, and I knew what it was. I stood up and took a pair of nitrile gloves from my pocket and snapped them on, then crouched down again and gently scraped the dirt away from the yellowed artifact, and I knew we were mere seconds away from making the call.

"Good boy," I said and sighed with sadness and no little amount of disbelief. I patted his head, then carefully scraped away the dirt until, at last, I could see the small human skull nestled among the leaves on the forest floor.

Anne knew, I thought. *She really did know... I wonder what else she knows.*

Chapter Twenty-Four

July 14, 2023
12:35PM

I tugged on Samson's leash, backing him up as the cadaver dogs came crashing back through the property, having located two more sets of remains. The crime scene unit swarmed the rural hunting grounds, and I watched in silence as the county stepped in and took over. I was pissed, but after all, we were out of our jurisdiction, and the only thing linking this crime scene to Chattanooga was Anne Robar.

I glanced at Anne, who was standing beside me. She had a distant look on her face that caused me to frown. I could only imagine how hard it must have been for her to witness this gruesome scene... for a second time.

"Would you like to sit in the car for a while?" I asked her. "It's getting pretty warm out here."

She sighed, pushing her blond hair from her face. "I'm

fine," she replied. "I just... I wonder if one of them is Emma Jacobs."

"We won't know until they run tests," I replied, knowing I was telling her something she was already well aware of, but at that moment, I was at a loss for words. I felt I should've trusted Anne's memory, and I was still coming to terms with the fact that we'd located *three* bodies.

Three, I thought.

We didn't have files for three missing kids. If two were Emma Jacobs and Louise Hackett, it meant we had an unknown third. And that meant there was another family out there still waiting for answers more than three decades later. I folded my arms across my chest as a familiar face appeared from behind me.

"Kate Gazzara," Doc Sheddon greeted me. "Now, why would you be way out here?" he asked as he trudged through the knee-high grass to where Anne and I were standing.

"It's..." I began, not knowing quite how to explain it. "We're here because... because it's connected to a case we're working," I said, knowing I should probably offer more details, but I wasn't ready for the blowback I was sure to get from Doc; his sense of gallows humor was something I didn't need, not at that moment. Not after finding the remains, and I'd fallen into something of a detached state of mind and thought trying to explain it all seemed... daunting.

"Cold case, I assume?" he asked, peering into the nearest of the shallow graves, which was several feet away from where I was standing.

I nodded. "It's not so cold now," I said. "And what are you doing here? This is Sequatchie County, not your usual purview."

Doc Sheddon chuckled. "Well, Sequatchie doesn't have an ME, so Sherrif Lock called and asked me to attend rather

Annie

than have to wait for State to send someone from Nashville. So, of course, I agreed." He paused for a moment. I said nothing. Then he continued. "It's not often someone stumbles across not one, but three sets of remains. And they're old, which means, if I'm reading the signs correctly, there are probably multiple dumping grounds?"

I blanched at the thought, but deep down I knew he was right.

"Maybe so," I said, glancing at Anne. She was staring at Doc, her face ghastly white, and that was when I knew it was time for me to take her off the case. She'd already had to muddle through a long and traumatic statement for the sheriff's office, and now she was having to listen to Doc as he casually theorized that we were probably dealing with a serial killer who had been operating for... God only knew how many years.

"Well, these are always the hardest," Doc said. "I'm going to go take a look. Would you two like to join me?" He had that... I wanted to say giddy, excited look on his face, but that really wasn't it. It was dedication, a sense of urgency, a look I knew well. I nodded and handed Samson's leash to Anne.

"Take him over there, out of the way," I said. "I'll join you when we're done."

Anne didn't protest. She bent down, patted Samson's head and said, "Come on, boy. Let's get out of here."

Doc handed me some Tyvec booties. I slipped them on and followed him to the graveside, the first one where Samson had found the skull, and I couldn't help but wonder what Anne must have experienced all those years ago.

She was only ten years old, I thought as my stomach tightened at the thought. *No kid—or adult, for that matter—should ever have to witness something like that.*

"Anne looked a bit off," Doc Sheddon commented.

I nodded but didn't reply.

"These were all we found in this location," a crime scene tech said as she stood up. "There's not much left, as you can see. There's been a lot of animal activity."

Doc nodded. "Indeed, there has," he said. "What we have here is a small child, age to be determined. Most of the long bones are missing, by the look of it. The body cavity is still partially intact, as is the left arm—the humerus, ulna, radius... several ribs, the clavicle, sternum and... yes." He leaned in to get a closer look. "See that there?" he asked, touching something with a forefinger. "That's the hyoid bone. And it looks like it's broken. Now..." He paused, squinting. "That might not mean what you think. It could've been broken post-mortem. I'll have to run some tests on that. But..."

"But it means she was probably strangled," I said through gritted teeth.

"She?" he asked. "You think it's a she? Hmm. Possibly, but yes, in all likelihood, this child died either by ligature or manual strangulation."

He looked at the tech and said, "Nice job so far, but keep digging. See what else you can find. We're going to take a look at the other two."

She nodded, and Doc straightened. *With no little effort*, I thought. *The old boy's feeling his years.* I did not know how old he was, but I knew he had to be at least in his sixties. He'd been around long before I enlisted.

The trees above us swayed and rustled in the light summer breeze. Had it not been for the gruesome situation, it would have been a beautiful day.

The canopy overhead was thick and lush, allowing only glints of sunlight to filter through, and the forest floor was virtually free of undergrowth due, I imagined, to the lack of

Annie

sunlight. *But the roots,* I thought. *It would have been difficult to dig here, especially in the dark.*

"Strange place to dump a body," Doc said as if reading my mind. "Can you imagine how difficult it would be to dig a hole?"

I nodded, staring up into the canopy. "It would be a lot of work, but the trees would have been much smaller and probably not so numerous thirty-seven years ago," I said, trying to imagine how in the world Anne had been able to find her way back after all this time.

"Thirty-seven years?" Doc asked as he stopped walking. "How on earth do you know that?"

"It's a long story, Doc," I replied, "and one for another day, if you don't mind."

He grunted and continued on.

"Ah, this one seems to be more complete," he remarked as the two techs stepped to one side.

He was right. The body was small and, as far as I could tell, almost complete.

I've seen a lot of death during my years as a homicide detective, but the thought that Anne could have been one of these bodies still twisted my gut into knots.

Doc knelt down beside the body, shook his head and sighed as he pointed to the broken hyoid bone. "It's not as easy as you might think to break a hyoid, even if the victim is a child, as we have here. The surrounding muscles protect the hyoid, you see, so it takes a considerable amount of force, such as generated by anger or… sexual gratification, to break it."

I frowned but nodded.

"There are no signs of any other wounds," he added. "No signs of blunt force trauma to the skull. Hmm, well, we'll see. Let's take a peek at number three."

We stood up. I turned away and closed my eyes. The cool

breeze wafted across my face, and a shiver rolled down my spine. The temperature seemed unseasonably low for July, but I put that down to the trees blocking out the sun.

I stood for a moment, inhaling the damp, woodsy scent of decaying leaves, and I actually shivered.

"You coming?" Doc said, breaking into my thoughts.

I opened my eyes, heaved a sigh, nodded, and followed him to the third shallow grave.

The third skeleton was also near complete, and, once again, the hyoid bone appeared to be broken.

"It appears we have a pattern," Doc said, his voice somber, missing its usual air of quirkiness. "Smaller than the other two, though."

I looked at the pathetic little pile of bones, nodded, and said, "And younger?"

"Perhaps," he replied, then shrugged and continued, "It's hard to tell without a reconstruction." Doc sighed, pursed his lips and furrowed his brow. "What kind of evil bastard does something like this? It's always the little ones that get to me."

"It's tough," I agreed, turning to look for Anne and Samson. I couldn't see them from where I was, but I could imagine her standing beside Samson.

I need to get her out of here, I thought.

As much as I wanted to stay and get a solid feel for the scene, what was done was done—and I would have to wait for Doc and the Sequatchie County crime scene team to send us their findings. Lucky for me, I had an in with Doc and Mike Willis, the head of our crime scene investigation unit, so I'd be able to get the information I needed as soon as it was available.

"I think that's about all I can do for right now," Doc said. "I'll talk to Sheriff Lock to see how he feels about me taking the bones with me for evaluation... You say this is about a cold case you're investigating?"

Annie

I nodded. Then said, "At least one of the bodies, perhaps two. We won't know until the remains are identified."

"Well, you know as well as I do how long it can take to identify..." He trailed off and shook his head, then continued, "I'll talk to Lock and see what we can do."

"I think we have a place to begin," I began. "If I'm right, one of them is Emma Jacobs, and another is Louise Hackett. The third... I don't know. It has me wondering, as you said, if my perp moved on to pastures—or perhaps I should say burial grounds—new. You'll call me, right?" I asked.

"Of course," he replied. "Take care, Kate." And with that, he turned away and shuffled through the long grass to where Tony Lock was standing with his hands on his hips, talking to two deputies.

Me? I took one last look at the remains of the small child and shuddered. I heaved a deep breath, blew it out through my lips, then turned and walked away and out of the woods to where Anne and Samson were waiting for me beside the car.

"Was Doc Sheddon able to tell you anything?" she asked as I walked around to the passenger side rear door and let Samson jump in.

"I'll drive," I said. And without waiting for an answer, I climbed in behind the wheel.

I hesitated as she climbed in beside me, then I started the motor and turned and looked at her and said, "They were strangled." I was brutal, I know, but there was no other way to say it. "All three of them."

"Oh my God. That's awful," she said, covering her mouth with her hand.

I nodded and almost told her about the third victim being smaller than the others, but I didn't. I didn't want to make it any worse for her than it already was.

Not yet, anyway.

Chapter Twenty-Five

July 14, 2023
3:30PM

We made the drive back to the department in good time, stopping through the McDonald's drive-thru to grab cheeseburgers and cokes. Anne was silent for most of the drive, and I couldn't find the right words to break it. That is until we pulled into the parking lot.

"Anne," I said without looking at her. "I think you should take some personal days. Give yourself a chance to process it." I took a sip of my Coke and waited for her to say something.

"I've told you already, Kate. I'm not taking any time off because of this." Her voice was sharp as she pushed open the passenger side door and jumped out. "You already drove me back in my own car. I think that was enough of a break."

I took a deep breath, fighting the urge to argue with her, but I stopped myself. This was no time to scold her for the way she'd spoken to me.

"I'm sorry," Anne said after a few moments. "I shouldn't have snapped at you. I know you're trying to look out for me, and I get it. I do."

"And I completely understand why you want to stay with it. But it's too personal. You're too close to it, Anne, and that's not good. You know that."

Samson whined. I got out, went to the rear door and let him out.

"I know, and I appreciate it, Kate," she said as she rounded the car, and together, we walked toward the station doors. "But I need this. Please don't take me off the case."

I stopped at the door, my card at the reader, and I looked at her, hesitating over what I was about to say next.

I nodded, looked at my watch, then said, "It's three-thirty. Are your folks at home, d'you think?"

Anne paused, glanced at her own watch, then said, "They should be. My dad hates the afternoon traffic."

I nodded, made my decision, and said, "I think I'll stop by and have a chat with them. You go on in."

"You're going now?" she asked. "You don't want me..." She caught my look and said, "Oh, I see. Okay. I'll text you their address. It's only about thirty minutes from here. I'll... go on in, then, and update the others on what we found... if you're sure."

"I'm sure," I replied, though I hesitated, half-tempted to grab my partner, Corbin. But I didn't. Instead, I said, "We'll meet up in the morning. In the meantime, I want you to get some sleep. Understand?" I looked at her sternly, and I meant it. I was in no mood to argue with her. I was a hair's breadth from removing her from the case altogether.

She nodded. We said our goodbyes, and Samson and I went to my car.

The heat of the afternoon was setting in, and I found

Annie

myself missing the cool breeze of the woodland crime scene. I let Samson into the passenger seat, then started the car and waited for it to cool down.

A minute later, my phone pinged. Anne had sent me the address.

It was almost thirty minutes later when I pulled into the driveway, noting the upper-middle-class home. And I wondered if Anne had let them know I was coming. I parked in front of the three-car garage and stepped out. Samson scrambled over the center console and down to the ground. I shortened his leash and walked around the front of the car toward the front door. Before I could get there, it opened, and an older woman in a pair of white slacks stepped out onto the porch.

"You must be Captain Gazzara," she greeted me with a sad smile.

Her resemblance to her daughter was striking. Her eyes, nose, and high cheekbones were almost identical to Anne's.

"Annie sent me a text. She said you were coming by to chat. I'm her mother, Anita Smithson. Please come in."

She looked hard at Samson for a second but said nothing. She took a step back and held the door open.

It was a... pleasant home. I could smell lavender as I stepped across the threshold. I paused and waited for her to close the door before she led us into the white-carpeted living room, again looking at Samson. I smiled and looked down at him.

"Please, sit down," she said, gesturing toward the white leather couch, and I did. Samson sat at my feet, staring intently at Anita Smithson.

"So," she said after sitting down in a matching easy chair, "Anne said you found some remains today."

"That's true," I replied and changed the subject. "Is your husband home?"

Anita's lips flatlined but then curved up into a slight smile. "He is, but he's walking on the treadmill. I'm sure he'll join us in a minute. Would you like something to drink?"

"No, thank you," I said. "Look, I know this must be difficult for you, but I'd like to talk about what happened in 1986. Anne doesn't remember much, so anything you can remember could be helpful."

She frowned. Her outlook darkened. "What I remember," she said angrily, "is that the police didn't seem to give a damn. They said she was a runaway! Can you believe that? She was ten years old, for God's sake, and her sister was there. I'll never forget it. Not till the day I die."

I looked at her, slowly nodding my head, not quite knowing how to respond.

"I'm so sorry," I said finally. "I can't change the past, but maybe, with your help, I can find the person responsible and—"

"Don't you dare use the word closure," she snapped. "Nothing... nothing will ever erase the memories of those horrible days."

I didn't answer. I mean, what could I say? Instead, I stayed silent and waited for her to continue.

"It was a day just like any other," she said after a moment or two of silence. "She and her sister, Lillian, were riding their bikes, as they did almost every single day. They didn't always ride together, though." She paused, her hands clasped together in front of her, staring down at the carpet. Then she looked up at me and sighed. "Lillian is three years older than Annie, and she had her friends. She liked to ride with a boy in the neighborhood."

Annie

I took out my notepad. "D'you remember his name?" I asked.

"Oh dear, goodness," she said, frowning and shaking her head. "Let me see... Was it Ronnie? No." She shook her head. "I don't remember. I'm sorry." And she fell silent again, staring at the carpet. And again, I waited. The room was quiet. I could hear the clock ticking on the mantlepiece.

Finally, after what seemed like a full minute, she continued, "The other little girls that had gone missing were never really spoken of. Just a few stories on the local news, and then they were forgotten. And I have to be honest, I didn't think too much of it, not until Annie was taken. Nobody seemed to care. Nobody. It was... awful... as if they were just trying to sweep it all under the rug. The police..." She trailed off, slowly shaking her head. "I can only tell you what Lillian told me."

I nodded. "I understand," I said. "I'd like to talk to her. Can you give me her number?"

"Of course," she said, "but she's a busy woman, and she doesn't like to talk about it. I think she blames herself for what happened to Annie."

She gave me the number, and I made a note of it. It was then that a tall, heavyset, white-haired man wearing a dark gray sweat suit entered the room. He looked at me, then at Samson, dabbing his face with a sweat towel. Samson looked up at him, his tongue lolling out of his open mouth.

"So you're Anne's boss, then?" he said sourly. "You know, I never could understand why in the hell she wanted to go off and join the people who failed her so damned completely. It makes no sense to me at all." And he sat down in the chair opposite his wife.

"Oh stop, Jim," she chided him. "She wanted to make a difference. You know that." She looked back at me and said, "Anyway, Lillian found Annie's bike just a couple of houses down from us. She thought maybe she'd left it to go play. We..." She looked at Jim. "We were both at work."

"It wasn't until we got home that we realized Annie was gone," Jim Smithson added. "We didn't wait. We phoned the police right away, and it all went downhill from there. It was the most frustrating, awful thing I've ever experienced. This detective showed up and barely wrote a single thing I told him!" He gritted his teeth at the memory.

"Do you remember his name?" I asked, though I already knew the answer.

"Detective Watson," Anita answered quickly. "I'll never forget it. He was absolutely worthless. He promised us he'd find her, and then he did nothing. We didn't hear from him again until after Annie came home. The only thing that saved my little girl was Annie *herself*. Thank God."

"And the man who found her on the road," Jim added. "He was a Good Samaritan, that's for sure."

I perked up, thinking back to the lack of information in the file. "You wouldn't know his name, would you?" I asked.

"Oh hell," Jim scoffed. "Let me think. He was an off-duty police officer, I believe."

"Vinny," Anita said. "Vinny Romano. He was living just a couple of streets over from us. I often wondered, what were the chances of an encounter like that?"

Me, too, I thought dryly. *There's that name again.* "Did either of you know him?" I asked.

They both shook their heads, and then Anita said, "We didn't know many people in the neighborhood..." She paused for a moment, then said, "We moved soon after..." She paused again and then continued, "We were so lucky Annie was able to escape. She was so badly hurt..." Again, she paused. I said nothing. Neither did her husband. "She wasn't able to tell us anything. She wouldn't talk about it at all. Not even to the police."

"She still doesn't remember much," I said, more for something to say than anything else.

"She started having night terrors," Jim said, wiping his face with the towel. "That lasted for years. We took her to a therapist, two, in fact, but they couldn't get anything out of her, either. We figured she'd talk about it in her own time."

"And she never did." Anita sighed. "I think back to that day and wish that we'd not been at work or that her sister would've been with her, but that's... just... wishful thinking. She's been... I don't know, happy enough with Alex and the kids, but I know she's still suffering. And I suffer for her. We'll never get over it. Will we, Jim?"

Jim stared dourly, unblinking at Samson, seemingly reliving the past. Then he straightened up, took a deep breath, smiled at me and said, "I hope you get the bastard, Captain, and if you do, I'd appreciate you giving me five minutes alone with him."

I couldn't help but smile to myself at that. How many times had I heard it before? Too many to count, but I understood the sentiment, so I nodded and said, "You can rest assured that I'm going to do everything in my power to find him. Unfortunately, the five minutes you need... well, I wish I could oblige, but I can't. Is there anything else you remember that might help?"

They both shook their heads.

"Anne won't talk to me about the investigation," Anita said suddenly. "How is she? Is she... Is she coping?"

"I honestly don't know," I said. "But she's a strong woman, stronger than most. She'll cope." *Until she doesn't,* I thought as I rose to my feet, as did Samson.

They also rose to their feet, and I dug a card out of my pocket and handed it to Jim but said nothing.

He looked at it and nodded.

I bid them goodbye, and they showed me to the door. I stepped outside and stood for a moment. I heard the door close quietly behind me. I took a deep breath and tried to shake off the eerie feeling that had suddenly overshadowed me. I looked up at the sky. Dark clouds were billowing in from the west, reflecting the feeling of foreboding that I couldn't shake. I looked down at Samson and said, "Looks like we're in for a storm, buddy." And I meant it literally and figuratively.

Why was Vincent Romano on the road that night? I thought as we walked slowly back to the car. *Was it just a coincidence? Or was it something else? So many questions. So few answers.*

I looked at my watch. It was just after five-fifteen. *Geez,* I thought. *How time flies when you're...* I shook my head and headed home for the day. I checked my phone, hoping Doc Sheddon might have made some leeway with the identifications. It was a forlorn hope, I knew, but what else was I to do? And no, he hadn't made contact. It would take time, that I knew. It always does. It could take months to identify the bodies.

But I also knew I didn't have months. I didn't even have weeks. I wanted to know now!

Chapter Twenty-Six

July 14, 2023
6:15PM

It was well after six that evening when Samson and I arrived home. Any other day I would have gone for a good long run, but not that day. It was hot and still, and the sky was darkening. I could smell rain in the air. So I opted to let Samson outside in the backyard while I dug through the freezer to find something enticing, but all I found was a tub of leftover beef stew from back in January. I held it for a moment, stared at it, sighed and dropped it back into the freezer.

I took what was left of a bottle of Pino from the fridge, poured it into a glass, and smiled as it filled the glass almost to overflowing. I set the bottle down on the kitchen counter and carefully raised the glass to my lips, and took a big sip—no, not a sip, a damn great swallow. I held it in my bulging cheeks for a moment, savoring the taste, then gulped it down, gasped, sucked air, coughed and almost choked. *Stupid...* I thought, staring at the glass. *Oh, screw it,* and I took another huge mouthful. This time it went down smoothly, and I literally collapsed onto a kitchen chair. I was suddenly bone tired and... pissed off isn't the way I'd put it, but it was close. I'm sure you know the feeling.

And so I sat there for a long moment, pondering the events of the day. It had been one hell of a day, but one thing stuck in my mind, and strangely, it wasn't the discoveries of the morning. I was still stuck on Vincent Romano's appearance as the Good Samaritan who had picked Anne up that night. Why in the world would it have not been in Anne's file? I mean, he was a police officer, the perfect person to make a statement, right? So why didn't he make a statement? And if he did, what the hell happened to it? And will Anne recognize him after all these years?

"Yikes," I muttered as I stood up and looked down at the now half-empty glass, rubbing my forehead as I tried to keep everything straight in my head.

I went to the back door and looked out. Samson was at the far end of the garden, his nose to the ground, running back and forth. *A rabbit, I shouldn't wonder*, I thought, *or maybe a squirrel.* I needed a shower. I pondered whether or not I should leave him out, but the sky was darkening even further, as was my mood, so I opened the door, called him in, went back to my wine, sat down again, and stared at my silent phone; it stared malevolently back at me, and I knew I was soon going to find myself in a whole heap of trouble.

This was a doozy of a case, and it wasn't just the fact that it was cold and involved young girls. It was the mysterious finger pointing back at the department. I had a feeling, to paraphrase Hamlet, "something was rotten in the State of Denmark," of that I was pretty damn sure. My gut was telling me so, and so were the facts, or rather the lack of them.

Annie

I took another swallow, reducing what was left in my glass by half. I held it by the stem, tilted it sideways and stared at it.

What was going on in the department all those years ago? I wondered. It made no sense, and the more I thought about it, the angrier I became. *Bruce Watson won't talk,* I thought. *Why not? Floyd Harrison is dead, murdered. A coincidence? I think not. The files have been stripped. By whom? And why was Vincent Romano on the road that night? And... he was the same officer who responded to Emma Jacobs' missing person report. It frickin stinks. All of it.*

I picked up my glass and emptied it, then slammed it down on the table, went to the fridge, grabbed another bottle and poured myself another huge glass. I knew I was headed for a drunk, and I didn't care. I had an awful feeling that for the first time in nearly twenty years as a detective, I was out of my depth, and I didn't like it worth a damn.

I squeezed my eyes shut tight and tried to remember when Romano had been charged with sexual assault and battery.

"This case is a wreck," I muttered to myself as Samson scratched at his empty bowl.

I slid off the chair and refilled his water bowl, then overfilled his bowl with kibble.

"Whadda you think about it, Sammyo?" I asked him as I grabbed a protein bar for my evening meal. I'd drunk that first, brimming glass of Pino in just four swallows and had already started on the second, and, having barely eaten that day, I was beginning to feel the effects.

Samson paused, stopped chewing, and peered up at me, tilting his head. I waited for him to smile at me, but he didn't. And that, to me, was all I needed to know.

"So you think this is a mess, too, huh?" I said. "And you know what, buddy? I trust you more than I do most humans. I need a shower."

I took another swallow of wine and rose a little unsteadily to my feet.

"If you hear a crash," I said, chuckling like an idiot, "it'll just be me taking a header into the bath. You come and get me, okay?"

He didn't answer. He just stared up at me, stoically.

"Okay," I said, "be that way." And with that, I headed up the stairs, topped-up glass in hand, singing softly to myself. *When duty calls me, I must go. To stand and face another foe. But part of me will always stray. Over the hills and far away.* Yes, I'd been watching a lot of the Sharpe movies lately, and that chorus had been wallowing around inside my head and wouldn't go away. Or was it the wine?

I took a quick, cold shower. Afterward, I pulled on a pair of black cotton shorts and a white T-shirt, leaving my damp hair to fall around my shoulders, and went back down to the living room, stopping along the way to grab my cell phone from the kitchen table.

I flipped through Netflix and was about to begin watching *Sharpe's Enemy,* hoping it would take my bleary mind off the case, when my phone rang. My heart jumped in my chest, and under my breath I found myself whispering, *Please don't let this be work. Please, please, please.*

Much to my relief, it wasn't. It was Thomas.

"Hey," I answered, the sound of fatigue in my voice borderline startling. "Am I glad it's you. How's your day?"

"Not too bad," he answered, not sounding nearly as cheery as he usually did. "I caught word through the grapevine that you happened upon a discovery today."

"So you have contacts in the Sequatchie County Sheriff's Office, too, then, huh?"

"One or two." He laughed, but it sounded empty. "Any-

Annie

way, I just wanted to call and see how your day went. We don't have to talk about work if you don't want to."

"I don't," I admitted. "And I've already had too much to drink, but it's so nice to hear your voice. When are you coming home?"

"Soon," he replied. "And I promise you, when I do, we're going to have the nicest dinner Chattanooga has to offer, and the best wine, too."

"Deal." I laughed. "I miss you, Thomas."

"I miss you, too," he said and was quiet for a moment, then said, "What's wrong, Kate? You're not yourself, I can tell."

"Nothing," I replied, frowning. "Well, maybe a little. It's this case, but I want to forget it, just for tonight. Let's talk about you."

And we did. We chatted for the best part of an hour, mostly discussing the weather and the mundane intricacies of life. I was aching to tell him what I was really feeling, but... well, that wasn't me, and so I didn't, and finally we hung up and I went back to Sharpe.

"King George commands and we obey. Over the hills and far away..."

Why was Vinny there to pick up Anne that night? I couldn't help but wonder. *And what about Bruce Watson? Would he be open to a chat, off the record?*

Chapter Twenty-Seven

July 15, 2023
4:45 AM

I woke up long before my alarm went off. I stared at the clock. It was four-forty-five. Samson looked up at me from his bed, then closed his eyes again. I rolled onto my side and closed my eyes, trying to will myself back to sleep. It didn't work.

At five o'clock, I gave in, flipped back the covers, and rolled out of bed. I dressed quickly in a pair of running shorts and a white T-shirt, put my hair up in a ponytail and looked at Samson, who was, surprisingly, still fast asleep.

I didn't like the idea of going on a run without him, but I also didn't like the idea of making him get up this early if he didn't want to. So, I told myself he would be fine, chugged a couple glasses of water, and then slipped out into the early morning hours.

It had indeed rained sometime during the night, and the air was still damp and heavy, but the darkness brought with it a coolness to the air that I knew would evaporate with the rising sun, still more than an hour away.

I took off at a fast clip, heading north along the pavement, choosing not to wear my earbuds. My tennis shoes squeaked with each stride in the morning's stillness.

Some people avoid running in the darkness, but I enjoyed it. It cleared my head, something I needed in the worst way. It also brought an air of peace, and four miles later, I was back on my front porch breathing hard, feeling exhilarated and, yes, ready for whatever the day might bring. I stepped inside and went straight upstairs to the bedroom.

"You ready to get up yet?" I said as he gazed up at me lazily. He slowly stood up, stretching his paws out in front of him, then his back legs, yawning widely.

"Good," I said. "Come on. Let's get you outside."

I let him out, made him his breakfast and then started my coffee, popping a couple of slices of bread into the toaster.

I waited till the coffee finished brewing before I grabbed my mug and filled it almost to the rim, then stepped outside onto the back patio to watch Samson schnauzing around. It was time for me to mow, and I made a mental note to take on that task that evening.

Samson came jogging up onto the patio, and I let him inside. Me? I sat there for a few more minutes, enjoying the cool morning air, the sound of the birds singing in the trees, and... my coffee. We had plenty of time, though I still needed to take a quick shower and get dressed. I downed the rest of my coffee and then smeared some jelly on the toast. Samson gobbled up his kibble, and I inhaled the toast.

I checked my phone as I headed back up the stairs to my bedroom, and for a brief moment, I thought about what it might be like if Thomas and I got serious enough to live

Annie

together. It was a fleeting thought, but my heart still skipped a beat at the idea.

I do like him, I thought to myself, smiling. *Of course, I like him. I'm just too old to go through the puppy love phase. Maybe... Oh, I don't know.*

I took a quick, cool shower, put my hair up in a bun—a rather severe look for me—and opted for a pair of dark blue jeans, a sage blouse, and a tan linen jacket.

"Ready?" I said to Samson as I made it back to the kitchen. "If we go now, we'll be right on time."

He wagged his tail, and I slipped his harness on, clipped my badge and holster to my belt and filled my to-go cup with coffee. We then headed out into the garage and climbed into the car.

I was feeling pretty good as I backed out onto the street. Somehow, in the peace of the early morning, I'd been able to avoid the previous evening's dread of what was sure to come, but as I made my way to work, that same sick feeling returned.

"I don't like it when cases take the kind of turn that makes me second guess the detectives and department that worked on them," I told Samson. He was sitting next to me in the passenger seat. "Not only does it look bad for the department, but Chief Johnston doesn't want us ruffling any feathers. But it's hard not to do that when all the signs are pointing to one of your own."

Samson tilted his head at me, his tongue lolling out the side of his mouth. He didn't get it, I was sure, but he was a good sounding board. A dog can't lie, cheat, or manipulate. All Samson can do is to be true to himself and to me, which he always was, and that's the greatest gift one person can give another. And yes, I do regard him as a person, as my friend and protector.

I pulled into the lot and parked, taking my time as I helped

Samson down to the ground. He has a tendency to want to leap over the center console to the ground, and I'm always scared he's going to hurt himself, but he didn't.

The air was heavy, muggy, and as I gazed up at the dark clouds, I chided myself for not checking the weather. I almost always gave it a quick peek in the morning or evening, but that day... well, I hadn't. But I shrugged it off, even as the thunder cracked in the distance. *Another omen?* I wondered as I led Samson into the building.

We were greeted, one after another, by several uniformed officers as we made our way to the second floor, and even as I made it to my office door, I could see several members of my team were already waiting for me inside. I put a pleasant look on my face and stepped in to see Anne, Ramirez, Corbin, Hawk, and Cooper. The only person missing was Jack.

"Good morning." I gave them a nod as I unclipped the leash from Samson's harness and set it on my desk. "Any updates from yesterday?"

"Not that I'm aware of," Ramirez said. "We've been working to get the information from the owners of the hunting property, but they've only owned it since 2013. So not much hope there."

"We need to find the person or persons that owned it back in eighty-six," I said before taking a sip of my coffee.

"We're already on it," Cooper said. "I'm supposed to get a call from the courthouse today. But it must have changed hands several times, and then there's the fact that whoever took Anne out there that night... Well, it doesn't mean they owned the land, does it?"

"It could have been anybody," Corbin said. "Probably was. Maybe even a local who was familiar with the area. It's like looking for a needle in a haystack. It was July. Out of season." He shrugged.

Annie

I took a deep breath and took a seat at the table. "I have something to share," I said as I eyed Anne, wishing I could've talked to her before I told the rest of the team.

"What is it?" Anne asked and leaned forward. "Mom said you stopped by. Is it something they told you?"

I nodded. "Do you remember who it was that picked you up that night?"

She frowned. "No... I really don't."

"Your mother didn't tell you, or the police, nobody?"

"No. I've never talked to my mother about it," she replied, still frowning. "And I don't remember anyone else talking to me about it. Why? Who was it?"

"Yeah, who was it?" Ramirez and Corbin chorused.

"It was Vincent Romano," I said, watching Anne's face.

She looked dumbstruck.

"You're shitting me," Cooper said.

The shock on their faces was exactly what I'd expected.

Anne grabbed for her bag, riffled through it and pulled out a file. She set it down on the table, flipped through the pictures, and then eventually pulled out a mugshot. It was the one of Vincent taken at the time of his arrest.

She stared at it for a moment, then shook her head. "I don't recognize him," she muttered as she ran a finger over the picture. "But..." Her voice trailed off. "Maybe I do."

And we waited for Anne to work it out. In the meantime, I was trying to decide who was going to visit Romano. I knew Anne would want to go. However, as she looked up and was about to speak, my phone rang. I held up my hand and took it from my jacket pocket. It was Doc Sheddon.

"Doc?" I said, still holding up my hand and my breath, hoping for some good news.

"Kate, I've got you one ID," he began. "I was able to get

hold of Emma Jacobs' and Louise Hackett's dental records. Number two is Emma Jacobs."

"Whew…" I blew out a long breath. "How about Louise Hackett?"

"Nope," he said. "Neither of them is Louise Hackett," he said carefully. "Which means we now have a fourth victim. The cause of death in all three cases is manual strangulation, and though it's difficult to be absolutely certain, they all died within months of one another. That's all I have for you for now, Kate. I'll be in touch."

"Thank you for letting me know, Doc," I replied. "I appreciate it more than you know."

"You're welcome. Goodbye, Kate."

He hung up the phone, as did I, and I set mine down on the table and stared at it. Everyone seemed to be eagerly waiting for me to speak.

I took one sip of coffee and then set my cup down, looked at them, and said, "One of the bodies is Emma Jacobs. Neither of the other two is Louise Hackett. So now there are four."

Chapter Twenty-Eight

July 15, 2023
9:00 AM

"Four," Corbin said.

"Four," Anne whispered.

"We'll have to let Greg Jacobs know," Corbin said. "It might be a good idea for me and Tracy to do it. A fresh pair of faces for him and a chance for us to ask him some questions, especially about that property. Maybe if he, by some odd chance, knows something about it—"

"And if he does," Cooper said. "That would be more than a coincidence, right?"

"Let's not get ahead of our—" I began, but Anne cut me off.

"You'd better be careful how you ask him about that," Anne said, pursing her lips. "Get it wrong, and he'll assume that you're trying to point the finger at him—trust me. He's paranoid."

"We can be careful," Corbin said.

"Someone needs to talk to Vincent Romano," I said. "I think he knows a lot more than he's ever let on. He keeps popping up on the radar, and it's time we chased down that lead. Does anyone know where he's at now?"

"Yep," Hawk spoke up for the first time. "It took some time to track him down, but after he served his time in prison, he moved out of town to Spencer, near to where Floyd Harrison used to work."

My brows rose. "Really?"

"Yeah," he said and nodded. "There's nothing suspicious in that, though, Kate. Most folks move out of the city to escape when they come out of jail. It's the way of things. Nobody wants to keep running into... old friends, shall we say?"

He said old friends with a certain amount of sarcasm.

"From what I can tell," Hawk continued, "Vincent Romano has led a quiet life since they turned him loose. He hasn't had any more run-ins with the law, or with anyone else."

"What's he doing now?" I asked.

Hawk glanced down at his notebook. "Last anyone heard, he was working on a horse ranch? Maybe he owns it? It's not clear. We can figure that out once we speak to him."

"So he was convicted and served time for the assault?" I asked, thinking back to seeing the charges but nothing else.

"No," Hawk said. "He wasn't. The case was dropped for lack of evidence."

"So what did he go to jail for?" Cooper asked, frowning.

"I don't know yet," Hawk replied, "but I'm still digging. Trouble is, I can't get my hands on any of the court records."

"Big case to just drop," Anne muttered. "I can't believe I rode in the car with someone like that..."

"You and I are going to go see him, Anne," I said, "but

Annie

you're going to have to go into the interview with an open mind. And I—"

It was at that moment that Chief Johnston entered my office and cut me off in mid-sentence. "I need to talk to you when you're done," he said. "It might take a while."

I nodded, my stomach tightening. "Of course," I replied. With that, he slipped out and I let out a sigh. "I don't want you to wait for me to do this interview," I said to Anne, "so why don't you and Cooper go chat with Romano? Are you up for it?"

Anne was hesitant but then nodded and said, "I can handle it. Cooper will be there to back me up. He can handle him if something goes awry."

Cooper chuckled. "Absolutely."

"Also," I said, "I want you to ask him about Floyd Harrison. That's still an open, active murder case, and we have no leads. We need to do what we can to keep moving it. Including Harrison, we've got four bodies and one missing child, and I think they're all connected."

Everyone nodded, and I wrapped up the meeting, sending them off on their separate ways. Hawk said he would continue digging into the hunting property, as well as Vincent Romano's background. Me? I was disappointed I was going to miss the interview with Romano, but duty called, and when the chief tells you to jump, you don't ignore him.

I left Samson in my office, locking the door behind me, and headed for the elevator, hoping that whatever it was that Chief Johnston wanted, it wasn't to tell me to back off. The media still hadn't caught wind of the discovery we'd made on the hunting property, which was a good thing and a miracle in and of itself.

I knocked twice on the outer office door and stepped

inside. Christy, Johnston's PA, looked up at me from behind her desk, smiled, and then nodded toward the inner office door. "He's waiting for you," she said.

I knocked once on his door, opened it and stepped inside.

"Hey, Chief," I said brightly. "You wanted to speak with me?"

Johnston nodded. "Close the door, Kate, and sit down."

I did as he said. I sat down in one of the two chairs in front of his desk and crossed my legs.

Police Chief Wesley Johnston was, to me, both an enigma and a mentor. He was a big man, an imposing man of average height with broad shoulders and a barrel chest. He was, as usual, impeccably dressed, his uniform sharply pressed, head shaved, and his Hulk Hogan mustache perfectly trimmed. He was also something of a martinet, confident and humorless. Rarely did he smile, and when he did, it was usually ice cold and reminded me of a barracuda about to strike. But he was also a fair man, and though we'd had many a run-in, he's always been fair with me.

He looked at me.

I looked at him. "What can I do for you, Chief?" I asked.

He leaned back in his chair and folded his arms across his chest. "I need an update on everything you have so far on the Emma Jacobs case and all cases you think may be connected to it."

With a nod, I brought him up to date, and it took me more than fifteen minutes to do so, during which he sat silently listening to me. I told him we'd identified Emma Jacobs' body, that we now had a fourth victim, as yet unknown, and that off-duty cop Vincent Romano was the person who picked Anne up that night.

"Vincent Romano," he said thoughtfully. "I've never heard

Annie

of him. Before my time. I doubt he had something to do with the abduction of the girls, though."

"I'm not sure I agree," I said. "He was also the responding officer when Emma Jacobs was reported missing. That's quite a coincidence, don't you think?"

He gave me a wry smile and said, "I trust your instincts, Kate. Always have, but coincidences do happen, you know?"

I shrugged, waiting for him to continue, and he did.

"I must say I'm curious why there's nothing from him in Robar's file. There should at least have been statements from the parents and the sister. It makes no sense."

"I guess maybe they got lost," I said flatly. "As did the contents of the other two files, Jacobs' and Hackett's. And why don't we know about the fourth victim we found up there on that hunting property? The only answer I can think of is that the kid disappeared in another jurisdiction, probably Sequatchie County."

"And you checked everywhere for the missing content?" he asked.

I nodded my head and said, "Well, there's nothing in the basement and there's nothing in the evidence locker. I can only think it must have been checked out at some time in the distant past and..." I paused for a second, reluctant to say what I was about to say, but what the hell? I took a deep breath and continued, "And the jackets were returned sans content."

He stared at me for a long moment, during which I did my best to keep my expression blank.

"You realize what you're implying?" he asked.

I merely nodded, not wanting to elaborate further.

"Robert Milton was chief at the time," he said without pushing me further. "Maybe he can point us in the right direction, though I hear he's senile." He shook his head and lapsed into silence, staring at me.

I shifted uncomfortably in my chair, then locked eyes with him and said, "I need to talk to Bruce Watson. He was the investigating officer. He would've been the one who took Vincent's statement that night. He won't talk, and there's no reason he wouldn't unless..."

Chief Johnston let out a long, heavy sigh, rubbing his chin. "I get it, Kate. You think it's internal, or it was?" He narrowed his eyes until they were mere slits, "And I don't like it. Harrison, so I understand, was an excellent detective—"

I opened my mouth to speak, but he held up his hand and continued, "Watson?" He shrugged. "Average. Kate, we have to be very careful. We stir this rusty old pot and we do not know what sludge we'll find at the bottom. We get it wrong; they come for me, and it's taking everything I've got to keep this mess out of the media as it is. I don't know how they haven't yet caught wind of the bodies you found."

I didn't answer. Instead, I widened my eyes and pursed my lips.

"Our best witness is Anne Robar," he said. "She was there." He frowned and then shook his head. "It's a shame she can't remember anything."

"She remembered where the killer buried the bodies," I said. "That's a win."

It was quiet. I could hear the rain beating on the window. I turned to look at it, seeing the raindrops coursing across the glass.

"They solved some big cases, those two," Johnston said thoughtfully. "I wonder what the hell happened here. Geez, what a mess."

"Let me talk to Watson, Chief," I said earnestly. I uncrossed my legs and leaned forward, my elbows on my knees, hands clasped together. "We have good reason. We found three bodies, and one of them is Emma Jacobs. It would

Annie

be a nice thing for him to know, don't you think? I mean, it *was* his case."

Chief Johnston eyed me wearily, and I thought, for a moment, he was going to deny me, but he didn't. Instead, he said, "Fine. Okay. We'll go talk to Bruce Watson."

I raised my eyebrows in surprise. "You... and me?"

He chuckled. "You betcha," he said, rising to his feet.

Chapter Twenty-Nine

July 15, 2023
10:25 AM

I was stunned. Gobsmacked. It was the first time in my entire career that Chief Johnston had accompanied me into the field, much less to an interview.

"I'll be back," he said to Christy as he stalked through the outer office.

Christy smiled at me as I followed him to the door and shook her head.

"I'll be just a minute, Chief," I said. "I have to go get Samson."

"Hurry up, Captain," he replied. "I don't have all day. I'll be waiting at the front desk."

"What's going on?" Corbin asked as I hurried through the situation room.

"Don't even ask," I said as I rushed past him. "I'll fill you in later."

Less than five minutes later, I was back in reception, where Chief Johnston was chatting to the desk sergeant.

"Ah, there you are," he said. "Lead the way, Captain."

And with that, he followed me out into the parking lot. And I have to tell you, I was more than a little uncomfortable with his presence.

I loaded Samson into the backseat of my unmarked cruiser while the chief slid in on the passenger side.

"I think, to begin with, you'd better let me do the talking," Chief Johnston said as I pulled up outside Watson's house.

"I can't think why he would be pissed off," I said, frowning. "Well, I can..." I caught the look on the chief's face and quickly changed the subject. "Most detectives love to talk about their old cases, and we have good news, so..." I tailed off.

"And most detectives retire with their egos intact," he replied. "Watson? Maybe not so much."

I huffed, shook my head, opened the car door, and stepped out into what had turned into a gray and dismal morning. The rain had stopped, but the ground beneath our feet was soaked. I let Samson out and slammed the rear door, then gestured to Chief Johnston to lead the way, and he did. He strode briskly along the cracked concrete driveway with Sammy and me at his heels.

I hope he treats the chief better than he did me, I thought as we stepped up onto the small concrete porch. I had no idea how the chief was going to handle his approach. Had it been me, I was in no mood to take any BS from the retired detective. He'd either talk to me or I'd haul his ass downtown. But who am I when the exalted one is handling the interview?

Johnston thumbed the doorbell, and we waited. Johnston turned to look at me, his eyebrows raised, and then he thumbed it again.

A moment later, I heard the lock click, and the door

Annie

opened to reveal a wide-eyed, petite elderly woman, who I assumed was Watson's wife.

"Yes? What can I do for you?" she asked, taking in the chief's perfectly pressed uniform and eyeing Samson with a worrisome look.

"I'm Chief Wesley Johnston, and this is Captain Gazzara. We need to speak with Mr. Watson."

"Well..." She glanced back behind her, and I knew by the body language that Watson was, indeed, at home.

"He... He is here," she said hesitantly. "But he's not been feeling all that good and—"

"Oh, for God's sake, just let them in," a gruff voice called from somewhere inside.

Her cheeks flushed crimson and she stepped aside, gesturing for us to enter.

Chief Johnston led the way through the house into the living room, where Bruce Watson was sitting in front of the television.

He rose to his feet and turned to face us. His face was drawn and pale, and he looked angry.

"Detective Watson," Chief Johnston greeted the old man. "You're before my time, so we've never met, but it's good to see you." He stuck out his hand. Watson eyed it for a second, then grudgingly shook it.

"Chief," he growled. "I can't say the pleasure's all mine, but you'd better sit yourselves down, I suppose."

He glared at Samson. "There was no need to bring a K-9." And he glared at me.

I said nothing. The Chief sat down on the couch opposite. I sat on the opposite end of the couch. Samson parked his rear on my left between the chief and me.

I took in the dusty, outdated home, and I felt as though I was stepping back in time, thinking the couch upon which we were sitting must be as old as the case we were trying to solve. I noted several framed photographs on the walls, officers in uniform, and one of a uniformed officer flanked by two male detectives I recognized as Watson and Harrison. The tall man in uniform had four stars on his collar, so I assumed it was Chief Robert Milton.

"I thought you'd be interested to know we've found Emma Jacobs' remains," Johnston began, and I watched Watson's expression morph into one of shock. Or was it panic? It was hard to tell. It came and went too quickly.

"Really?" he said quietly. "Where did you find it?"

"Sequatchie County," Johnston replied. "Wild country. Hunting land. Remote."

He was giving him just enough information to make it appear we were being transparent with him.

"There were two more bodies," Johnston continued. "Three in all."

Bruce was silent for a moment, then said, "Just three?"

Just three? I thought, my hackles raised. *What the hell does he know that we don't?*

"There should have been more?" Johnston asked quietly.

Watson looked away to his left, a sure sign he was about to lie. As experienced a detective as he was, I thought he should have known better.

He was silent for a moment, perhaps realizing his mistake. "I... I don't know," he said finally. He looked away, across the room. He was looking at a desk in the far corner of the room. It was stacked high with papers, and I had to wonder if the missing information was among them.

"Bruce, I'm going to lay it out for you," Johnston said, leaning forward. "We need your help. It was your case, so no one knows it better than you. You were there when it was happening. We have little to work with. The information is

Annie

missing from the files. It's a mess." Johnston was using the soft touch.

Watson looked down at his hands, then at me, then at the chief. He took in a deep breath, then another, and said, "Listen." There was a sharp edge to his voice. "Whatever I say in this room is off the record. You hear me?" He glared at us. "No recording. No chasing it back to me. Deal?"

"Deal," Johnston said.

I nodded.

"So, you're obviously not going to give it up, are you?" He didn't wait for an answer. "And it's clear you're not making any headway. So ask your questions. I'll answer as best I can."

Watson folded his arms across his chest and leaned back in his chair.

Johnston looked at me and said, "Kate?"

"Your old partner, Floyd Harrison," I began. "He was murdered. Any ideas?"

Bruce chuckled. "Not surprising, really, and if we're shooting it straight, you should know Floyd was a damn good detective, but he was a weak link. He took it hard when we couldn't solve the case, but he didn't stop pushing. But we all know that the harder you push, sometimes things come back to bite you. I think the past came back to bite Floyd, which is why you two are going to leave here when this is over and *never* speak of me again. Not to anyone. And damn sure not to anyone on the force, or even previously on the force. I don't know who killed him, but I hope you find the son of a bitch."

It was an answer. Not one I liked, but I could see he was telling the truth. So I pressed on,

"Do you think Vincent Romano was involved?"

Bruce's face flashed a shade paler. "What, that kid... He... Floyd, you mean? I don't know."

"I'm not sure I'm following you," I said, frowning.

"Listen," Bruce cleared his throat. "I'm going to just bypass all this and tell you what you need to know. One, Greg Jacobs didn't kill his daughter. He was with some woman, Patricia Gillian, and it was impossible for him to be involved in the others." He sighed, rubbing his wrinkled forehead. "And the other thing to know is that a damn predator took all those girls. All of them. And there ain't just three of them. There are a whole lot more."

"More?" What d'you mean, more? How many more?" Johnston asked.

"That, I couldn't tell you," Watson said angrily. "But I *can* tell you who the first one was. Her name was Linda Warsaw. She was eleven years old and a bit of a delinquent. Everyone pinned her as a runaway."

"I've never seen that case file..." Chief Johnston commented.

"Because there ain't one anymore." Watson laughed. "And if you two haven't figured it out yet, then that's on you. Come on. You're not stupid. The pickings are slim, I know, but listen here. Linda was my first missing girl case. There was *one* witness. *One.*" He leaned forward in his chair, his voice lowered. "And I thought it was a hell of a good lead."

I was on the edge of my seat. "What'd they say?"

"The little old woman used to sit on her front porch and sip tea in the afternoon," Watson continued. "She saw Linda riding her bike down the street, which was apparently something the kid did all the time. So the old woman saw a patrol car pull up alongside them. She didn't think nothing of it, not then." He paused, his eyes flickering with emotion. He was angry. "She went inside to refill her glass," he continued, "and when she stepped back out, guess what? All that was left was Linda's bike lying on the sidewalk."

"When was this?" I asked.

Annie

Bruce leaned back in his chair. "1979, August 25, to be exact. Everyone said she was a runaway, but why the hell would she run away and leave her bicycle lying there on the roadside? She wouldn't, would she?"

My gut churned at what he was implying. "Do you know who that officer was?"

"No!" he replied.

"Could it have been Vincent Romano?" I asked.

"Nah," he said and chuckled. "He was a freshman in high school when this took place. He wasn't even a blip on the map. In fact, what was even more troubling is that there *wasn't* a patrol officer in the area when the abduction took place, but the woman *swore* it was a Chattanooga cop. I had no idea what to make of it, and most of the guys were on call when it took place. The ones who weren't? They were eating at a diner on the other side of town."

"So, was someone impersonating an officer?" Johnston asked, his eyes narrowed.

"Either that or it was an off-duty cop," he replied. "Or maybe... Maybe we'll never know because any evidence there was has disappeared. But you know what they say, right?"

"What's that?" I took the bait.

"If you stick your damn hand in a hornet's nest, you're bound to get stung." He shrugged his shoulders. "You might oughta keep that in mind as you dig deeper into it. I hope you solve it, but I hope like hell I'm dead before you do." With that, he coughed violently. "And I think y'all should be on your way now. I'm gettin' one of my headaches."

Johnston and I exchanged a glance. He nodded, and we rose to our feet. There were a million more questions I wanted to ask, but I settled for just one.

"I'll ask you again. Do you know who killed Floyd Harrison?"

He looked up at me, a sadness in his eyes. "No, I sure don't, but I am sure that it was someone from the past trying to silence anyone who ever knew anything. I promise you, that monster is still out there, and they might be getting old, but they ain't dead."

I nodded, sighed, and twitched Samson's leash. I made it a point to walk around the far side of the living room to exit, which allowed me to take a quick peek at the desk, and I was disappointed to see the stack of papers was just a heap of bank statements.

I followed Chief Johnston out of the house, and we stepped back out into the muggy heat of the late morning. I looked up and down the street, spotting a black nineties model Chevy taking off from one of the other houses.

I turned to Johnston as I opened the rear driver's side door for Samson. "D'you think he's right, that it's internal?"

Johnston sighed, popping the door handle. "I think he thinks it is," Johnston replied, noncommittal.

"Do you believe him?"

Chief Johnston hesitated, then said, "I don't have a reason not to."

I nodded as I slid in behind the wheel. The air inside the car was blistering hot.

I sat for a moment with the motor running, my hands on the wheel, staring at the speedometer.

"Kate?" Johnston asked, frowning.

"The last thing I wanted to do, Chief," I said, "was to begin an internal investigation, but it looks like that's exactly where this is headed. There's nothing more sickening than a monster hiding in a uniform."

"You need to get to the bottom of this, Kate," Johnston said. "And quickly."

Chapter Thirty

July 15, 2023
12:15PM

It was just after noon when Chief Johnston, Samson, and I arrived back at the police department. The rest of my team were still out in the field, but, one by one, over the course of the afternoon, they checked in and I told them we'd reconvene in my office on Monday morning at eight-thirty.

Bruce Watson had given me a lot to think about, as had the chief now that he was semi-onboard with the idea that we were dealing with a serial killer who might or might not be an ex-police officer.

Linda Warsaw, hmm, I thought as I sat at my desk, pondering the conversation with Bruce Watson. *I wonder.*

I turned to my desktop and did some digging into departmental history in general and the supposed delinquent runaway Linda Warsaw in particular. Unfortunately, Watson had been correct; there was no file. I searched the department database: nothing. Not a single mention. Weird!

I turned my focus to the department during the years the girls went missing, beginning with Linda Warsaw in August 1979. Pat Rhodes, now deceased, had been the chief at the time, so that was a dead end, no pun intended. Robert Milton became chief when Rhodes retired in 1981. Robert Milton! I stared at the name, knowing I'd need to get permission from Johnston before I went barking up that tree. The department was busy during those years, as it always is, and to imply that Milton hadn't been doing his job... Well, that wasn't something to undertake lightly; Milton was a highly decorated police chief.

Beyond that, I compiled a list of the officers and staff who worked for the department from 1979 to 1987. It was a substantial list. I stared at the computer screen, dismayed by the enormity of it. I shook my head, then deleted the female officers. That reduced it somewhat, but it was still an impossible task, so I turned my attention to the senior officers. There wasn't a single name I was familiar with. *Geez,* I thought, staring again at the name Robert Milton. *Really?* I thought. *Hmm... Where are Linda Warsaw's parents, I wonder? I need to talk to them.*

I did a quick search of the name Warsaw and found nothing. *That's weird,* I thought, sitting back in my chair. *There has to be something, right?* I thought. *I mean, a kid disappears and there's no record of it... or the kid's parents.* I need Jack.

But Jack was, unfortunately, on vacation somewhere in Arizona and wasn't due back for another week.

I looked up at the ceiling and squinted, then rubbed my eyes. "Whew!" I muttered with a sigh.

I looked at Samson. He was lying on the floor with his backside in his bed, staring at me with a furrowed brow.

Annie

"Yeah," I said. "It's all right for you. You don't have to figure out this crap."

He blinked but otherwise didn't move.

"You're no help," I said and turned to look at the screen again. Then I looked at my watch. It was almost two o'clock. And it was Saturday afternoon. *Hmm, I wonder?* I thought.

I leaned forward, picked up my phone, stared at it for a moment, then hit the speed dial.

"Kate," Harry said. "To what do I owe the honor?"

"Hello to you, too..." I said, then after a brief pause, continued, "I need a favor. You at work? You busy?"

"Yes, I'm at work, and no, not especially," he replied. "What d'you need?"

"Actually, it's Tim I need. Is he busy?"

"Tim?" he asked. "Why d'you need Tim?"

"I need to trace a family that seems to have dropped off the map. The only name I have is Warsaw. I'd have Jack do it, but he's on vacation."

"Shouldn't be a problem," he replied. "Hang on, I'll put you through."

The line went dead, and then, "Captain Gazzara," Tim said. "Harry said you need a favor. What can I do for you?"

I told him what I needed. He was silent for a moment, then said, "I can find nothing on Linda Warsaw. There is a Jennifer Majors. Her name was Warsaw before she got married. She was born December 7, 1972."

That's not..." I began, then changed track and said, "Unless... She would have been seven when Linda was abducted. Could she be a younger sister, I wonder? Do you have an address?"

"I do, and a phone number." He gave it to me, and I scribbled it down on a notepad.

"Thanks, Tim," I said. "What about the parents?"

"Both deceased."

I thought for a moment, then thanked him and hung up.

I picked up the notepad, leaned back in my chair, and stared at it. The address was north of the river on Tucker Street.

I sucked on my bottom lip for a moment, then picked up my phone and dialed the number.

She answered on the fourth ring, "Hello?"

"Mrs. Majors?" I asked.

"Yes. Who is this?"

"My name is Captain Kate Gazzara, Chattanooga Police Department. Do you have a minute?"

She was silent for a moment, then said in a hard voice, "What's this about?" And I knew it wasn't going to be easy.

I took a deep breath and plunged in. "Before you were married, your name was Jennifer Warsaw. Is that correct?"

Again, there was a brief moment of silence, and then she said, "Is this about Linda?" And I heaved a sigh of relief.

"It is," I said. "I—"

"I can't help you," she snapped. "And I want you to leave me alone. I'm going to hang up—"

"Wait," I jumped in. "I know this is painful, but you're all I've got. Other than Linda's name, I have nothing. Please. Please, just give me a minute and then I will leave you alone, I promise."

And I waited for what seemed like an age, then, "I don't know anything," she said, finally. "I was only seven. My parents wouldn't talk about it, ever. I don't even have a photograph of her. As far as I'm concerned, she never existed, and I don't mean that in a bad way. It's just a fact."

I sighed audibly, and she heard it.

"It killed my mother," she said. "She committed suicide."

Annie

"Oh my," I said. "I'm so sorry." I didn't have the heart to ask about her father.

"It's okay," she said. "It was a long time ago. I don't remember her... I wish I did, and I wish I could help. I really do, but I can't. They wouldn't talk to me about it. They took me out of school and my mom home-schooled me... until I was twelve. That's when I found her dead. She took an overdose of sleeping pills. I was devastated, and so was my dad. He started drinking and... He fell down the stairs. I was eighteen... I'm sorry. I've told you... I don't know anything about my sister or what happened to her. I have to go—"

"Wait," I said, "Just one more question before you go. Who was your dentist when you and Linda were children?"

She was silent for a moment, then said, "It was Doctor Hall. Doctor Jason Hall. Now, I have to go."

I thanked her, gave her my number and then hung up, wondering how it could have happened. Bruce Watson hadn't lied to us. The slate had been wiped clean.

I sat for a minute, thinking about the two unidentified bodies, then I called Tim.

"Kate?" he said. "You need something else?"

"Linda Warsaw," I said. "Her dentist was a Doctor Jason Hall."

"Hold on," he said. He was silent for a moment, then said, "I found a Doctor Sarah Hall. She's a dentist, but I can't find any others."

"Do you have a number?" I asked.

He gave it to me, and I thanked him and hung up.

I looked at my watch. It was almost three. I took a deep breath and punched in the number.

"Doctor Hall's office," a female voice said.

"My name is Captain Gazzara, Chattanooga Police," I said. "Could I speak to Doctor Hall, please?"

"May I tell her what it's about?"

"I need some dental records," I said.

"Hold on, please."

There was a moment of silence, then, "This is Doctor Hall. How can I help you?"

I explained who I was, confirmed that her father was indeed Doctor Jason Hall, and then I told her what I needed. After that, I shut up and listened.

"Our computer records only go back as far as 2000," she said. "But my father threw nothing away. If Linda Warsaw was his patient, the records would be in the file cabinets in the basement. I still have patients to see, but I'll send someone down to see if we can find them. If we do, do you want me to send them over to you?"

I looked at my watch. It was almost three-thirty.

"No," I said. "It's rather urgent. I need you to send them to the Medical Examiner's office on Amnicola, care of Doctor Richard Sheddon. Can you do that for me? This afternoon?"

"Well, I don't know," she replied. "It's getting late, but I'll do my best. If we find anything, that is."

"Good," I said. "I'll call him and tell him to expect them."

I thanked her, gave her my number, then hung up and called Doc Sheddon.

"I have a function this evening," he said when I'd finished explaining. "I can wait until six, and then I'll have to leave."

"Come on, Doc," I said. "This is important."

"So is my function," he replied testily. "Six o'clock. No later."

It was fifteen after six when he called me back.

"Got them," he said. "I have to go. I'll call you on Monday morning." And, with that, he hung up.

I smiled as I looked at my watch. *You're the best, Doc,* I

Annie

thought as I gathered my things. It was time for me to call it a day.

* * *

I drove home with Bruce Watson's words gyrating around in my head. *What if he was lying?* I thought. I didn't think he was, but hey, stranger things, right? *Could he be trying to point the finger away from himself?* I wondered.

"Maybe," I said and glanced at my canine partner riding high in the front passenger seat. "I don't know what to think, do you?" I glanced to my right and met his chocolate eyes. "Geez, I wish you could talk."

I shook my head, thinking sadly about Jennifer Majors. And I couldn't help but wonder how much leeway Johnston would give me to go digging into the department. He'd stepped out of the box and gone with me to talk to Watson. That was a first, but it didn't mean I had free rein to start an internal investigation. That was out of my purview. True, everyone involved was either dead or retired, but I'd still have to tread lightly.

My mind was still wandering when I pulled into my garage and saw immediately that the interior door *was wide open*. I cut the engine, grabbed my Glock, slid out of the car, ran around to the passenger side and turned Samson loose. He bounded out of the seat and into the house, letting out a deep, throaty growl.

I followed him through the door, gun in hand, and we cleared the house room by room. We scoured every nook and cranny of my home, but there was nothing out of place. I stood for a moment at the kitchen door, thinking hard.

"Did I forget to close the door this morning?" I asked Samson. "I don't think so."

He sat still, his head tilted to one side, looking up at me as if to say, *I don't think so either, but we can't be sure.*

In the end I gave up, sighed and began my evening routine, though I kept my gun on my hip. Paranoid? Maybe, but the last thing I needed was to be caught off guard.

I filled Samson's bowl with fresh water and gave him his kibble. How many times had I promised myself to give him something healthier? *I need to go to the store,* I thought. "We need to try some of that fresh food. What d'you think?" He didn't look impressed, but I promised myself I'd do it tomorrow.

I stuffed an Italian pasta TV dinner in the microwave and waited for the ding. I ate it standing at the bar. Geez, it was... bland. *Damn, you can do better than this, Kate,* I thought as I threw the bulk of it into the trash.

I let Samson out into the backyard, then grabbed a glass of wine and joined him. I took a seat on the deck and watched him lollygagging around in the grass, sniffing and rolling.

"I'm going to have to give you a bath if you don't stop," I warned him as he scratched his back, belly up, for the fifth or sixth time. He paused, looking up at me, his tongue lolling out. He rolled over, sprang to his feet, shook himself violently, then trotted back and up onto the deck.

We spent the next forty-five minutes or so sitting quietly together before heading back into the house. I took a shower, dressed in pajamas, went down to the living room and turned on the TV, still feeling more than a little uneasy. And I couldn't decide if it was because I'd come home to an open door or if it was the conversation we'd had with Bruce Watson.

Or maybe both, I thought as I flopped down on the couch, thinking that if what he'd told us was the truth, then it was more than likely he was clean.

Annie

"I don't know what to think," I told Samson as I crawled into bed.

Needless to say, I slept little that night.

Chapter Thirty-One

July 17, 2023
9:30AM

Sunday passed without incident, but I woke late that Monday morning and had to rush around to make it to the office on time.

I made a quick stop at McDonald's to grab a coffee and a couple of sausage biscuits, which would make me even later. My phone rang as I pulled into the lot at the Chattanooga Police Department, home sweet home.

"Doc," I greeted the medical examiner as I parked the car and got out. "You have some good news for me?"

"I do," he quipped and chuckled. "Unfortunately, I haven't yet been able to ID body number three, but we do have a match for body number one."

"Oh?" I said, surprised, remembering how few remains there were. I got Samson out and juggled my coffee and

McDonald's bag, the phone pressed to my ear with my shoulder.

"The dental records supplied by Dr. Hall were the clincher. Would you believe those records were over forty years old?"

"Come on, Doc," I said impatiently, heading toward the PD. "Don't keep me hanging. Who is it?"

"It is indeed Linda Warsaw," he replied.

I can't say it was a surprise, but I stopped walking toward the building and said, "Not the one I expected, but it's a relief. Now we have only one unidentified body." I sighed, then continued, "I'll let her sister know. Thanks, Doc."

"So, what d'you know about her?" he asked.

"Not much," I replied. "According to Detective Watson, Linda was the first, which probably accounts for the scattered remains." I continued on toward the door, carrying the brown bag and my coffee, and somehow managing to hang onto Samson's leash. "According to him, she was reported missing in 1979. I was able to trace the sister, hence the dental records. Both parents are dead. That's about all I know. The case file is missing."

Doc was silent for a few beats, and by then I was at the door struggling to find my key card.

Thankfully, one of the uniformed officers opened the door for me, and I was able to slip through.

"I'll continue digging," I said. "D'you have anything else for me?"

"No," he replied. "We're still working on body number three, of course. Hopefully, I'll have something for you sooner rather than later. Have a good day, Kate. If you need me, you know where I am." And with that, he hung up.

I stepped out of the elevator, spotted Corbin at his desk, and asked him to get everyone together in my office.

Annie

"Running late, huh?" Corbin said, grinning at me.

"Don't be a smart ass, Corbin," I said. "Ten minutes. My office, okay?"

I closed the office door behind me, went to my desk, set my coffee, brown bag and phone down on the desktop, unclipped Samson's leash and flopped down in my chair. Then I took a sausage biscuit from the bag, unwrapped it and tossed it to Sammy, feeling more than a little guilty. I tried not to feed him too much junk, but desperate times called for desperate measures. I took a sip of my coffee, then a bite of my biscuit, and it was so good I closed my eyes.

Two minutes later, there was a knock on my door. It opened and Corbin walked in, still grinning.

"What?" I asked, my voice muffled by a mouthful of food.

"How long have I been your partner, Kate?" he asked, then continued before I could answer, "Five years? Six? This is a first. You're rarely late, and never more than ten minutes. It's nine-thirty. What happened?"

"I overslept," I replied. "Get over it. Where is everybody?"

"On their way," he assured me.

And, sure enough, one by one, they appeared, all of them grinning, and took their seats at the table.

I shook my head, crumpled my now empty wrapper, and dropped it in the trash can beside my desk.

I took a sip of coffee, set the cup down, stared at each of them in turn and said, "Body number one is Linda Warsaw."

"I have no idea who that is," Cooper said, frowning. "Should I?"

"Linda Warsaw was reported missing on August 25, 1979," I said, and then I quickly filled them in on the interview Chief Johnston and I had conducted with Bruce Watson.

"So, that's where we are now," I said, wrapping it up. "Let me break it down for you. We have two bodies, identified as

Emma Jacobs and Linda Warsaw. And we have one unidentified body and a missing child, Louise Hackett. We have three files that appear to have been cleaned, and one is missing completely. We think, the chief and I, that there may have been a uniformed officer involved in the abductions. Either that or someone impersonating an officer, though that seems unlikely, as someone with access evidently was able to get to the files. I think we can eliminate Watson, Harrison and Jacobs as suspects. Which leaves us with..." I stared around the table, my eyebrows raised. "Nothing!"

There was a moment of silence, and then Anne said, "How were we able to identify Linda Warsaw? There was so little left of her."

"It's a long story," I said, "and one we don't have time for right now. Let's just say dental records and leave it at that."

"Family?" Hawk asked.

"A sister, Jennifer," I replied. "I've already talked to her. She was only seven when Linda disappeared and barely remembers her. So no help there."

"Parents?" Anne asked.

"Both dead," I replied.

Anne shook her head, pursed her lips, and took a deep breath.

"So," I said, "moving right along. How are you doing with the hunting parties, Hawk?"

"Still trying to trace the lessees for the years 1985 on," he replied. "And I'm not having much luck."

I nodded. "You need to go back to 1979," I said.

He nodded, grimacing.

"Corbin?" I asked.

"Well, first off, we let Greg Jacobs know we'd found Emma's body," Corbin spoke up. "He took it quietly with little emotion, then he demanded we find out who killed her. We talked for... I dunno, maybe thirty minutes. I don't think he had anything to do with her death."

"Watson doesn't either," I said. "He also said he checked his alibi. He was with a Patricia Gillian when she was abducted. We could see if we can find her, but there's little point, I think. If Watson cleared him, I think we can go with it, too."

Corbin nodded.

"So. Anne," I said, "how did it go with Vincent Romano?"

"Horrible," Anne grumbled. "He was... uncooperative, to say the least. He spent most of the time telling us to find someone else to bother."

"It's true," Cooper said and sighed. "It took us half the day to find him, and when we did, he spent the first twenty minutes yelling at us that we had the wrong guy. After that, he shut down. Not sure what to think about him. One look at us, and he was done."

I frowned. "So you got *nothing* out of him?" I asked, scarcely believing what I was hearing.

"He wouldn't even admit he picked up Anne that night," Cooper said, gesturing at her.

Anne's lips were set in a hard line before she chimed in. "He was adamant he didn't help any little girl, but his face went white when I told him who I was. But he still wouldn't admit it."

"Oh yeah?" I snapped. "Where does he work?"

"At a construction site across town," Cooper answered.

"Corbin," I said. "You and I are going to pay him a visit. He knows something, and we're going to squeeze it out of him." I took a sip of coffee as I gathered my thoughts.

"As for the rest of you," I said, "my best guess is still that the answer lies in that hunting property." I thought for a moment, then continued, "Tracy, Coop, I want you to widen the search.

I want you to research missing girls in the tri-state area from 1979 to 1990. Pull every case you can find and check our database for missing children during those years. Check in with Sheriff White and the other county sheriffs. Hawk, I want you, Anne, and Ramirez to continue digging into the history of that hunting property. We need to find the lessees, and we need to interview them. Someone has to know something. We need names. Names, people. We're looking for an ex-cop. If you find anything, *anything* at all that points to someone in the department, bring it to me before you act on it. Everyone good?"

Everyone was.

"Good," I said, rising to my feet, "then let's get to work. Corbin, you're with me."

I waited until everyone had left the room, then said to Corbin, "I need to swing by Chief Johnston's office before we go. Give me a few minutes, then meet me in the hall outside his office."

"Got it," he replied. "I'll get Samson ready."

I slipped out and headed down to Chief Johnston's office.

Two minutes later, I stepped into the chief's outer office and said to Christy, "Is he in?"

She nodded and picked up the phone. "Captain Gazzara is here to see you."

She listened for a moment, then hung up and said, "You can go on in."

I knocked on the door, opened it and stepped inside.

"Sit down, Captain," he said. "What can I do for you?"

I sat down, looked across the desk at him and said, "I thought you'd like to know... body number one is Linda Warsaw.

He removed his black metal-rimmed glasses, took a tissue out of the box on his desk and began to wipe the lenses. He stared at me for a moment, then said, "Well, it seems Bruce Watson knows what he's talking about."

"You think he knew we'd find her there?"

Johnston pursed his lips, then shook his head and said, "I get what you're implying, but no. I don't think so." He paused for a moment, obviously thinking, then continued, "I tried to call Chief Milton yesterday evening, but he was golfing. He's supposed to call me back. I'm hoping he can shed a little light... Kate, I don't like how this is shaping up."

"Neither do I, Chief," I said, shaking my head. Then, not knowing what else to say, I said, "I'm on my way to interview Vincent Romano."

He nodded.

"We done then?" I asked.

He nodded again.

"Thank you, sir," I said and rose to my feet, turned, and walked to the door.

"Oh, and Kate?"

"Yes, sir?" I glanced back at him.

"Be careful. And watch out for Detective Robar."

I nodded and then stepped out, closing the door behind me. I nodded to Christy, then stepped out into the hallway where Corbin and Samson were waiting for me.

The chief was right. Floyd Harrison was already dead. Did he know too much? I didn't know, but I was pretty sure he did, as did Bruce Watson and, of course, Anne, though she couldn't remember much, though that wasn't to say she wouldn't. And she'd already put herself in the spotlight by leading us to the bodies.

We need to protect her, I thought as I took the leash from Corbin and led the way out into the parking lot.

"So what makes you think Romano is going to talk to us

when he wouldn't talk to anyone else?" Corbin asked as we stepped out into the heated July morning.

"Nothing." I chuckled. "We're just not going to stop bugging him until he does—but I'm thinking maybe we can convince him we're on his side. If he thinks the police kept getting it all wrong, we'll let him think we think the same."

Corbin nodded as he opened the passenger door of my unmarked car. "But *do* we think the same?"

I met his gaze over the top of the car. "Maybe."

He frowned and climbed inside while I got Samson settled. Once done, I got in and typed the address of the construction site Anne had sent me into the GPS. Noting it was only about twenty minutes away, I punched the *go* button.

"Do you think there are more girls?"

I kept my expression neutral. "Bruce Watson intimated there might be, and Linda Warsaw was found in the same place as Emma Jacobs."

"But Louise Hackett is still missing."

"She is," I agreed. "There's a monster out there somewhere, Corbin. And we have to find him."

Chapter Thirty-Two

July 15, 2023
10:50AM

It was almost eleven when we stepped out of the car onto the construction site that Monday morning. The site office was a small, rundown job site trailer to the left of what appeared to be yet another low-income rental property. I'd parked in front of the trailer next to a work truck.

"Well, shall we?" Corbin chuckled, then nodded to a group of men in florescent work vests who were standing by idly watching us, and I wondered if Vincent Romano was among them.

"What do you want?" One of them called to Corbin as I opened the back door to let Samson out.

Corbin flashed his badge and said, "We're looking for Vincent Romano."

"Vinny?" one of them questioned, giving the two of us a

funny look. "What d'you want with him? He ain't gonna be happy to talk to the fuzz again."

"He's an ex-cop, and we need to talk to him," Corbin said. "Where is he?"

"He was a cop?" They all started laughing, and then one of them pointed to the trailer. "He's in there. Good luck."

With that, they turned away and went back to whatever it was they were doing, if anything.

I mounted the wooden steps, pushed the door open, and stepped inside.

"What the hell?" a voice said.

He was a tall, gray-headed, olive-skinned fellow in his early sixties. His hair was cropped short and almost completely gray.

"You're cops!" he stated. "Well, you can piss off. I already told those other two I don't know nothing. You're making me look bad in front of my crew."

"You're full of shit, Romano," I said. "You know plenty. It was you who picked up that girl back in 1986. You denied it to her face. Now, you're either going to talk here or we'll take you in. What's it to be?"

At that, he seemed to calm down. He looked at me, then Corbin, then at Samson, who gave him a smile.

"Your dog okay?" he asked, frowning.

"It seems he likes you," I said, "though I can't think why." And I meant it.

Vinny took a deep breath and then gestured for us to sit down.

"I guess you're not gonna quit, huh?" he said. "Okay, I'll tell you what I can, off the record. You ain't gonna be writing my name down or recording anything."

"Got it," I agreed, as his words took me back to the conversation with Bruce Watson.

Annie

He got up from behind his desk, went to the door and locked it, then returned to the red, beat-up leather chair, sat down and folded his arms across his chest.

"Okay," he said. "What do you want to know?"

"Why did you tell Anne it wasn't you who picked her up that night?" I asked.

"Okay. It was me," he said. "I picked the kid up. I found her wandering along the side of the road. She was bleeding like a stuck pig, so I took her to the hospital. I didn't know she was the missing girl, but I... I just... It happened."

I narrowed my eyes and stared hard at him. "Do you know where it was you picked her up?"

He shook his head. "No, I didn't, not exactly, but..." He ran a hand over his face. "Okay, so here it is," he said and leaned forward. "There were all those girls going missing in my neighborhood. The neighborhood I grew up in. I was twenty-four, not much more than a rookie. I don't think I'd stepped beyond the city limits, much less outta state, or whatever. But, look, it just seemed to me like something was really wrong, so I was kind of doing my own investigation outside of work. I was just a patrol officer, so I didn't have no right to be digging into it. I'd talked to a couple of people who had seen a car—the light green one—but they didn't know make or model. One of them said he thought he'd seen it before, out west of the city, so I followed the lead. It was dark. I was on my way back..." His voice trailed off as he stared unseeing at the wall behind me. "That's when I found her."

"Did you go back and look?" Corbin asked, frowning.

"No," he muttered, shaking his head. "I never got the chance. I thought she was gonna die, so I took her to the hospital, and then all hell broke loose and they arrested me."

"They... what?" I gaped at him.

"They frickin' arrested me on suspicions of kidnapping,

but I bet that ain't in the file, is it? Just like the charges they brought against me for which I lost my job. Some girl I ain't ever met shows up and says I assaulted her. I never did no such thing. I always wanted to be the good guy, a cop, but apparently, good deeds don't go unpunished."

I listened to him, disbelieving what I was hearing. When he finished, I said, "Who accused you?"

"It seemed like the whole damn force," Romano snapped, but then he paused, pulling out a pack of cigarettes, took one out and lit it. "Maybe not the *whole* force," he continued, "but back then there were more rotten apples than good ones. That's for sure."

"Who?" I asked. "I need names, Vinny."

Vinny eyed me. "I don't know about giving no names, but I'll tell ya this. It was the mayor's daughter who accused me of assaulting her. My folks hired an attorney from Nashville to avoid any crossings or payoffs. There wasn't a lick of DNA that pointed to me, no rape kit. Nothing. It was all hearsay, and it got dropped. But she went straight to the chief to take care of it. Her daddy and Chief Milton were close; buddies."

That raised my hackles and my eyebrows. "Chief Milton?" I said. "He's a decorated officer with a history of philanthropy and—"

Vinny burst into laughter, cutting me off. "Oh yeah, damn right, and I'm sure he loved the damn payoffs it brought with it. I wouldn't be so fast to jump to conclusions if I were you, Captain."

I made a mental note. "What about Floyd Harrison? What can you tell me about him?"

His smirk faded. "One of the good ones. They ran him off just like they did me. We both had solid alibis, what with work an' all, so it was impossible to pin much on either of us. But

Annie

Floyd, he just didn't bounce back from it. I think he knew more about what was going on than I did. They may have discredited me, but that guy... that guy knew something, and they kept a close eye on him."

"Who are they?" Corbin asked.

"I wish I knew." Vinny's voice lowered. "I had my suspicions back in the day. I thought Bruce Watson might have been crooked, or at least wishy-washy enough to stay silent and go with the corruption. I knew that bastard Milton running the place was, at a minimum, turning a blind eye to it all. But I got run out before I ever could get to the bottom of it. The rotten apples silenced me, and the good ones believed 'em."

"What about the missing girls? Emma Jacobs? Linda Warsaw? Louise Hackett?" I asked. "There's not much in the files, and the Linda Warsaw file is missing."

He looked at me, smiling, showing his teeth. I almost shivered.

"That it?" he asked. "That all you got? What about Kelly Barlow, Nina Hall, and Winona Christianson?"

I swallowed the bile in the back of my throat and stared at him, stunned.

"I bet you don't have files for them either," he said, his voice so low it was almost a whisper. "And there were more whose names I don't remember. They were disappearing all over Chattanooga. Most of 'em were runaways, delinquents, loners, foster kids—and, you know... I wasn't sure if they were *really* missing. That was, until Anne Smithson and then Emma. Whoever was doing it got brave."

Corbin furiously scribbled down the names.

"None of those names are in the database," I said.

"Of course they aren't, because whoever it was doing it..."

He paused, drew deeply on the cigarette, blew a cloud of smoke out of the corner of his mouth, then continued, "They knew what they was doing. They knew who'd be missed, and who wouldn't. My guess is the sick pedophile was right there under our noses. I wouldn't have been fired so fast if he wasn't."

"And you don't have any idea who was behind the abductions?" I asked.

He grinned slyly, slowly shaking his head. I didn't believe his response, but I had a deep-seated feeling he wasn't going to give us anything more.

"Do you stay in contact with anyone from the force?" I asked.

He chuckled. "With all due respect, ma'am, I try to stay the hell away from y'all. I don't trust a single one of you." Vinny paused. "Except maybe that girl you sent to talk to me. It was quite a shock to see that little girl all grown up and lookin' for answers. Annie was her name, as I recall. But I couldn't bring myself to say any of this in front of her. It was like explaining to a child that there really were monsters in the closet when we'd told them there wasn't."

Corbin and I fell silent. I didn't know about Corbin, but I knew I was done, and I was just about to say so when the phone rang. Vinny picked it up, listened for a moment, then said, "I'll be there in a minute."

He hung up, looked at me and said, "I gotta go do my job, but good luck to you, Captain. I hope you catch the bastard, and I hope you don't end up like Floyd." He rose to his feet, puffing out a cloud of smoke, and then said, "See yourselves out." And he walked out into the rain.

Corbin and I stared at each other, not saying a word, as the door slammed closed behind him. As much as I wanted to call his story a load of BS, I couldn't... I believed him.

Annie

I rose to my feet. So did Corbin, and together we went to the door. Corbin opened it and then stepped to the side to let Samson and me through.

It was then that my phone rang.

Chapter Thirty-Three

July 15, 2023
1:05PM

"Captain," Chief Johnston said, his voice low. "I'm at Bruce Watson's house. He's dead. So's his wife. I need you here, ASAP."

"I'm on my way," I said, stunned. "Thirty minutes, no more."

"Soon as you can," he replied. "Doc Sheddon and Mike Willis are already here." He hung up, not offering any further details. I knew that meant it was bad—and probably complicated. I slid my phone back into my pocket, then turned to Corbin and said, "Come on. We've gotta go. Watson and his wife are dead."

I quickly loaded Samson into the rear seat, fired up the engine, turned on the lights and siren, and pulled out of the construction site onto the street.

But how could anyone have known he'd talked to us? I

thought as I floored the gas pedal. It didn't seem possible. *Maybe it was suicide? I mean, he said he hoped he was dead before the truth came out. Was that because he was involved somehow?* I couldn't wrap my head around it.

I headed through downtown on Market, siren blaring, lights flickering, weaving in and out of the traffic, over the bridge into North Chattanooga. I turned left onto Cherokee Boulevard and then made a sharp right onto West Bell.

"Hah! Kinda quiet, don't you think?" Corbin said, breaking into my thoughts.

He was right. There were only two cruisers, Doc's SUV, Mike's van and the chief's Cadillac. There were no officers out on the street, no media milling around, and there were just a couple of neighbors standing on their doorsteps.

I pulled up at the curb and cut the engine.

I looked at Corbin. He looked back at me, his eyebrows raised in question.

I nodded, took a deep breath, and said, "Let's do this." And with that, we piled out of the car. Samson was whining as I let him out. I looked down at him. "What's wrong, buddy?" I asked him.

He looked up at me plaintively, I thought, and for the umpteenth time, I wished he could talk.

I reached down and patted his head.

"Good afternoon, Captain," Officer Harris greeted me at the front door. "The chief is waiting for you."

I nodded, and Corbin and I slipped through into the house. I was immediately struck by the overpowering smell.

Gasoline, I thought, frowning, as I continued on into the living room, where Chief Johnston, Mike Willis, and Doc Sheddon were standing together. I didn't have to look around to see that the room had been ransacked.

Annie

"Wow," Corbin muttered, wrinkling his nose. "Someone was going to burn this place down."

"You think?" I said sarcastically.

"Maybe they forgot matches," Corbin joked, but I didn't laugh, and his half-smile faded quickly into a frown.

"Kate, Corbin, and Samson," Doc Sheddon said brightly. "Nice to see you."

"Always a pleasure," Corbin nodded. "Well, mostly."

"We'll never know," Mike Willis said. He was talking to the chief. But then he turned to me and said, "I was telling the chief that we'll never know what was taken, if anything. The only people who would know are no longer able to tell us."

"It looks to me like someone was looking for something?" Corbin said, scanning the living room. The desk drawers had been pulled all the way out. The desk itself had been flipped over onto its top, and the papers were scattered everywhere. The couch and chair cushions had been cut open, and the stuffing scattered. The books on the shelf had also been scattered around the room. The pictures had been ripped off the walls, and... well, you get the idea. The place was a mess.

"Hard to say," Johnston said thoughtfully. He looked at me and said, "They're in the master bedroom. They look as if they died in their bed, but I doubt they did. So whatever this is, it probably took place post-mortem. And yes, I think it's safe to say that whoever did this was looking for something."

"How about the victims, Doc?" I asked. "Homicide or murder-suicide?"

"There are no obvious signs of trauma," Doc said, shaking his head as he looked up at me. "They're lying in bed as if they'd fallen asleep. I won't be able to give you a cause of death until I've performed the autopsy, of course. I can give you a rough time of death, though. Considering the liver temperature, the advanced rigor and lividity, it would have been around eleven last night, give or take an hour."

"Who called it in?" I asked.

"Anonymous," the chief replied, "to the 911 center, from here, the landline."

"But—"

The chief cut me off. "I know," he said. "Who and why? Something's going on here, Kate, and I want to know what it is."

"Are there any cameras?" I asked. "Doorbell cameras?"

"I doubt there are any of those around here," the chief muttered, almost to himself. "I had Harris go looking for them. The closest neighbor with a camera is five houses down, and the battery was dead."

"How long have you been here?" I asked, surprised. "You should've called me sooner."

"I needed to know what we were dealing with before I brought you in," he said. "If it's what I think it is, we have a real problem." He let out a sigh. "This can't be a coincidence. You know it, and I know it."

I nodded and then turned to Doc. "I need to look at the bodies."

Doc nodded. "Of course," he replied. "If you'll follow me?"

I handed Samson's leash to Corbin and followed Doc to the master bedroom.

"Odd, don't you think?" Doc commented as we walked along the hallway. The other two bedroom doors were wide open and the rooms appeared to be untouched. I paused to take a look.

"This doesn't fit with the theory that someone was looking for something," I said, shaking my head.

"Neither does the heavy use of gasoline, but no fire," he

agreed. "It's almost as if they botched whatever it was they were trying to do."

"Or they were disturbed in the process..." I thought aloud. "Or maybe this is how they intended it. A warning to someone, perhaps."

"I don't know what that means," Doc said, sliding on a fresh pair of latex gloves. "Here, put these on," he said and handed me a pair.

The two figures were lying side by side on the bed, on their backs.

"And this is how you found them?" I asked.

"It is," Doc answered. "I removed the covers. Those were pulled up around them as if they were sleeping. I doubt they felt anything." He gestured to the peaceful expression on their faces.

"How odd," I said. "What could be the cause?"

He made a face, then said, "It's hard to say. Poison, perhaps. An overdose of sleeping medication. I'm not at all sure if it's homicide, though."

I rubbed the back of my neck. There was something tugging at my mind, and I had a gut feeling I should know more about what I was seeing. What we all were seeing. It was there, but I couldn't put my finger on it. Nor could I wrap my head around how someone could kill these two, seemingly without touching them.

"What about carbon monoxide?" I thought aloud. "Would that be possible?"

"No," he replied. "Not unless it was induced into the house from outside. The house is all electric."

"So why did they ransack the living room but not the rest of the house?" I muttered. "This is a first for me, Doc."

He nodded but didn't reply.

Was Watson trying to tell us something? I wondered as I

walked slowly around the tidy bedroom, pulling out drawers and looking around. There wasn't much to find. *So why was the living room in shambles? Did Watson do it himself and pour the gasoline? Is it some kind of message?*

I stepped into the en suite bathroom and looked at the vanity. "Whoa, what's that?" I said aloud to myself as I caught sight of three large and obviously empty prescription pill bottles. One by one, I picked them up. They weren't labeled. I shook my head and sighed. *More questions*, I thought as I replaced the bottles.

"Hey, Doc," I called. "Come and look at this."

And he did. He picked up one of the bottles, looked at it, and said, "Now that's strange."

"I wonder what was in them?" I said as he held the bottle up to the light.

"And I wonder who prescribed them," Doc said. "I'll have Mike bag and test them." He turned away and disappeared, calling out for someone to bring an evidence bag to the bathroom.

I looked at the three bottles one last time.

Did you do this to yourself, Bruce? I thought. *Or did someone stage it to make it look like you did?* I pursed my lips and stood to one side as the tech bagged the bottles while I tried to make sense of it all. There were a lot of things I didn't know. I was sure of that, but one thing I was certain of... *Whoever did this knows we're closing in on them, and they're watching us.*

Chapter Thirty-Four

July 15, 2023
6:15PM

The rest of the day went by in a blur as the crime scene was processed and the bodies transferred to the medical examiner's office while the next of kin were notified of the Watsons' deaths.

Me? I returned to my office. There was little more I could do until we knew the cause of death.

Nothing other than the ransacking of the living room indicated foul play. There was no sign of forced entry, and I left the site wondering if Watson himself had carried it out. All I could do was wait for the CSI team to finish up and submit their analysis.

At five-thirty that afternoon, I packed up my things and headed home, opting to pick up some Chinese takeout. I needed a night to decompress, and while I wanted to keep working on things right then and there, I figured the time away from the chaos might do my brain some good.

It was six-fifteen when Samson and I got home. I put the takeout in the fridge and changed into my running gear while Samson tanked up on fresh water.

It was warm outside, but I knew a run would do me well. I stripped Samson of his harness and opted for a long leash so he could run on the grass verge.

We took off down the street at a fast clip to Mozart playing in the earbud in my left ear. I pounded the pavement, my arms pumping, breathing hard, sweat pouring down my face as we made it through the first mile, with waves at several of my neighbors who were braving the heat to mow their lawns and prune their bushes.

We pushed through another half mile, making it to the thick, gnarly woods where I'd met foul play once before. But Samson and I reached the three-mile point without incident. I brushed my forearm against my cheek to wipe away the sweat, and as we made the turnaround, I realized I was suffering from a slight headache, and it dawned on me that we'd skipped lunch because of the crime-filled afternoon.

Well, the assumed crime-filled afternoon, I thought as we ran toward home. That the Watsons had died at the hands of a killer was still up for debate. Had it not been for the ransacked room and gasoline, I would have opted for murder/suicide. Could Watson have done that himself? Of course, but why would he? It seemed like a far-fetched notion to me, but stranger things, right? And I was still fighting the nagging feeling we were supposed to find something there.

"But what?" I asked.

Samson looked up at me but offered no indication that he'd understood the question.

What about his wife? I thought, chiding myself for not

Annie

speaking with her, though she'd made herself scarce the moment we'd shown up. But it was on me that we hadn't thought to question her.

It was a little after seven-fifteen when Samson and I made it home. I locked the doors, freshened Samson's water bowl, gave him his kibble and then went upstairs to shower.

Once out of the shower, I pulled on a pair of white knit shorts and a gray T-shirt. I toweled off my hair but left it damp to air dry, then returned to the kitchen to heat my food. Then, I poured what was left of my last bottle of wine into a glass.

"Come on, buddy," I said as I grabbed the tray. "Let's go watch some TV, huh?" He spun around, dashed off to the living room, jumped up on the couch, plopped down with his head between his paws, and looked up at me. I followed him, tray in hand, sat down on the other end of the couch and turned on the TV.

"What do you feel like watching today?" I asked.

Other than his eyebrows, which alternated up and down, he didn't move. I shrugged. I was in no mood for anything serious, so I settled for a mind-numbing sitcom.

I ate my dinner in silence, pausing now and then to exchange text messages with Thomas. He was still in California, trying to put the last pieces of his own case together. I would have liked to discuss the nuances of my case, but I didn't want to distract him, so even though he asked me how it was going, I brushed it off. It was after eight when I told him good night.

I picked at my sesame chicken. Try as I might not to think about my day, I couldn't help but think about the Watsons and the unnerving conversation I'd had with Vinny Romano.

I hope you two don't end up like Floyd. His words filtered through the mental barriers I'd erected.

I forked some rice in my mouth and chewed, frowning. It

wouldn't be the first time that I'd gotten myself into danger while working a case. Far from it. Despite the last time it almost killed me, I was pretty damn sure it wouldn't be the last. My job was fraught with danger, as that of every cop. Did it bother me? Of course it did, but not to the point where I couldn't do my job.

Things had changed since I signed up more than twenty years ago. Cops were respected then. Now, not so much. Only yesterday, two uniformed officers in Florida had died in an ambush while responding to a domestic.

But I knew what I had signed up for, though I had to admit it had been one hell of a ride. I had twenty-three years in. Two more years and I'd be eligible for early retirement. Was I ready for that? As I sat there staring at my dinner that night, I honestly didn't have the answer. I loved my job, but... Yeah, there's always a but. I knew I needed a break, but a vacation at that time—at any time—would have been a challenge.

Samson let out a huge sigh that drew me out of my thoughts, and I turned to him, set the tray down on the coffee table and said, "What's wrong, boy?"

He lifted his head and gave me a half-smile, scooting closer to me, and rested his head on my knee.

I smiled at him, put my hand on his enormous head, and ruffled his ear.

"Sometimes I think you can read my mind," I whispered.

He sighed again and looked at the clock. It was eight-thirty. I closed my eyes, breathing slowly, deeply, enjoying the moment.

I turned off the TV. The silence was deafening.

"Maybe we should head up to bed?" I said. "You can sleep with me, if you like."

He didn't react. His eyes remained closed.

Annie

"Come on," I said, and he jumped down off the couch and ran to the back door.

Five minutes later, I was in bed with Samson on top of the covers beside me.

I shut my eyes as Samson's breaths slowed, and I drifted off into a deep slumber only to be jarred awake what seemed to be only minutes later by the sound of my phone ringing. I sat up, rubbed my eyes, and glanced at the clock. It was two-thirty-three. And I closed my eyes in despair. A call at that time of night could mean only one thing: trouble.

I grabbed my phone from the nightstand and looked at the screen. It was Anne.

"Anne?" I said, the grogginess all but gone. "What's wrong?"

"Kate, I need you to come to my house." She sounded calm. "I just had a break-in, and I think I shot someone."

I blinked a couple of times, trying to process what she'd just said. "Oh, geez," I said. "Have you called 911?"

"Of course I have," she said testily. "They're already on their way. I'm outside. I've looked, but I can't find anyone."

I jumped out of bed. "Go back to the house. Now!" I shouted. "I'm on my way." I knew I was telling her to do something I wouldn't do myself, but that was different.

I hung up, looked wildly around, raked my fingers through my hair, and then pulled on my sweatsuit, grabbed my little Sig P938 and slipped it into my right pocket, my wallet and badge into the other pocket, then turned to Samson.

"Come on, buddy. We gotta go."

Chapter Thirty-Five

July 16, 2023
3:00AM

We hopped in the car and headed off in the middle of the night, lights flashing, and drove to Anne's house in record time.

She lived in a quaint two-story in one of Chattanooga's older neighborhoods on the north side of town. By the time I pulled up in her driveway, there were already two blue and white cruisers present.

I let Samson out, and we hurried to the front door and stepped inside to find her on the couch, her husband, Mike, beside her. Her Glock was on the coffee table in front of her, and two uniformed officers were hovering over her. Fortunately, both her boys were away at college.

"Captain?" the one closest to me said, frowning.

"Michaels. Wells." I greeted them. "I take it you haven't found anything."

"No, ma'am," Wells acknowledged. "It's too dark. We'll have to wait until morning to do a proper search."

I nodded, then looked at Anne. "Did you get a good look at him?" I asked.

She shook her head. "I barely saw him. He was wearing a mask. He was... tall. Maybe six feet, dressed in black. He was just a shadow in the dark, Kate."

She leaned forward, her elbows on her knees, her head in her hands.

Samson tugged at his leash. I let him run to her. She wrapped her arms around his neck and sobbed. Her husband, Mike, put his arm around her shoulder, then looked up at me and said, "What are you going to do about it, Captain?"

"There's not much we can do until morning," I said. "In the meantime, I'll have one of these officers park outside until it gets light."

I looked at Michaels. He nodded.

"Do you have a camera?" I asked Anne.

She looked up at me and shook her head.

"Do you think it could have been a random break-in?" I asked.

She leaned back and folded her arms across her black Rolling Stones T-shirt. "It could've been, right?" she replied, though I could see by the look on her face that she didn't think it was.

I looked at the two officers. "Can you give us a minute? Go take another look around the exterior. Make sure it's clear, but keep an eye open for evidence."

"We already—" Wells began.

"Let's go," Michaels snapped, cutting him off.

I waited until they'd gone before I took a seat across from Anne and her husband. "Tell me what happened," I said.

She looked at Mike. He nodded. "We were asleep," she

Annie

began. "Something woke me up. I heard something. Something like a creaky floor outside the bedroom door. I knew I'd locked all the doors; it's a routine I go through. I grabbed my Glock and aimed it at the bedroom door just as it opened. The guy flinched. I think he was surprised to see I was awake. He had something in his hand. I told him to freeze. He didn't. He took a step forward and to his left. I fired one shot, and oh, you have no idea how loud it was. My ears are still ringing."

"Mine, too," her husband said with a self-conscious smile.

"I think he staggered a little," Anne continued. "Anyway, he turned and ran, and that's... about it."

"And you pursued him," I said. *Of course you did,* I thought dryly, and not a little pissed off.

"Yeah," Mike said. "She jumped out of bed and ran after him."

She looked at him and nodded. "I did. I grabbed my phone and ran downstairs. But by the time I got to the back door, he was gone. I ran to the back gate and out into the street, but there was nothing. That's when I called 911, and then you."

I blew air out through my lips and shook my head. My first reaction was to take a mental step back and think about it. My second was to grit my teeth. I was even more pissed off when I thought about it. Someone was out to get Anne, and I didn't like it, not one bit.

"I called my sister Lillian," she said.

"Oh?" I said, not sure where she was going with this, so I waited for her to continue.

"I started thinking it might be better if they were all to go somewhere safe. I don't want anything to happen to her. She was a witness, you know."

"She what?" I said, frowning. "I thought she was riding her bike with her friend."

"Well." Anne took a deep breath. "She was, but she was..." She shrugged. "...close."

"I see." I watched as Samson laid his head on her lap. "Anne, are you now telling me she saw something that day?"

"I'm not really sure," she replied. "We've never really talked about it. Mom always said it wasn't good for us to keep reliving it, so... we... She... We haven't."

"So, what did she say when you called her?" I asked, not knowing how I felt about this new revelation.

"She said that she would come and talk to you—but only you." Anne frowned. "And that concerns me. I don't want her getting into something that could get her killed, and I told her so." She nodded once, then continued. "She said she'll meet us at the police department later this morning."

"Okay." I nodded, not sure what else to say. I'd been under the assumption that her sister had seen nothing that afternoon. That's what her parents had told us, but here we were, and I was... I don't know how I was. Angry? Yes. Disappointed that Anne had held it from me? Absolutely. But there was nothing I could say or do that would improve what was already turning into a problem—and an even bigger problem when I told the chief. Oh yeah, I'd have to tell him, and I sure as hell wasn't looking forward to that.

I thought for a minute, staring down at her, then said, "Officer Michaels is going to stay," I said. "I doubt the intruder will come back, especially if you winged him. I'll see you tomorrow... later, at the office," I corrected myself. "You two'll be okay?" I asked.

They both nodded. Mike was holding Anne's hand, but she already had that defiant look back on her face that told me she was over it and ready for whatever might come next.

"Yes," she said, "of course. I'll be in by eight-thirty, as always."

Annie

I nodded, twitched Samson's leash, and headed out to my car, brushing off my fatigue as I climbed in behind the wheel, Samson at my side on the passenger seat, and I drove away, wondering if I should give Chief Johnston a call. I decided not to. And then I wondered if Chief Milton had gotten back to him.

As much as I knew Chief Johnston wanted to avoid questioning the veteran cops, especially the higher ranks, I knew it was now time to start reeling them in and making them uncomfortable. We were under fire and... *screw 'em,* I thought. And then I had another thought: *Lillian, Anne's sister. What the hell? If she saw something... If... Geez, I dropped the ball. I should have talked to her. But her parents... Oh, come on, Kate. Now's not the time to make excuses. I know,* I thought, *but why didn't Anne say something? We might have been able to avoid all this mess.*

Damn! Damn! Damn!

Chapter Thirty-Six

July 16, 2023
8:00 AM

It was just before eight that morning when Samson and I exited the elevator into the situation room to find that Anne was already there at her desk.

She must have heard the elevator ding because she looked at me, stood up, and waited.

"You okay?" I asked, wondering how she'd coped after the events of the night.

She nodded and raised her eyebrows, opened her eyes wide and looked at me, her lips clamped together in a thin line.

"You said eight-thirty," I said.

She nodded. "I couldn't sleep," she replied. She paused, then said, "Lillian called. She's on her way."

"Good. I need to get Samson settled," I said, "so give me a few minutes. In the meantime, if she arrives before I'm ready, put her in one of the interview rooms and give her some coffee; make her comfortable, then come and let me know."

I left Anne at her desk and went to my office, set my coffee down, turned Samson loose, then sat down at my desk, pursed my lips and stared at the two whiteboards.

For several moments, I sat there, unmoving, sucking on my bottom lip, my mind whirling.

It's beginning, I thought. *They're worried. They're taking chances. First Harrison, then the Watsons, now Anne. Something's about to break.*

I took a big sip of coffee, leaned back in my chair and continued to stare at the images on the boards: Anne, Emma, Louise, Linda. I thought about the others Vinny Romano had mentioned, *Kelly Barlow, Nina Hall, and Winona Christianson. Where are they?* I wondered.

"She's here," Anne said, poking her head through the door. "I put her in room two."

I nodded, took a deep breath and said, "Come on in."

She pushed the door open and stepped inside.

"Sit down, Anne. Has she said anything?"

Anne shook her head. "No. She doesn't look well. She wouldn't look at me."

I picked up my coffee, took a sip, and set it down again.

"There are more," I said.

She frowned, narrowed her eyes, and stared at me.

"More?" she asked quietly. "What d'you mean, more?"

"More kids," I replied. "And the Watsons are dead. Both of them."

She stared across the desk at me, her eyes wide, and then she said, "More kids?"

I nodded. "That's what Romano said. I don't have time to explain now. I need to talk to your sister."

I rose to my feet, picked up my laptop, looked at Samson,

Annie

who was in his bed under the window and said, "You stay here, Sammy. Be a good boy, okay?"

He stared back at me, his head between his paws.

By then, Anne was also on her feet, and she followed me to the door, then we stepped outside.

I locked the door, then turned to her and said, "Anne, I want you to sit this one out—"

"No!" she snapped, cutting me off. "I need to know what my sister knows."

I let out a deep breath, inwardly shaking my head, then I nodded and set off across the situation room.

I stopped at Corbin's desk, tapped him on the shoulder, and jerked my head toward the elevators.

Lillian Cruz rose to her feet as we entered the room.

"Mrs. Cruz," I said. "Thank you so much for coming. I'm Captain Gazzara, and this is Sergeant Russell. Please... sit."

Corbin and I sat down at the table opposite her. Anne sat down in one of the two chairs set against the wall off to the left side of the table.

I looked at Anne, frowned at her and shook my head, a silent warning to keep quiet. Then I looked at her sister and said, "Anne said you have something to tell me."

She looked at Anne, bit her lip, then looked at me and nodded. "I was there when Anne was abducted. I saw it happen."

Anne gasped. I turned my head and frowned at her.

"Please tell me what you saw, Mrs. Cruz," I said.

"We were riding our bikes," she began. "I was out in front, maybe fifty yards away, down the street. Anne had stopped. She was on the sidewalk. I'd also stopped. I was waiting for her. The green car pulled up alongside her, and two boys got out of the back seat and began talking to her. I couldn't hear what they were saying. She said something to them and then..." She paused, glanced at Anne, and then looked back at me and said, "The older boy grabbed her and pulled her off her bike, and the other boy grabbed her and then dragged her to the car and was trying to shove her in. She was struggling and screaming. I dropped my bike and ran to help her. By the time I got there, she was half inside, her feet still on the sidewalk. The smaller of the two boys was inside, trying to drag her in. A man was shouting 'Hurry up!' as I grabbed the older boy. He punched me in the face and I fell down, and he kicked me in the stomach. Then he shoved her into the car, slammed the door, jumped into the passenger seat, and the car drove off."

She stopped talking, stared at Anne, tears rolling down her cheeks, and she said, "I'm sorry, Anne."

"Why didn't you tell me?" Anne whispered.

"I wanted to," she replied, "but Mom told me not to, not ever. She said it was a good thing that you couldn't remember."

"That's... It must have been awful," Corbin said. "You were fourteen, right?"

Cruz nodded, still looking at Anne, and wiped her eyes with the back of her hand.

"And the police interviewed you?" he asked.

Again, she nodded but didn't reply.

"Why didn't you tell them?" he said.

"I did," she replied. "I told the detective. I told him what I just told you."

Corbin looked at me, his eyebrows raised in question. I gave him a small shake of my head. We both knew there was no such interview in Anne's file.

"Do you remember the detective's name?" I asked, opening my laptop.

"No, there were two of them," she replied. "They came to the house. I... I... don't remember either of their names."

Annie

I opened my laptop and pulled up an image of Bruce Watson, then turned it until she could see it.

"Was this him?" I asked.

She leaned forward and stared at it for a long moment, then said, "He looks..." She shook her head. "It could be. It was so long ago."

I nodded, pulled up a photo of Floyd Harrison and said, "How about him?"

Again, she stared at the photo, then looked up at me, her eyes welling with tears. She shook her head and said, "I'm sorry. I'm not sure."

I stared at her for a moment, then turned the computer back to me again and pulled up a photo of Vinny Romano.

"Have you ever seen this man?" I said. And again, she shook her head.

"Tell me about the two boys," I said.

She thought for a moment, then said, "The bigger boy was tall, heavy, overweight. He was about my age, I think. He was wearing shorts, a T-shirt and big boots. The other boy was younger, Anne's age, I think... That's... it."

"You said you could hear a man inside the car telling the boys to hurry up," I said. "What can you tell us about him?"

She paused for a moment as if trying to remember. "Nothing physical. I just heard his voice. He sounded angry. I heard him shouting 'hurry up' and then for the older boy to get in, and he did, and then the car drove away. That's all I remember."

"You should have told me," Anne whispered.

Cruz looked at her, bit her bottom lip, and then said, "I've told you everything I can remember. I want to go home now."

She was trembling. I closed my eyes, took a deep breath, and thought for a minute. There was no point, I realized, in pushing her further. She looked drained, and I was sure she was.

"I understand," I said. "Thank you. You've been a great help." I handed her my card. "If you remember anything else... I'll have someone show you out."

I stood up, went to the door, grabbed a passing uniformed officer, and asked him to show her out.

She stood, looked at Anne and opened her mouth to speak, but Anne looked away. Cruz bit her lip, stared down at her for a moment, then turned and followed the officer out of the room.

"She should have told me," Anne said, more to herself than to us.

"Anne," I said. "You've been up all night. I think you should go home and try to rest."

She shook her head.

I took a deep breath. I could have ordered her to go, but then I thought about how I would have felt. So I gave in and said, "I need a moment with Corbin. Have the rest of the team assemble in my office in fifteen minutes."

She nodded, rose to her feet and left the room without saying another word.

"She's too close to it," Corbin said. "She shouldn't be on the case."

"Oh, yeah?" I said. "Put yourself in her shoes. How would you feel?" He didn't answer.

"I thought so," I said. And I brought him up to speed with the events of the night. He listened intently but had little to say other than he wasn't surprised. "So, what about Cruz? What d'you think?"

"I think we just made ourselves another target," he said. "Other than that, we know she was taken in a green four-door and that there were three of them, including two kids. How

Annie

bizarre is that? We also know she made a statement. Two detectives interviewed her, but we don't know who they were, though it's likely it was Watson and Harrison. How about you?"

I made a face, then replied, "You said it."

I heaved a sigh, then said, "Go on up. I have to bring the chief up to date on what happened last night. I'll be up in a minute."

It's time we talked to Milton, I thought as I exited the interview room, made a right, and walked three doors down the hallway to the chief's suite of offices.

Chapter Thirty-Seven

July 16, 2023
10:00AM

Johnston, now thoroughly in the loop and a de facto member of my team, if only temporarily, accompanied me to my office, where the rest of the crew were already assembled.

"Good morning, everyone," Johnston said as he sat down behind my desk.

Hawk nodded to him.

Corbin said, "Good morning, Chief."

Anne also nodded.

Ramirez nodded and said, "Good morning."

Cooper just looked at him in awe.

I took a seat at the table facing him, set my laptop down in front of me, opened it, tapped several keys, and looked up at the chief, my eyebrows raised in question.

He merely nodded, so I cleared my throat and began.

"Good morning," I said and, without waiting for a

response, dove right in. "First," I said. "I don't know what Anne may have told you about last night..." I looked at her and raised my eyebrows.

She shook her head.

"Nothing, so it seems," I said. "So..." And I quickly filled them in on what happened—the short version. Any other time I would have taken my time, but with the chief sitting there... Well, let me put it this way. He's not the most patient of men. I also filled them in on the strange deaths of the Watsons, and then...

"Corbin," I said. "Did you fill them in on our interview with Vinny Romano?"

"I was just about done when Anne came in," he replied.

I looked at Anne. I knew she didn't know about the Romano interview. So I said, "I'll fill you in later."

She nodded but didn't reply.

I looked at Johnston and said, "Chief? Would you like to say something?"

"I would," he replied.

He looked around the table, then took a deep breath and said, "You may be wondering why I'm getting involved in your case, and I understand. So I'll tell you. This is something I rarely do." He paused, looked around again, then locked eyes with me and continued, "Two things, well, three really: One, you should know and believe I have every confidence in Captain Gazzara, and I am not here to take over your investigation. Nor do I intend to usurp her authority. But this thing is getting out of hand, and it involves several of our own. Retired though they may be, Detectives Watson and Harrison were long-serving officers with exemplary reputations. Harrison was murdered. Ambushed. Watson is also dead. So is his wife; the cause of death as yet unknown, but it's certainly suspicious."

The chief ran a hand over his bald head, then continued,

Annie

"Two: someone has to talk to Chief Milton, and protocol requires that he must be interviewed by an officer of equal rank or above, so that would be me."

He looked at Anne. "And three, but not least, Detective Robar was attacked in her home last night. That is intolerable."

He looked at me, nodded and said, "I'll interview Milton today. Detective Cooper will accompany me if you agree, Captain."

"Of course, Chief—" I was going to say more, but the phone rang. I looked at the screen. It was Mike Willis.

I looked at the chief and said, "It's Mike Willis. I need to take it."

Johnston nodded.

"Mike," I said, "you have something for me?"

"I'm still at the Watson residence," he replied. "I've found something. Kate, you need to see this."

"What? What have you found?" I asked.

He was silent for a moment, then said, "Not over the phone, Kate. You need to come."

I looked at my watch, then said, "Okay, but I have to finish up here first. An hour?"

"Of course," he replied. "I'll be waiting."

I hung up and looked at the chief. "You probably got the gist of that," I said. "Willis has found something."

Johnston nodded. I looked at Hawk. "How are you coming along with the hunting leases?" I asked.

"I've found all the lessors," he replied. "There were only eight. They're clean. Nothing stands out. I just got a list of lessees for the years 1986 through 1989, so I'm going after them."

"Good," I said. "Anne, Tracy, I want you to go through the lists of sworn officers from 1975 through 1988. Yes, I know," I said, holding up my hand, "it's a lot of people, but it needs to be done. See if anyone stands out."

Tracy nodded. Anne just stared at me. God only knows what she was thinking.

"Are we good, then?" I asked.

We were, and the chief rose to his feet and said, "Keep in touch, Kate. I want to know what's going on hour by hour."

"You can't be serious, Chief," I said.

"I'm not," he said caustically. "Every other hour will do fine." And with that, he beckoned to Cooper, who looked more than a little intimidated, and then the two of them walked quickly out of the office.

I, too, rose to my feet and said, "Corbin. You're with me."

"That's what I figured," he said with a grin.

Chapter Thirty-Eight

July 16, 2023
11:15AM

Mike Willis was waiting for us on the front porch when we arrived at the Bell Avenue crime scene some twenty minutes later.

Lieutenant Mike Willis is one of those enigmatic characters one never really quite gets. He's been a CSI since he graduated from the academy, and CPD's CSI supervisor for more than twenty years. He's a strange little man in his early fifties, eccentric, short, stocky, untidy. He shaves his head, has thick, bushy eyebrows and over-large hands, and he always seems to be in a hurry. That being said, he's an infinitely patient man and always takes the time to make sure we understand exactly what he's talking about, and he does like to talk.

"Kate, Corbin," he said, glancing at Samson as he pushed the door open for us to enter. "Thanks for coming so quickly.

Sorry you had to brave the weather. The hangover from Don, I think."

He was talking about Hurricane Don.

"If you'll follow me," he said as he led us through to the kitchen. "It's in the basement. We were finishing up when I had a thought. You'll never guess what I found. I was stunned. I can tell you. Careful, now," he warned as he opened the basement door. "The stairs are a little rickety, so one at a time. We don't want an accident, do we?"

He grinned at me as he stepped aside to let me go first.

"After you, Mike," I said. And I watched him step carefully down the ancient flight of wooden steps. I waited until he reached the bottom, turned to Samson and told him to stay, then I followed Mike. I reached the bottom step, stepped down, staggered, and almost fell. The bottom step was at least three inches higher than the other twelve.

Mike grabbed my arm, steadied me, and said, "Sorry, Kate. I should have warned you about that. I almost broke my neck the first time I came down. Homemade, by the look of them, by an amateur, I'd say. Didn't know how to measure, I guess." He looked up at Corbin, who was carefully making his way down, holding on to the single wooden handrail, and said, "Watch out for the last step, Sergeant. It's a bit of a drop and will take you by surprise."

He'd been talking incessantly from porch to basement, almost without taking a breath, so it seemed, but as Corbin stepped down onto the concrete floor, he stopped talking and looked at us expectantly.

"So?" I said.

"What d'you see?" he asked.

I looked around. It was a large basement, unfinished, with a low ceiling, a furnace, several benches—one piled with pots and pans and other bric-a-brac, another with cardboard boxes

Annie

and yet another with old and dusty computer elements: monitors, inkjet printers, two ancient towers, several keyboards and—

"Not that," Mike said, somewhat impatiently. "Over there."

He pointed to a rack of steel shelving set against the far wall. It looked heavy and had a wooden back. The shelves had nothing on them.

I shrugged and looked at him. "So?" I asked. "Shelves. What did you do with the stuff?" I asked as I looked once more at the clutter on the benches.

"Stuff?" he asked, frowning. "What st...? Oh, I see." He grinned at me and then said, "There was no stuff, not on those shelves. Come, take a closer look."

I followed him to the shelves. They looked ordinary to me. I reached out, grabbed one of the uprights, jerked it, and then pulled it. Nothing. It was fixed firmly to the concrete wall.

"So?" I said.

He was grinning from ear to ear, but he said nothing. Instead, he reached past me, under the steel frame of the middle shelf and... there was a click, and with little effort, he pulled, and the left side of the shelving swung away from the wall.

"It's a door," Mike said, stating the obvious. "I couldn't understand why, with all the clutter down here, the shelves would be bare. I'd given them only a cursory glance, but something was niggling at me. I'd been down here a half-dozen times since we'd been here, and each time they'd caught my eye. Anyway, I decided to take a closer look and, voila, there you are." He raised his hand, palm up, and said, "Shall we?"

And with that, he stepped through the opening into the darkness. He flipped a switch, and the room, for that's what it was, was flooded with light from two fluorescent lamps attached to the ceiling.

Corbin and I stepped inside a windowless room twelve feet by twenty, with concrete walls and a wooden ceiling supported by wooden beams; the floor to one of the upper rooms, I assumed. The furniture comprised a large kitchen table with a laptop computer on it. There was also a simple, inexpensive office chair and a stack of cardboard boxes in the corner. A large air cleaner and dehumidifier whirred quietly in the corner to the left of the door. The table was covered with papers and photographs. All interesting stuff, and from just a cursory inspection, I knew I was looking at some of the missing content of the files from our current cold cases. But what really caught my eye was the wall in front of the table. It was covered with photographs.

For a moment, I simply stood and stared at it from the doorway. Then I stepped closer, around the table, stood in front of it and stared at the photographs. I counted them. There were twenty-five; most of them were young girls. My mouth went dry. I licked my lips, swallowed hard, put my hand over my mouth, and turned and looked at Corbin.

He was standing on the other side of the table, his face pale, his lips parted.

"Corbin?" I said.

He just shook his head. He was speechless. Mike was standing off to the right of the table, his arms folded, his expression serious.

"Now you know why I couldn't tell you over the phone," he said.

I turned again to the wall. The photographs included Linda Warsaw, Emma Jacobs, Louise Hackett, Anne and twenty-one more young girls; twenty-five in all. At the center of it all was a large photo of... Chief Robert Milton. The same

Annie

image as the one on the PD lobby wall. His photo was flanked, one on either side, by photographs of two men who appeared to be in their late forties, early fifties. They were labeled Robert "Junior" Milton and Nelson "Bubba" Milton.

"Twenty-five," I muttered as I fumbled for my phone and hit the speed dial to call the chief. It went straight to voicemail. I left him a message to call me. I called Cooper. He didn't answer either. I left him a message, too.

I turned to the table. It was piled high with documents. Some of it from the files, the rest pertaining to missing girls from counties all over the tri-state area from Monroe in the north, Bledsoe, Sequatchie and Marion to the west, Murray in Georgia and DeKalb in Alabama, and going as far back as Linda Warsaw in 1979 to... "January of last year," I muttered.

I turned to the laptop, tapped the spacebar, and the screen lit up to reveal a Word file. I sat down in the chair and began to read.

This is my true and accurate confession— "So he was involved," I muttered and continued reading.

But he wasn't involved. He was being blackmailed.

I read through several more paragraphs, then snapped the laptop closed, disconnected it from the power supply, and rose to my feet.

"I'm taking this with me, Mike," I said—

"You can't," he snapped. "It's evidence. Give it to me."

I hesitated for a moment, then handed it over to him and snapped back at him, "Print that confession and have it on my desk within the hour. Understand?"

He nodded, his face white. I'd never, in all my years on the force, spoken to him like that before, but I didn't care. Desperate times call for desperate measures.

"Come on, Corbin," I snapped as I rushed to the door. "We're going to Milton's home. We have to find Johnston and

Cooper before—" I didn't bother to finish, and by then I was almost at the top of the rickety stairs, taking them two at a time, to where Samson was waiting, staring down at me.

"It's okay, boy," I said. "Come on." And I ran to the door with Samson and Corbin close behind.

"You said something about a confession," Corbin said as I turned onto Cherokee Boulevard, lights flashing, siren blaring. "What was that about?"

"I didn't read it all," I said tightly. "Just enough to..." I shook my head, took my hand off the wheel, and glanced anxiously at my watch. It was eleven-forty-two. Johnston had left almost an hour ago.

"He would have gone right away," I said. "But he would have had to at least check in with Christy, maybe make a couple of phone calls—"

"What are you talking about, Kate?" Corbin asked, gripping the handle above the door as I weaved the car through traffic, sometimes taking the hard shoulder.

"The chief!" I snapped. "The chief. He was planning to interview Milton, remember?"

"You need to slow down, Kate," he replied. "You'll kill us at the rate you're going."

I didn't answer him. And I didn't slow down.

Ten minutes later, halfway to the Milton estate, having calmed down a little, I said, "Milton was blackmailing Watson. Back in the day, Milton and Watson were partners. Apparently, Watson shot and killed an unarmed Hispanic kid, a drug dealer. Milton was a sergeant in his mid-thirties. Watson was twenty-five, a rookie detective. Anyway, Milton put a throw down in the kid's hand, made sure the kid's prints were on it, and then dropped it beside him. He covered up for Watson, and apparently Watson's been covering for Milton ever since—"

Annie

My phone rang, cutting me off. I picked it up out of the cup holder and glanced at the screen. It was Anne.

I swiped the screen with my thumb and took the call.

"Kate, it's me," she said, breathlessly. "I know who it was. I was going through the officers for 1980 and saw a photograph of Sergeant Milton. It was him, Kate. I remember. It was him. I'm certain of it. We have to tell the chief. He's on his way to interview him. I tried to call him, but he's got his phone turned off. So does Cooper."

"Calm down, Anne," I said, though I was feeling anything but calm. "I know. We're on our way to Milton's home—"

"So am I," she said, cutting me off. Then, before I could answer, she hung up.

"Damn! Damn! Damn!" I shouted.

Chapter Thirty-Nine

July 16, 2023
11:55AM

It was almost noon when we arrived at the Milton home, a large four-bedroom, two-story house built, judging by the style, sometime in the early 2000s on a seventy-five-acre parcel of woodland. The house itself was set back from the road some fifty yards or so, with a gravel drive leading to the wrap-around porch.

I raced the car up the drive. Johnston's car was parked outside. I slid the car to a stop, shoved the door open, leaped out, dragging my Glock from its holster, and ran to the porch and up the steps to the front door.

Samson must have leaped over into the front seat and out the open door because he was on my heels all the way.

Corbin joined me at the front door a moment later.

I grabbed the handle, depressed the latch and pushed; the door was locked.

"Damn!" I yelled and hammered on the door with my fist. Nothing. The house was quiet.

"Break it open," I snapped at Corbin.

He hesitated, then caught the look on my face, nodded, took a step back, then bolted forward and hit the door with his shoulder; the door held. It took two more hits before the doorframe split and the lock gave.

I ran into the house, Glock in both hands. Corbin followed at the crouch, also a gun in hand. Samson? He stepped inside, sniffing the air, then he sat down.

It took but a few minutes for Corbin and me to realize no one was home and the house was empty, something Samson must have known the moment he stepped inside.

I holstered my weapon and stepped back out onto the front porch, put both hands on the rail and wondered what the hell I was going to do next.

I didn't have to wonder long because, as Corbin stepped up beside me, Hawk called to tell me that Milton's name was on the list of lessees of the hunting property in 1984, '85 and '86. I quickly told him what we knew and that we were at Milton's house, that Johnston's car was there, but he and Cooper were nowhere to be found, and that, much to my dismay, Anne was on her way.

"Damn!" he said when I was finished. "I'll send backup. I'm on my way." And he hung up.

Two minutes later, Anne's car screeched almost to a stop, then turned sharply into the driveway, accelerated hard, throwing up a shower of gravel as she fishtailed toward the house.

She stopped the car. "Get in!" she shouted through the open window. "It's back there. Come on, come on!"

We ran to her car and jumped in, all three of us, and before I'd even shut my door, she was on the move, gravel

Annie

flying, around the house and onto a dirt track leading away to the east.

"That house wasn't there, then," she said through gritted teeth. "The drive was, but it was just dirt. I remember. He brought me here after he was done burying..." She trailed off, shaking her head. "There's an old house back here, somewhere," she continued, leaning forward over the wheel as she drove, looking from side to side; then, "There!" she shouted and took her hand off the wheel and pointed out the passenger side window. "See it? I can see it. Look, there, between the trees."

And I could. I could see the roof and a tall brick chimney.

The dirt track made a sharp turn to the right and Anne almost went off into the trees, but somehow she made the turn, the car sliding sideways, wheels spinning. And then we were there.

It was an old house, large, two stories, with tall wooden columns supporting a covered balcony that stretched along the front of the house. The house had, sometime in the long-distant past, been painted white, but most of the paint was long gone, leaving the house a dirty gray color. It had that dilapidated, abandoned look about it. Thinking back on it, to me... it looked... evil, haunted, even.

Anne hit the brakes. The car slewed to a stop next to a late model Ford 150 and a black Ford Expedition.

Before I could stop her, she was out of the car, gun in hand, and running up the steps and into the house.

I, too, jumped out, drew my weapon, and before I'd gone three steps, I heard Anne scream.

"Oh, my God," I shouted as I ran. I ran up the steps, stopped, held up my hand to stop Corbin and Samson, listened, heard voices, and stepped carefully inside into a huge, dark and dirty living room. It was like stepping back in time. The only light was coming from a single floor lamp beside a large, over-stuffed easy chair in which sat a very old-looking Robert Milton.

"Come in, my dear," he said. "Your friends, too. And please lower your weapons. You, too." He nodded at Anne. He paused, then said in a voice that was much less genial, "I said, lower your weapons, all of you. If you don't..." He looked to his right where one of his sons, the older one, Robert junior, was holding a shotgun to Chief Johnston's head. The other son, Bubba, was sitting awkwardly on a couch, his right leg stretched out in front of him, his pant leg soaked in blood. He was pointing a handgun at Cooper.

I lowered my weapon. So did Corbin. Anne didn't.

"It's over, Chief," Johnston said.

Chapter Forty

July 16, 2023
12:10PM

"It's over when I say it is—" Milton snarled. He would have said more, but I could hear sirens in the distance, and so could he.

"Watson was covering for you, wasn't he?" I said. "Did you know he kept records of *everything?*"

He laughed, wrinkled his nose, then said, "I'm not surprised. Bruce was a good detective, but you don't have the bodies, do you? And before you mention those you found in Sequatchie County, you'll have a hard time proving it was me that put them there."

"I frickin' saw you," Anne screamed at him.

He shook his head, smiling. "You think you did," he replied, "but didn't I hear you've been seeing a quack who specializes in repressed memories? Fiction, my dear. You made it up. You saw nothing because I wasn't there. It never happened."

"Screw you, you sick bastard," Anne yelled and braced herself, her finger on the trigger. "I know what I saw."

"You know what you think you know," Milton replied quietly, still smiling. "Now put that gun down and stop being silly. As for these two..." He motioned to Johnston and Cooper. "They were trespassing. My boys didn't know who they were, nor did I, for that matter. I've never met you, Chief, much less the kid you brought with you. Now, let's all calm down and figure this out before it gets out of hand."

Anne stared at him. She was stunned by his apparent lack of concern. "What about him?" she yelled, waving her gun toward the wounded son. "I shot him."

Milton looked at her and frowned. "There you go again," he chided her, "conjuring up falsehoods. Nelson had an accident just before these two arrived. Now... put... the... gun... down!"

But she didn't. Instead, she raised it higher and aimed it at his face. He stopped smiling. He swallowed and stared at her.

"The bullet," she said. "They'll compare it."

He shook his head and said, "Through and through."

"If so," she snarled, "they'll find it in my house and do a DNA comparison. I'm going to kill you for what you did to me and the others, you sick bastard," she snarled.

"Anne—" I began, but she cut me off.

"Shut up, Kate," she snapped. "He has this coming. They have guns on the chief and Cooper. I'm in fear for their lives."

At that, Milton turned to his boys and said, "Lower your weapons, lads. I'm sure the chief and his partner meant no harm."

The two men did as Milton said, slowly. They lowered their weapons, looking fearfully at Anne.

Annie

"Now, Anne... That is your name, isn't it?" Milton said calmly. "You're no longer in fear for their lives, so you, too, can lower your weapon, can't—"

But before he could finish, he was interrupted by a low growl as Samson rocketed across the room, leaped at the elder son, Robert Junior, and clamped his jaws over his right wrist. And I flinched as I heard the sickening crunch of breaking bones. He screamed, dropped the shotgun, and toppled over, Samson on top of him, still worrying at his wrist.

I almost missed what happened next, so taken up was I with what Samson was doing, but I caught most of it in my peripheral as Cooper spun around and kicked Bubba in the thigh. The kick landed right on target, on the gunshot wound. Bubba howled, dropped his weapon, and passed out.

I rushed forward. "Samson," I shouted. "Off!"

He let go of Junior's wrist instantly and backed away, leaving RJ lying on the floor, wailing and holding his wrist, blood streaming through his fingers.

Samson whirled around, trotted around behind me, and stood watching him, his tail between his legs.

"Good boy," I said, my Glock now trained on the old man.

"Corbin," I said. "Do something with him." I nodded toward Robert Milton Junior, the man with the shattered wrist.

Corbin stepped forward but stopped when Anne spoke.

"I'm still going to kill him," she said. "He deserves to die... All those kids."

Milton looked at her. He didn't seem bothered one bit, and he wasn't, for he looked up at her and said, "That would be a blessing, my dear," he said. "You see, I'm already dying. Too many smokes. Lung cancer. Stage four. So go ahead, put me out of my misery."

Johnston turned and stepped up to Anne, the muzzle of

the Glock almost touching his chest. Gently, he put a hand on her wrist and pushed it down. "He's not worth going to jail for, Anne," he said, then he reached down with his other hand, took the gun from her, wrapped his other arm around her and pulled her to him. And she buried her face in that crispy uniform shirt and began to cry.

I turned to the old man and began the routine: "Robert Milton, I'm arresting you on suspicion of the murder of..." At that point, I almost stopped. I mean, whose murder was I going to charge him with? Then I smiled and continued, "The murder of Emma Jacobs."

As I was reading him his rights, I could hear, in the background, Cooper reading Bubba his rights, charging him with the criminal trespass of Anne's home.

I wasn't sure what we were going to do with Robert Junior. He was, after all, an accomplice to Anne's abduction, and so was Bubba, for that matter.

Hawk arrived a moment later, followed by two blue and white cruisers.

"Damn!" he said, looking around, frowning. "I missed all the action."

Chapter Forty-One

I stepped forward and took the old man by the arm, helped him to his feet and led him out of the house to one of the cruisers.

"You can't prove anything, you know," he said as I helped him into the car. "You'll never be able to pin those crimes on me. No one can prove that I buried those three bodies out in Sequatchie County."

"How did you know there were three?" I asked.

"A little bird told me," he replied, smiling up at me.

"Watson left a confession," I told him, leaning on the open car door.

"The ravings of a bitter old man," he replied confidently. "He was just pissed at me because I knew he killed that kid in cold blood. He was just trying to get even by blaming me for the kids. But you need to ask yourself this, Captain: how did he know, huh? Makes you think, huh? Reasonable doubt, I think. And he's dead, isn't he? So he can't testify. You have nothing."

"I have an eyewitness," I replied.

"Hah," he snorted. "That crazy bitch in there? My lawyers

will have a field day tearing her apart. You should spare her the agony."

I nodded. "We'll see," I said. And I took a step back, slammed the car door, and turned to the driver.

"Put him in a cell by himself. I want him kept separate from his sons. I'll be there soon to book him."

Then I turned again to the old house. Corbin was leading Junior down the steps, his wrist wrapped in a towel.

I turned to the driver of the second cruiser and said, "Take him to the emergency room and stay with him until they've fixed him up, then put him in a cell by himself." Then I turned to Corbin and said, "Have you called for an ambulance? That gunshot wound Bubba has looks pretty bad."

"Yeah, there's one on the way," he replied. "Should be here in a few minutes."

"You'd better go with him," I said. "I want an officer outside his door twenty-four-seven. Make sure you arrange it."

"You got it, boss," he replied.

"Don't call me that," I said absently, still staring at the house. "Where are they, I wonder?" I said, more to myself than to Corbin.

I heard the two cruisers pull away and turned my head to watch them go.

"That old man's something, isn't he?" I said. "Denying everything to the end."

Corbin didn't answer.

Anne stepped out onto the porch, followed by Chief Johnston. He pointed to Corbin and then beckoned him.

Corbin looked at me, then walked quickly to the porch and up the steps.

Johnston said something to him. I couldn't hear what it was, but Corbin nodded and went inside.

Johnston said something to Anne, then came down the

steps and joined me. He stared at me for a moment, his hands on his hips, then he smiled at me, something he did only rarely, and said, "So, it's over. You think we can make it stick?"

I pursed my lips, thought for a moment, and then said, "I think so. We have Watson's confession, but..." I turned away slightly, "...this." I waved my hand in a wide arc, taking in the house and the surrounding woods. Then I shook my head, locked eyes with him and said, "Seventy-five acres?"

"We'll call for mutual aid if we have to," he replied. "And when this gets out..." He paused, looked around, and then continued. "We'll have the FBI breathing down our necks."

I nodded. "For sure," I agreed. "Nine counties, including Georgia and Alabama."

He blew out a breath, shook his head, and said, "And that's the last thing I need." He was silent for a moment. I didn't interrupt him. Then he said, "Good work, Kate. Let's see if we can wrap it up before that happens. I'll get Mike Willis and every CSI I can find out here ASAP. We'll also need the cadaver dogs; can we borrow Samson?"

I looked down at Samson. He was sitting quietly at my feet, blood still around his muzzle. "Of course. I'll clean him up first. He's used to Walker. I'll have him bring him out here."

Johnston nodded. "Good," he said. "I'll see you back at the office. You done here?"

I shook my head. "No, I'll wait for the ambulance. I also want to look around the house. How's Anne doing?"

"I don't know," he said. "I told her... I ordered her to take two weeks off and get some rest. She wasn't happy about it, but I insisted, so she agreed. She needs help, Kate. We need to see that she gets it."

I nodded, staring at Anne still up on the porch. "I'll send her home," I said.

"Good," Johnston said. "I have to go. I need a ride back to my car, please."

"I'll be there in a minute," I shouted, then did as Johnston asked.

By the time I returned to the old house, the ambulance also arrived. There was another entrance to the estate off Binkley Road, a hundred yards to the rear.

The EMTs loaded Bubba onto a stretcher and then into the ambulance and drove away; Corbin went with them, leaving me with Hawk, Anne and Cooper.

"Hey," I said to Anne, who was talking to Hawk. "I hear you're officially on vacation."

She opened her mouth to speak, then thought better of it and closed her mouth again.

"It's tough, I know," I said, "but it's for the best."

"No!" she snapped. "You don't know. You'll never know. I don't need a vacation. I need to work. I need to finish this."

Oh, she was angry. And for the first time in my life, I realized I was facing a situation I didn't know how to handle.

I thought for a moment, staring at her. I could have sympathized with her. I could have argued with her. I did neither.

"Go home, Anne," I said. "Now!" I looked at Hawk and said, "You drive her. I'll have someone take your car to the office. Call me when you get there and I'll have someone pick you up."

He nodded.

I looked at Anne. There were tears in her eyes. She looked at me, and, without a word or a backward look, she turned and walked down the steps and got into the passenger side of her car.

Epilogue

The next two weeks passed quickly.

Sammy was on detachment with Officer Walker and the cadaver dog team for the first four days. It didn't take them long to locate bodies of eighteen young girls on the Milton property. The other three are still missing, and those are only the ones we know about. Linda Warsaw, the first victim we were aware of, disappeared in 1979, over forty-four years ago. The most recent victim had been taken less than two years ago. I had a strong feeling there were more, many more.

Chief Robert Milton was right. He didn't live long enough to stand trial. He died three months after his arrest. He remained silent to the end.

As to the two brothers, they did stand trial, and Anne testified against them in court. The evidence against them was overwhelming: Watson's confession, which turned out to be a suicide note—both he and his wife died from barbiturate poisoning—and the eighteen bodies found on the Milton property. Anne's eyewitness account of her kidnapping. DNA evidence found in the old house, along with numerous items of clothing, even jewelry. They were both found guilty of twenty-four counts of kidnapping, twenty-four of first-degree murder, and a litany of lesser crimes. Bubba was also convicted of the home invasion and attempted murder of Anne Robar. Finally, Anne gave her victim impact statement. It was pretty damn moving. I know. I was there.

Robert Milton Junior and Nelson Milton were sentenced to life imprisonment without parole. It was over...

Well, not really. Anne is not the same woman she once was. Shortly after the arrests, she took early retirement. After the sentencing, she and her family moved to Florida. For almost a year, she did nothing. Oh, we kept in touch, of course, and I still hear from her now and then.

Anyway, it was early in January 2024 when I received a call from the Palm Beach County sheriff. She'd given him my name as a reference. She'd applied for a detective's position. We talked for a few minutes, and then two weeks later, she called and told me she'd gotten the job. She sounded happy. But we didn't talk long. We never do. Something's missing between us, and I hate it. I don't think she ever forgave me for sending her home that day.

The investigation into Floyd Harrison's death goes on, but I'm not holding my breath. We all think we know who killed him—my money's on Bubba—but it's a forlorn hope.

Chief Johnston held a press conference which, of course, I had to be a part of. He offered an apology on behalf of the department for what happened while Milton was in office. He didn't mention Watson by name, but he apologized for the corruption and the cover-up. He gave me most of the credit for solving the case. It was something I didn't want and didn't feel

Annie

I deserved, but like it or not, I'm the face of the department, and that's how it is.

You may be wondering about my relationship with Thomas. He did take me out to dinner, as promised, upon his return to Chattanooga. I'm still seeing him. I like him—a lot—and he seems to like me. Where is the relationship going? I have no idea. Time will tell, I guess.

Sadly, the case Thomas was working on in California ended up being deemed a suicide. But that didn't stop him from creating a compelling podcast about the young woman's life and bringing awareness of suicide prevention to his listeners.

Samson? He did his part in helping to find the remains of the girls Milton had murdered. He's doing well, but he's not getting any younger, and I worry about him. I've promised him I'll buy all-natural dog food from here on out.

Uh-oh... Sorry. I have a call. It's Chief Johnston. That can't be good. Here we go again.

* * *

Thank you for taking the time to read **ANNIE**, the Twentieth Book in the Lieutenant Kate Gazzara Murder Files. I hope you enjoyed it. If you did stay tuned as the Next book in this series is **underway!**

WHILE YOU WAIT CHECK OUT MY OTHER BOOKS!
ALL ARE AVAILABLE AT BlairHowardBooks.com

Have you read Jasmine?
Genesis?
How about Harry Starke?

Blair Howard

Do you enjoy Spy Thrillers?

* * *

SIGN UP For Announcements & great deals!

PLUS you'll Unlock 20% Off

Get Exclusive Deals (As Part Of "The Family")

Visit www.BlairHowardBooks.com

If you don't see the pop up above, just click the blue unlock 20% off icon and enter your details.

Don't forget to confirm your email and whitelist (save as contact)BlairHoward@blairhowardbooks.com to your email system.

From Blair Howard

The Harry Starke Genesis Series

The Harry Starke Series

The Lt. Kate Gazzara Murder Files

Randall And Carver Mysteries

The Peacemaker Series

The O'Sullivan Chronicles: Civil War Series

From Blair C. Howard

The Science Fiction Sovereign Star Series

About the Author

Blair Howard is a retired journalist turned novelist. He's the author of more than 50 novels including the international bestselling Harry Starke series of crime stories, the Lt. Kate Gazzara series, and the Harry Starke Genesis series. He's also the author of the Peacemaker series of international spy thrillers and five Civil War/Western novels.

If you enjoy reading Science Fiction thrillers, Mr. Howard has made his debut into the genre with, The Sovereign Stars Series under the name, Blair C. Howard.

Visit www.blairhowardbooks.com.

You can also find Blair Howard on Social Media

Made in United States
North Haven, CT
27 August 2024